KT-461-262

For D325

CHAPTER 1

The wind howled as it administered a series of stinging slaps to his face. It had been a long, hot summer, the days warm and balmy, but tonight the weather had broken, and it was unusually stormy.

'What's wrong with you, uni boy? A wee bit of wind and you're burrowing into your tunic like a ragged-arsed mole digging for his life. Tell me, what the fuck did you join the Glasgow polis for anyway?'

Thoroughgood couldn't have answered this question even if he wanted to, but before he had time to think up a suitable reply his inquisitor spoke again, raising his voice above the icy gusts that seemed to slice through their woollen 'monkey suits'.

'You fuckin' students are all the same – think you can turn up with your bloody degrees and run the show before the ink has dried on your warrant cards but...'

Thoroughgood ground to a halt, aware that his tormentor was no longer next to him. As he turned around, the senior cop jabbed a finger into his shoulder, a breath of stale alcohol washing over the rookie. He found himself mesmerised by Davidson's mouthful of rotten teeth, which resembled a blown fuse box.

'It don't work that way out here, you wanker. It is what I say that goes and it is me that calls the shots. When I say jump, you ask how high, because doing what I say is the only way you're gonnae stay alive on these streets. Do you understand me, uni boy?'

Thoroughgood attempted to provide an answer but found words hard to come by for a second time and settled instead for a nod of his head.

Davidson glared at Thoroughgood, but the probationer, a mounting anger at his treatment at the hands of his tutor cop rising inside him, met the older man's spiteful stare with a seething resolve that he would not be cowed. Davidson's hat sat at an angle that slightly covered a headful of straw hair; his eyes were cruel and grey, set into a pale and ghoulish face. As Thoroughgood stared back at him, their close proximity brought home the sense of latent violence that seemed to perpetually accompany Davidson.

'Now, listen good, *boy*,' hissed the senior cop. 'I don't like middle-class, sponging, student scum and I couldn't give a fuck whether you make it out the other side of your probation dead or alive, but what I do care about is keeping my own hide in one piece. So while you are with me you play by my rules. Your education, uni boy, starts right now.'

Thoroughgood attempted to subdue his shame that a male in his late thirties, whose physique was far from imposing and inclined to strain the silver buttons of his tunic, was indeed doing a very good job of intimidating him. While physically Davidson was no man-mountain, it was the experience and knowhow that he had gained on two tours of Northern Ireland during the height of the Troubles and his reputation for dealing out brutal and systematic beatings that kept Thoroughgood's mounting anger in check.

Davidson took another step closer. 'Rule number one for any beat cop is *know where you are*. Stay sharp, stay alive. You may have all the brains in the world, uni boy, but now we're gonnae find out if you have the wits to go with them, cos wits is what keeps you safe 'n' sound on the street.'

The senior cop's lecture was ended by the chimes of an ice cream van and within seconds a golden-roofed, blue-sided vehicle emblazoned with the words 'Mojito's Ices: Satisfaction Guaranteed' came into view at the top of Braidendmuir Street.

'Move it,' spat Davidson out of the side of his mouth, immediately setting off up the hill towards the van. About fifty yards from the vehicle he turned into the doorway of a derelict tenement close and gestured to Thoroughgood to do likewise.

Davidson's eyes remained homed in on the van before he eventually spoke. 'You never know what's drawn out of the woodwork by the icy. Did you know that junkies have a sweet tooth? Ice cream, chocolate and all that shite helps them fight their cravings.'

'Nope,' said Thoroughgood, taking his hat off and running the fingers of his right hand through his mop of black hair.

'Junkies equals warrants. So you stay awake and we might just get ourselves a body here.'

Within seconds the deserted street was teeming with kids and their mothers, high-pitched chatter and shrill cackling filling the air, but Davidson's hopes that any of the criminal fraternity would oblige him with an appearance were left unfulfilled.

As the last of the van's customers walked away, licking their purchases, the senior cop stepped forwards. 'Stay here,' he barked.

The rookie watched in fascination as the former soldier approached the driver of the vehicle, a young, dark-haired male who Thoroughgood put in his early twenties. There ensued an increasingly heated conversation, which ended with Davidson grabbing the driver by the scruff of his denim jacket and half dragging him out the vehicle sales window.

A combination of the blowing gale and distance meant, infuriatingly, that no matter how hard Thoroughgood strained his ears he could not hear a word of the exchange.

Having clearly made his point, Davidson propelled the obviously shaken ice cream man back through the window and, as he did so, a brown paper envelope found its way onto the service counter before being quickly scooped up by Davidson and shoved into his left-hand breast pocket.

Ten yards from the tenement close Davidson shouted, 'Time to move out, uni boy,' and without waiting for a reply marched off as the ice cream van sped down the road in the opposite direction.

CHAPTER 2

They continued to pound the concrete pavement between grimy, graffiti-stained tenements, some shuttered up with steel casing, others showing signs of life that looked anything but human.

Desperate though he was to ask the senior cop about what had just taken place, Thoroughgood decided he would be dammed if he would give Davidson the chance to slap him down again with one of his vicious rebukes. Besides, in Thoroughgood's eyes, it was obvious enough what he had seen.

The only sound breaking the silence was the metallic chink of Davidson's whistle, the chain entwined through the silver buttons of his woollen tunic. In Thoroughgood's mind it was like the sound of a cowboy's spurs, the noise echoing in time with Davidson's footsteps.

Thoroughgood had noticed that none of the other shift cops bothered to wear the whistle, which seemed to be strictly for ceremonial occasions, unless you were a probationer. Now he knew why the senior cop persisted in wearing his. What Davidson wanted to send out was a warning, before he was even seen, that the sheriff was in town. It only added to Thoroughgood's impression that this place they called Lennox Hill was more like the Wild West than a slum on the outskirts of Glasgow.

The area was widely regarded as the 'arse end' of the north of the city and one in which the heroin problem had turned half the population into feral zombies who would sell their grannies for a tenner bag of smack. To newly commissioned Constable Z325, Angus Thoroughgood, it felt like stepping into a parallel universe.

Having graduated from the University of Glasgow earlier that year, class of '89, Thoroughgood was not long into his probationary period in police service, having negotiated his disastrous basic training course at the Scottish Police College by the skin of his teeth. Already, his university life seemed like some kind of surreal dream from which he had been snatched, thrown instead into a company of wolves who were intent on administering their version of 'justice' on a population who hated and despised the police in equal measure.

The Lennox Hill station, or 'the Hill', as it was dubbed, was a five-man affair with one long-serving officer detailed as station constable and four others rotating on two-man patrols. The fact that the radio reception in the area was erratic and that there were several blank spots where there was no coverage had already led to the local cops being ambushed on more than one occasion by the natives. When the residents of Lennox Hill did not seethe in silent resentment, they indulged in their favoured pastime of playing the hundred-yard hero, brave enough to hurl abuse on a passing patrol only when the gap was big enough.

While he knew that Davidson, or 'Dangerous', as he was known to everyone in Zulu Land, as Z-division was nicknamed, was a source of valuable and potentially life-saving information, it was his constant sniping at Thoroughgood's former status as a student that really got under his skin – that, and Davidson's persistent assertion that the rookie cop was an information plant 'for the brass'.

After they had checked a row of shops, front and back, at the top of 'the Hill', Thoroughgood found it increasingly hard to concentrate, his mind drifting in the direction of the west end, where most of his mates would be out on the piss. Meanwhile, he was stuck pounding the streets with Glasgow's answer to Wyatt Earp.

His mind already longing for the 3 a.m. piece break, Thoroughgood couldn't help checking his wristwatch. He knew it was a mistake.

'Bored? Good, old-fashioned, honest coppering not what you

were promised when they signed you up, you smug little shite? Never mind the fuckin' time, where are we?'

Thoroughgood had switched off and the furtive glance he made around him for confirmation of his whereabouts revealed as much.

He felt the impact of Davidson's right forearm ram across his chest and then gasped in astonishment as he saw the glint of a knife, which had appeared from nowhere and was now just inches below his chin.

'What did I tell you five minutes back, uni boy? *Know where you are at all times.* Here we fuckin' are and you've switched off already. What happens if we get jumped and need to put out a 21-call for urgent assistance and you don't know where the hell we are?'

The pressure on his throat and the glinting menace of the knife just below his chin ensured that Thoroughgood remained silent, but in truth he had been left speechless by the actions of the man who was supposed to be tutoring him in the art of the beat cop.

A smile of malicious relish spreading across his face, Davidson drew his forearm back but quickly manoeuvred the sharp point of the knife into the flesh just under the probationer's chin.

'Where we are is the old gas works – and your grave, if I want it to be, uni boy. What would happen if I slit your throat and left you for dead, bleeding out and dumped in one of the old tanks? It'd be easy enough to explain – the smart-arsed graduate wouldn't listen to his senior man, stormed off and got his throat cut for his troubles by our friendly locals. And it'd mean one less headache for me to worry about.'

Thoroughgood eventually found his words, but when he spoke he didn't recognise the hoarse rasping of his own voice. 'You're a fuckin' madman, Davidson. You can't be serious – you're my tutor cop, for Chrissakes...'

The point of the blade remained lodged against the underside of Thoroughgood's chin as Davidson stared down the younger cop, the familiar scent of his stale, alcoholic breath filling the space between them.

'Jesus Christ can't save you, Thoroughgood, but I can. Or not…' Davidson let his words fade into an ominous silence before continuing. 'You know how I survived two tours of duty in the province, uni boy? By staying switched on and relying on my wits every minute of every fuckin' day. You walk the streets with Billy Davidson then you stay switched on, cos I'm not taking a blade in the back for some smartarse bookworm who's still wet behind the ears.'

The pressure from the blade increased until Thoroughgood thought his skin was about to break. His eardrums seemed about to burst as the hammering of his heart went into overdrive and he almost stopped breathing.

Then Davidson pulled the knife back, flicked the switchblade's button, recoiled the four inches of gleaming steel into its ivory handle and slipped it snuggly into the poacher's pocket that had clearly been custom-made inside the left breast of his tunic. A feral smile swept across the senior cop's features before he spat contemptuously onto Thoroughgood's immaculately polished shoes.

'Better get that gob cleaned off before the sergeant catches you, uni boy.'

But before Thoroughgood could react, the noise of a diesel engine filled the silence of the night. He saw an approaching Ford Escort Mark III, liveried in white with the red side stripes that had earned Strathclyde police vehicles the nickname of 'jam sandwiches'.

'Sergeant Rentoul is a stickler for the smart uniform, Thoroughgood, and he won't be happy with the bull on your boots being covered by a huge gob,' said Davidson, filling the air with his harsh laughter.

The police vehicle drew to a stop yards away and from the driver's door the hulking shape of the senior shift sergeant, Jimmy Rentoul, hoisted himself out of the motor and ambled his way towards the two cops. The creases in the sleeves of his tunic and fronts of his woollen trousers were razor sharp, the army service ribbon fixed to his uniform breast stood to attention, and the peak of his cap reflected Thoroughgood's features in it, such was the gleam of its shine.

'Well, well, Davidson and Thoroughgood. I'm delighted to see you're not dossing your way through the night shift.' Rentoul, who had been scrutinising Thoroughgood's appearance from top to bottom, stopped short as his gaze fell upon the slimy green substance on the probationer's right foot. Immediately a giant index finger bore into Thoroughgood's chest. 'What the fuck is this, son?'

Realising that whatever explanation he offered would be pointless, Thoroughgood played it straight. 'I'm sorry, Sergeant Rentoul, I must have caught it round the back of the gas works. Thought I'd heard a noise back there but it was nothing. Must've missed the gob shite on my boot on the way out. I will clean it off immediately.'

'Not before I've finished with you, son. Now listen to me, and listen good. If I ever see the uniform of Her Britannic Majesty's police service soiled in such a manner again I will have you up on a charge of neglect. Do you understand me?'

'Yes, Sergeant,' stammered Thoroughgood.

'Remember I know your story Thoroughgood. A smartarse just out of Glasgow university with a degree in – what was it again...'

'Medieval History, Sarge,' said Davidson.

'Aye, that's it. Thanks, Billy boy. Medieval fuckin' history, that's right. You tell me what use that's gonnae be to you out on the streets of the Hill?' Rentoul paused but before Thoroughgood could answer he spoke again. 'Absolutely no fuckin' use, is the answer you are searchin' for. But then we both know that – just like we both know the reason you're here.'

'Sorry, Sergeant, I don't know what you mean,' replied Thoroughgood, trying to control his nervousness at this new line of questioning.

This time the palm of Rentoul's left hand rammed into Thoroughgood's chest, propelling him back into the crumbling brick wall behind him. The probationer flung out his arms, just managing to keep himself upright.

'The reason you are here, you son of a bitch, is that you are a grass for the brass. You've been sent here to inform on my shift and to try and get some of the toughest cops in this man's army busted out of it. But let me tell you this, you snivelling little arsewipe, that's no' gonnae be happening any time soon. You are almost four months into your two-year probationary period and you know who's gonna have the biggest say in whether you make the grade as a cop?'

Thoroughgood knew the question was rhetorical and silently grimaced.

'Jimmy bloody Rentoul, is the answer you are looking for. Do you think I'm gonnae allow one of my veterans to lose his uniform for a nancy-boy university graduate who's touting to the bosses? No way, son. No fuckin' way. I will be watching you every step of the way. I will know, before you do, when you need to take a shite. Let me promise you, there is no way you are going to make it through the box of delights I have waiting for you, Thoroughgood,' Rentoul took another step forward, so that his face was millimetres away from the rookie's. 'Now get your fuckin' notebook out, shit-for-brains, and let your sergeant sign it.'

Thoroughgood tried to keep his emotions masked as he shakily flicked the breast button of his tunic open and pulled out the notebook, opening it at the day's tour of duty page. Before he could hand it to Rentoul the sergeant ripped it out of his grip.

In the background Davidson helpfully piped up, 'You not going to fill the location of the sergeant's sign-in before you hand it to your superior officer, Thoroughgood?'

Rentoul took a sideways glance at the senior cop and gave a disgusted, knowing nod of his head, before returning the black, plastic-covered notebook emblazoned with the words 'Strathclyde Police' back to Thoroughgood.

'Well... Fill the location in here, *Constable* Thoroughgood,' said Rentoul, drawing the last two words out with dripping sarcasm.

'Blackmill Gas Works, Blackmill Road, sergeant,' said Thoroughgood lamely as he wrote the date, location and time of the sign-in in a quivering hand and proffered the book back for his gaffer's supervisory signature.

Rentoul scribbled his name and slammed the book into Thoroughgood's right shoulder. Then, turning to Davidson, he asked, 'How long you give him, Billy boy? You think he'll make it to six months?'

'I wouldnae be betting your money or mine on that, gaffer,' Davidson replied gleefully.

CHAPTER 3

Their return to Lennox Hill station may have been undertaken in silence but the voice in Thoroughgood's head refused to stay quiet.

Twenty-four days after graduating from university, he had joined Strathclyde Police – and from day one the evidence was that it had been a colossal mistake. His nightmare at the Scottish Police College had left him with massive doubts about his decision. His inability to keep his mouth shut when faced with the most mind-numbing acts of authority from a succession of the training centre's sergeants had meant he had only been able to graduate from the course after receiving a massive bollocking and a final warning from the college commandant, who had questioned the future of 'a smart-mouthed student in a real man's world'.

After learning that he was being despatched to Z Division, in the north of the city, Thoroughgood's hopes that he could put the catastrophic basic training course behind him had almost immediately been ruined by the news that the shift he had been allocated to was one that operated very much to its own rules of engagement.

Tonight's clash with Davidson had been the climax of a simmering mutual antipathy between Thoroughgood and his tutor cop, whose contempt for the graduate seemed to represent the attitude of most of the other cops on the shift. The dressing down he had received from Sergeant Rentoul for the besmirching of his uniform was one thing, but the way the senior shift sergeant had used it to launch into accusations of Thoroughgood being an

11

informant to the division's senior officers was something that left the rookie bewildered and at the same time with very little hope that he could negotiate Rentoul's 'box of tricks' and make it out of his probation to become a fully fledged cop.

But while the dazed Thoroughgood had remained alert for the remainder of their tour of the Hill, ready for a repeat of Davidson's antics, there had been none. Instead, the former soldier had adopted an almost jovial approach that left Thoroughgood wondering if the incident at the gas works had actually happened, so surreal did it now seem.

But as he followed Davidson through the scarred, splintered and graffiti-daubed doors of Lennox Hill's station, Thoroughgood knew that the next part of his daily ordeal awaited. The corpulent figure of Brian Jones, the station constable, leaning on the charge bar in the office's reception foyer, loomed large.

'So the boy wonder has made it through another turn around the Hill, but by the look on his face he'd rather have been anywhere else. What have you been doing to him this time, Dangerous?'

'Just been teaching Pug here the rules. He's got a bit of homework to do back at that posh west end flat of his but I don't think he'll be making the same mistake again,' said Davidson, a slight smile playing around the corners of his mouth.

'Aye, the rule book according to Billy Davidson... You'll do well no to choke on that, Pug ma boy. I hear the gaffer was less than impressed with the bull on your boots. You've a lot to learn, son,' said Jones, almost sympathetically, before erupting in an explosion of laughter that saw every one of the many folds of flesh under his jaw shake like a plate of giant jellies.

Thoroughgood looked from one to the other of the senior cops, fighting to restrain his own anger along with the tongue that had consistently landed him in trouble ever since he had started to wear the black woollen suit of Strathclyde Police. But his face would not cooperate and, as it betrayed his inward emotions, Jones's laughter died, his two giant forearms – a legacy of his time as a champion weightlifter – disappearing under the counter of the reception. When he drew his arms back up, gripped in his massive, fleshy hands were two machetes. He threw them up in the air, allowing them to somersault 360 degrees before catching them by their handles and ramming them into the scratched and rotting reception counter. The two-foot-long blades quivered in the wood, producing a curious whirring noise.

'See these two fuckers, boy? They were taken off the locals the last time they jumped the lads in one of the radio black spots. Listen and listen good, Pug. No one is expecting you to like any of us but what we fuckin' well do expect is that you listen to every word and learn from it, cos it might just save your life. And if you're alive, so's your neighbour,' said Jones. Then he ripped the machetes free and hurled them, one after the other, either side of Thoroughgood and into the wall behind him. The impact loosened the handset on the public phone – the only one in Lennox Hill – and it fell from its holder, banging against the wall as the buzzing from the receiver reverberated on and on.

Thoroughgood stared at Jones. He knew he was being tested and this time he was determined not to fail. 'Fuck you both,' he snapped, booting the two internal reception doors open before disappearing into the rear of the station.

Behind him, laughter filled the air.

CHAPTER 4

'So what're you gonnae do now, Gus? It's bad enough trying to learn the job when your senior man is on your side but when he's threatening to slit your throat and dump you in a disused gas tank and your gaffer thinks you're an informant for senior management... Well, I just don't know where you go from there, pal,' said McNab, taking a thirsty gulp of his Becks.

Thoroughgood was perched on a bar stool at the top end of Bonhams bar, in Byres Road, the venue that he and his new best mate had referred to as 'HQ' since meeting during their basic training course at Tulliallan. But while Thoroughgood had barely made it through his introduction to the joys of the police service, McNab had skated through the initial training programme before being posted to the eastern city division, where his amiable and laidback personality had already earned him the nickname of 'Nicey'.

Thoroughgood turned his gaze on his fellow rookie. 'It gets worse, mate...'

'Meaning?'

'Davidson is on the take,' he replied flatly.

'How do you work that one out?' enquired a shocked McNab.

'I watched him clear as day taking a brown envelope off an ice cream man after he'd just about pulled him clean out the sales hatch and throttled him.'

'What was the name on the ice cream van?'

'It was a bizarre one – Mojito's Ices. I didn't know there were any Mexican ice cream van owners in Glasgow!'

'There aren't. Mojito is Bobby Dawson the club owner's nickname and,' McNab paused to make quotation marks with his fingers, 'respected businessman. He owns Tutankhamun's round on Great Western Road, the club with the Camel in the foyer, and the new place opening at the bottom of Byres Road, which I think is going to be called Vesuvius. He's known as Mojito after his favourite cocktail. No cop in his right mind is going to mess with one of Dawson's vans, whether he's tooled up with a flick knife or not.'

'I know what I saw, and if Davidson's on the take what's the bets the rest of the shift are too? Problem is that thinking you know something and proving it are two very different things. Especially when you're on your own. To make matters worse the bastards have now slapped a nickname on me too,' groaned Thoroughgood.

'Yeah, why are they calling you Pug anyway?' asked McNab, revealing that news of Thoroughgood's disastrous start to life in Z Division had already spread across the border to the east.

'Brilliant. I might have known it would be all over the place. Apparently they think I'm the spit of Robert Mitchum, the old Hollywood movie star who's in *The Winds of War* on TV,' said Thoroughgood with a disgusted shake of his head.

McNab looked singularly unconvinced. 'You sure about that? I mean, that nose of yours could be described as a bit of a pug!'

'Hi-fucking-larious,' said Thoroughgood over McNab's loud guffaw. 'But that isn't any help. I'm months into this shit and already it's obvious I've made the biggest mistake of my life. For crying out loud, Rentoul and Davidson have a bet going I won't even make it to six months, never mind the two years I need to make the grade as a cop. Christ, if only I'd got a first class then I would be over *en France* studying private archives on the Hundred Years' War... Paradise.'

Before McNab could answer, a lithesome female presence materialised behind the bar and a delicious scent filled the air.

'Do you two ever do any work? I thought cops were supposed to be on the job every hour of the day but the pair of you are never out of here,' said Anna, the svelte blonde manager of Bonhams bar.

McNab, as usual, was first to react to a female presence. 'Gus here is having a bit of a time of it out at his new station in Lennox Hill, Anna, and we couldn't think of anywhere better to try and sort out his problems than the best boozer in the whole of the west end – and of course the bar with the best looking manageress in Glasgow.'

'Your patter is mince, McNab,' replied Anna, a smile creeping across her face nonetheless. She turned her attention sympathetically to Thoroughgood. 'Nice place, Lennox Hill. Is it that bad, Gus?'

'Worse,' was Thoroughgood's wretched reply, before he quickly recovered himself. 'But like I always say, Anna, all my problems go away when you're behind the bar in Bonhams.'

'Never mind giving Anna the chat, big boy, what have you got here in the Slaters bag? To be fair, it didn't take long for you to make the most of the interest-free accounts available to the job,' said McNab, tugging at the black carrier bag liveried with the name of Glasgow's most famous gents' retailer.

A smile at last broke out on Thoroughgood's face as he opened the bag and pulled out its contents. Dropping a pair of sharply creased black trousers to their full length, Thoroughgood announced in triumph, 'These, my dear McNab, are Lancers, the substitute uniform trousers that are at last going to provide me with lightweight comfort rather than the sack-cloth excuse for woollen trousers we have to wear that turn into sodden blankets the minute there's a drop of moisture on them and the rest of the time chafe your legs till they're red-raw.'

The laughter that met Thoroughgood's triumphant announcement was, this time, of the female variety.

'Poor Gus, I didn't know you had such sensitive skin. If ever you need some moisturiser to stop your soft little legs chafing, just let me know,' said Anna as she dissolved into a fit of giggles.

Thoroughgood quickly shoved the Lancers back into the Slaters' bag, his embarrassment obvious.

'Can I say something, Gus?' asked McNab, in a way that made it obvious he was going to offer his opinion regardless of what his fellow probationer thought on the matter.

Thoroughgood shrugged his shoulders in resignation.

'How the hell do you think you will get away with wearing a pair of, what did you call them, Lancers, with a shift gaffer who seems more like a sergeant major when it comes to uniform and discipline and who's desperate for any excuse to bust you out of the job before you've even wiped your feet in it?' asked McNab.

For the second time, a look of triumph broke across Thoroughgood's drawn features as he ripped out a piece of paper from inside his black Harrington bomber jacket. 'As big Bob Mitchum would say, an ace beats a king every time. Feast your eyes on the medical certificate my doctor has just provided me with and one confirming that Lancers are the answer to a medical condition caused by a slight psoriasis of the skin that is painfully exacerbated by Strathclyde Police's woollen uniform trousers.'

Thoroughgood raised his half empty pint of lager in mock salute to his fellow probationer. 'For every problem they pose me I have to find an answer and,' Thoroughgood paused and patted the Slaters bag, 'this one has been provided courtesy of Ralphy Slater.' Then, for the first time that day, Constable Z325 Angus Thoroughgood laughed.

CHAPTER 5

Despite the warnings, Johnny Fox had almost completed his rounds with no problems. One look at the plastic tub he kept below the van's service hatch, packed full of crinkled tenners and twenty-pound notes, confirmed that.

Pulling up outside the Red Road Flats with his chimes on full pelt, Fox waited for the residents of Europe's largest high-rise dwellings, which were reputed to house a bigger population than the city of Perth, pile down for their ices and 'extras', as he liked to call them.

For the wads of cash that Fox had collected as he toured his pitch – to the tune of 'The Fields of Athenry' and a selection of pro-Irish anthems and ballads that emphasised the heritage of the van's owners, the McGuigans – had come from an illicit trade that he peddled under the legitimate front of ice cream man.

Taking a look at the queue that was starting to form at the front of his van, Fox, a forty-two-year-old hoodlum who had never amounted to more than a small-time enforcer and drug peddler, reflected that the lucrative nature of the McGuigans' under-the-counter trade looked like it would at last allow him to move from the damp gable end he currently occupied with his bidey-in, Irene, and their three weans, to a side door with a garden, even if it was a four-in-a-block.

Yet the pleasure he was taking at a job increasingly well done, one that was starting to allow him to finally believe he could make a better life for Irene and the kids, was tainted by a giant black cloud that had sailed onto the brilliant blue horizon. The verbal threats and counter-warnings that were ricocheting between his boss, Francis McGuigan, his son Gerry McGuigan and Bobby 'Mojito' Dawson, the man who was attempting to break their grip on the criminal empire the old man had built up over the last thirty years, was, Fox felt in his gut, showing nasty signs of escalating into something more lethal.

But the ice cream man silently chided himself for becoming so 'vexed', as his grandmammy Bella would have called it, and tried to concentrate on the prospect of another afternoon of lucrative trade. The junkies were easy to spot. All sunken-eyed, gaunt enough to look like they'd been inmates in a Nazi death camp, teeth either rotten or non-existent.

Fox fingered the hooped earring in his left lobe in anticipation of more cash crossing his palm. He didn't have long to wait for his first customer.

'Awright, Jonny? How's the Foxman? You got a Special 99 for the Dazzler?' asked Darrell McKenna, a hopeless teenage smackhead from the twelfth floor of 4 Red Road Court.

'You got the readies, Dazzler, and I'll have a 99 whipped up just the way you like it, son,' said Fox.

Despite the fact that it was a mild evening, McKenna had his shell suit zipped right up to his chin and the obligatory baseball cap was pulled down tight on his skinhead. His skin almost jaundiced, such was the severity of his habit, the self-styled Dazzler's right hand shot out onto the van counter and deposited a crumpled up ten-pound note and a one-pound coin.

Fox smiled knowingly and scooped some vanilla ice cream out of a container before using the handle end of the scoop to bore a hole into the ice cream, inserting a tiny cellophane wrap into the space and crowning it with a chocolate flake.

'There you go, Dazzler. Satisfaction guaranteed an' oblivion comin' yer way fast. Enjoy, wee man.' Fox watched as McKenna's eyes locked on the 99 in a way that suggested he didn't even know the ice cream man had spoken, such was the intensity of his craving for the smack that was the centre of his world and in the middle of his vanilla ice.

As the junkie turned his back on Fox without so much as bye or leave, the next punter stepped forward – but the walking stick, silver hair and almost double-glazing thickness of Agnes Sturrock's spectacles made it clear that Fox's latest piece of business was of an entirely legitimate nature.

But the ice cream man remained watchful. Fox couldn't help himself gazing at the pickaxe handle he kept for protection just inside the van's cabin, for he had no doubt that one day soon he would need it.

As the queue thinned out, Fox spotted a latecomer. He stuck his head out of the van hatch to make sure that no one else was about to see what his latest punter was bringing to the table in part barter for her score.

Maggie Brown was a well-known whore who plied her illicit trade from her top floor flat and anywhere else she could lie on her back and earn the cash she needed to feed her habit. With enough make-up on she could almost pass for a presentable young woman, until she opened her mouth and the sparseness of her teeth hinted at a more sinister cause for her dental decay, while her guttural voice spoke of her predilection to chase the dragon by smoking her heroin, such was the state of the limited veins she had left in her increasingly toxic body.

The weeping sores that spilled pus down her legs were a thing of horrific legend around the Red Road but Fox didn't care about any of that because she was a fantastic source of information for him and so for his McGuigan paymasters. And from time to time she helped exercise the frustration that built up in him with her serpent's tongue.

Maggie also peddled stolen car radios that some of her punters used to pay for her pleasures and that she in turn traded to Fox for her smack. The ice cream man could see from the plastic Spar bag in her right hand she had a couple of stolen 'diggies' with her for the horse-trading session they were about to conduct.

'Johnny the Fox, it's yer lucky day!' she said, in a rasping voice that would have made her the perfect choice for one of the crones from Shakespeare's Macbeth, and underlined that her nicotine habit was almost as heavy as her heroin addiction.

Fox smiled out from behind the van service counter. 'Why don't you come roon to the back o' the van, Maggie May, and see if we can sort something oot that works for the both of us.'

A moment later Fox opened the rear door. 'So how many diggies have you got for the Foxman, Maggie doll?'

'I've got half a dozen – four in the bag and two inside ma jaicket. How much shit you got left, Johnny, cos I'm needin' ma hit bad.'

'So you oot workin' the drag tonight or turnin' tricks up in yer midden?' asked Fox.

'What's it to you, Johnny boy? Just feelin' shitey and needin' something to get me through my punters.'

'I've always got plenty of good shit for my favourite tart, you know that, Maggie, but I'm needin' a wee relaxer back in turn,' said Fox, dropping his eyes down in the direction of his groin. 'Why don't you climb into the back of the van, shut the door, and we can take a wee turn roon the back o' the Broomy Tavern.'

Maggie smiled her gumsy, decayed grin but couldn't stop herself letting out a sigh of resignation – she knew what must come next if she wanted her smack.

CHAPTER 6

Fox lay on his back, groaning his pleasure, as Maggie paid for her habit.

Maggie's part of the bargain complete, the ice cream man grunted his satisfaction and zipped up his denims before articulating his gratitude in time-honoured tradition: 'The score bags are in the left-hand box. Thanks tae the six diggies you've given us, plus my little treat, we'll call it four score bags in return. That should get you well away wi' it and help you rattle through yer turns the night, doll.' Fox savoured the power he had over the whore and the pleasure she had just given him, however much she repulsed him.

Maggie wiped her face clean with several sheets of the toilet roll that Fox kept for just such encounters. Ignoring his words, she made no reply, such was her hunger for the contents of the cellophane wraps she was busy fingering out of the plastic container just underneath the vanilla ice cream, stuffing them inside the outsize, silky baseball jacket she wore.

'Aye, this'll do nice,' she rasped, clambering up from her knees while Fox grasped for the top of the service bunker as he attempted to pull himself up off his arse. As he did so a loud crack rang out and the ice cream van's rear door smashed open, rebounding off the service counter and sending Fox back onto his derrière.

In the doorway stood a stocky figure, his head sheathed inside a black balaclava, the rest of his clothing similarly dark. The visitor took one step forward and grabbed Maggie by her mop of brown hair. 'Out whore,' he spat, hurling the prostitute out the door with enough force to leave a clump of the tart's hair in his hand and the air filled with her tortured shrieks.

Fox stretched into the bottom of the van cabin and desperately tried to grasp the bottom of the pickaxe handle, but as he did so a booted foot slammed onto his wrist.

'Bastard,' yelped Fox in agony.

'Shut the fuck up,' said balaclava, hunkering down just above Fox and clasping his hand around the ice cream man's throat, slamming his head into the cold linoleum of the van floor.

'How many warnings do you Fenian scum need to stop encroaching? You're way off your beat and you know it, Fox. Now you're gonnae pay,' said the male, with a rotten, crooked smile.

'I dunno whit yer on aboot, pal, I'm just paid to drive a van and sell the ices, like.'

Another voice filled the vehicle and compounded the growing sense of doom that Fox could feel welling up inside of him.

'Listen to me, shit for brains,' said a second, similarly disguised figure, sticking his head through the service hatch. 'We've been watchin' you for the past half hour and we reckon you've supplied shit to three junkies from the Red Road Flats. And then we followed you round here while your smackhead tart performed a wee trick on you in the back o' the wagon. I'll bet you let her off wi' a tidy wee discount for her services and I'll bet your life that old man McGuigan doesnae know jack shit about her payment in kind, does he, bawbag?'

Realising the pointlessness of a reply and the desperation of his plight Fox stayed silent, though his breathing was coming in increasingly short, sharp pants as concern over his own fate mounted. The nicotine-laced breath of the man pinning him to the floor poured over him.

Then the male who had been at the hatchway came through the rear door and, while balaclava number one grabbed hold of Fox's wrists, produced a hammer and nails.

The lack of space in the service area, which was lucky if it was four foot by two, made the drama that was about to be played out in it a farce, although for Johnny the Fox its ending would be a tragedy.

'What are yous gonnae do with me? Look, help yourselves to the cash in the till. For Chrissakes, all I do is drive an ice cream van for the McGuigans and try and skim a wee bit extra to make a better life for my missus and weans. Your beef isnae wi' Johnny Fox, it's wi auld man McGuigan and his boy Gerry, for fuck's sake whit are yous gonnae dae?' asked Fox, almost beside himself with fear.

The second male spotted the plastic containers under the service hatch and then the knock-off digital radios that had been nicked from half a dozen motors by Maggie's clients and bartered by the prostitute moments earlier for her heroin supply.

Tipping the contents of the carton over Fox, balaclava number two rapped, 'Hold him tight and let's get the job done.'

The first male nodded and rammed Fox back into the linoleum flooring, his head now halfway into the driver's cabin.

Fox felt a sharp prick in the palm of his left hand and just as he looked up he saw that the second male was swinging the hammer down towards his palm.

Fox shrieked as a surge of pain shot through his paw and up his arm, confirming his worst fears. He looked down and stared in tortured disbelief that his hand had indeed been nailed to the van floor. He felt another sharp sting in his right palm and in dread looked up to see the hammer fall again.

There was more agony ahead and Fox was duly relieved of his Adidas Zamba trainers and white terry towelling socks as the process was repeated on his feet, leaving him crucified to the floor of his van.

Lying prone on his back, the van floor filling with pools of his own blood, Fox screamed. 'What the fuck are yous gonnae dae wi' me? In the name of the wee man just let me go.'

'Sorry, no can do, Johnny the Fox,' smiled the one with the nicotine breath. 'We need you to send a message to your bosses.'

A glimmer of relief spread across Fox's pain-wracked features. 'Just tell me what it is and I'll make sure Francis McGuigan himself gets it inside the half oor.'

But the masked male was no longer looking at Fox, who watched in horror as he sidled past the hulking figure of his confederate, who now stood over him with a spade.

'Break 'em,' he said, and the second male duly started to smash the spade down with cruel precision, first targeting Fox's hands and then going to work with a manic glee on his feet and shins as Fox's screams filled the van and echoed out far beyond it.

The smaller of Fox's two assailants stuck a fag in the mouth-hole cut in his balaclava, lit it, and took a long, lazy drag. Then he leant down and waited for Fox to stop screaming. As the ice cream man's desperation for one final crumb of hope stifled his terror, he whispered into his ear – 'Go to hell' – and smashed his right hand into the Fox's face.

'Time tae get tae,' said balaclava number two, and with that the pair jumped out of the van, leaving Johnny Fox broken, unconscious and bleeding out, nailed to the floor of his ice cream van.

CHAPTER 7

The last of the green, yellow and white ice cream vans had pulled into the depot building over an hour ago and the shutters had been firmly pulled down and locked, checked and double-checked by the building's security. News of the mishap that had befallen Johnny Fox had made its way around the McGuigan clan and their associates and left them jumpy about the safety of their prized fleet of wagons.

It was 3 a.m. in the middle of a moonless night. Two men sat inside an orange Morris Ital and watched the security guard continue on his rounds after once again checking that the former Scout hall was secure.

A fag dangling from the mouth of his balaclava, the smaller of the two males turned to his similarly masked associate. 'Wait till the light in the depot office goes back on and then we know that Mr Security Guard has got the kettle on, his feet up on the desk and is leching over page three, then we can hit him and get the turn done.'

'Sounds good to me, pal. If this doesn't help the McGuigans get the message that it's time to chuck it then nothing will. Christ, I wonder how Johnny the Fox is doin'? It'll be long and weary before he's up and walking.'

'Be even fuckin' longer before he's doin' anyone a 99!' retorted his pal and the Morris Ital rocked with laughter.

Jackie Deans sipped his tea and grinned with the satisfaction of a brew well made. The three sugars helped give him the extra energy to get through the night shift – he always found that halfway through his tour he badly needed the boost. He savoured the cup of Sailor's Tea, as he liked to call it in memory of his da, who had first made it for him as a wean and had served with the Merchant Navy running the Artic convoys during World War II.

As he took another gulp, Jackie started to dissect the day's events. He had been with the McGuigans long enough to know when a turf war was about to erupt. The signs were clear that the bastard they called Mojito was here to stay and was hell-bent on doing everything he could to take control of the drug-dealing empire that Francis and Gerry McGuigan had built into such a profitable enterprise. What his men had done to Johnny Fox was only the first step.

But, as Jackie knew full well, what had happened to Johnny would bring retribution from the McGuigans, and the hostility would escalate into a lethal tit-for-tat feud until only one of the two factions were left standing.

Jackie couldn't help himself putting his thoughts into words: 'Aye, Mojito, you wait and see what's comin' yer way from Francis McGuigan and ye'll wish you was never born. Bastard.' He spat onto the stone office floor in a reflex action of anger.

He dipped a ginger nut into the strong, tarry tea, waiting for a moment until it got soggy and then enjoying the sensation as the ginger nut dissolved in his gob. Grabbing hold of a copy of *The Sun* Jackie swung his feet onto the desk. 'Ooh aye, Sam, you've still got it darlin',' he said, savouring the curvaceous figure of Sam Fox, his favourite page three pin-up, but his moment of appreciation was spoiled by the ringing of the security office phone.

Jackie picked it up, knowing who it would be before a word was spoken from the other end.

'Awright, Jackie boy, how's everything? Have you checked the outside of the building and made sure the shutters are nailed down and locked tight? You didnae come across anything suspicious while you was doin' yer rounds outside?' asked Gerry McGuigan from down the line.

'Aye, Gerry, dinnae fret. It's all sorted. It would take an army tae get in here and the bastardin' British Army are up tae their eyes in it over in the Province, last I heard,' said Jackie, but McGuigan Junior was still not satisfied.

'Look, Jackie, I know you've got it all in hand but I've sent big Duncy Parkinson out to join you, just in case. He should be with you inside the half hour.'

Jackie tried not to let his irritation show at the slight he felt had been inferred by McGuigan's decision to send back-up and the suggestion that went with it that he couldn't take care of things at the depot like he'd always done. But he knew an argument would get him nowhere but on Gerry's wrong side so changed the subject. 'More to the point, Gerry, how is Johnny the Fox?'

'A right fuckin' mess and not likely to be up to much for fuck knows how long. Whoever did him knew what they wiz doin' and knew how to do it well. Two smashed paws, a fractured shin and a foot that's been turned into pulp by the sharp end of something nasty. The fuckin' rozzers have been no good either. I mean, no one saw a fuckin' thing in the middle of the day outside the Broomy Tavern? But then the cops are gonnae do fuck all to help us, aren't they. Nope, it's the work of Mojito and for it the fucker will pay a high price, I just have to decide what that price will be...'

Gerry McGuigan was interrupted in mid-flow by events at Jackie's end of the blower.

'What the fuck?' shouted Jackie, the alarm and fear in his voice cascading down the line before there was a click and the phone went dead.

In the depot security office Jackie's head was pulled back tight by a burly arm around his throat. A second man stepped in front of him, his lifeless grey eyes staring out from the holes in his balaclava.

'So what happens next, do you think, arsehole?' asked the man who had him in a chokehold.

Such was the pressure around his throat that Jackie could hardly find the breath to speak. 'I dunno, but whatever yous have got planned you better get a fuckin' move on cos the cavalry are comin' for you bastards,' spat Jackie as defiantly as he could, receiving a vicious backhanded slap from a gloved fist for his trouble.

'Tie him to the chair,' said the male in front of him and Jackie duly felt his arms being pinioned to his seat. His tormentor thumped a heavy jerry can down on the desk.

'Do you think we give a fuck whose comin' over the hill, you piece of shite? General Custer and the 7th fuckin' Cavalry could be riding to your rescue but it would still make fuck all difference,' said the man, stuffing a rag into Jackie's mouth.

He turned his back on his hostage and made his way over to the fleet of ice cream vans, parked about fifty yards away. There were twenty-five vans in total, parked in neat rows of five from the middle of the depot to the rear. Jackie watched with dread as he produced a jemmy and forced the fuel cap from the first vehicle, inserting a rag that had been soaked in whatever flammable liquid was inside the jerry can.

The first male was ably assisted by his bigger, more powerful partner, who had joined him after making sure that Jackie was bound to his chair both by his arms and legs. The process was repeated over and over again until each one of the McGuigans' vans had a doused rag inserted into the mouth of its fuel tank.

Jackie watched in helpless rage as the smaller of the two men lit the fag that was dangling from his mouth, took a draw and gave him a gleeful wave from the other end of the depot before applying the lit cigarette to the rag hanging out of the nearest vehicle's fuel tank. He gave a thumbs up to his number two, who held his lighter to the first van in the third row of parked vehicles.

The security guard felt a new feeling wash over him. For Jackie Deans knew that his hopes of escaping from this building were non-existent.

CHAPTER 8

Parkinson tapped the steering wheel of his black Ford Capri 2.8 Injection in time to the beat of Iron Maiden's epic guitar masterpiece 'Phantom of the Opera' as he anticipated the steaming mug of Sailor's Tea sure to be waiting for him at the depot.

'Aye, old Jackie makes a decent cuppa, I'll gie him that,' said the McGuigans' trusted lieutenant to himself. As Dave Murray's guitar work filled his motor with searing riffs, he turned the leather steering wheel of his powerful vehicle into Lennoxmill Street and felt the back end squirm slightly, the Capri's trademark wriggle on the wet surface.

Hooking up with Jackie would also give Parkinson the chance to talk over the day's events and the retribution Gerry McGuigan had planned for Dawson and his cohorts following their savage beating of Johnny the Fox who, it now transpired, was likely to lose his left foot. But Parkinson's mind was suddenly snapped back to the present as he clapped eyes on the huge orange glow that was lighting up the sky above the McGuigans' depot.

'Jesus H Christ,' said Parkinson out loud in shock. 'Bastards have only gone and torched the depot. Aw naw, Jackie boy...' He rammed his foot to the floor, accelerating the Capri forward at full pelt until he slammed on the anchors fifty yards from the front door.

Jumping out of his vehicle, he sprinted to the giant steel depot doors only to find the side entry next to the shuttered entrance locked.

'Jackie, you in there?' he shouted at the top of his voice as he became aware of the smoke that was starting to billow out from under the shutters. Then the whole building seemed to shake as an explosion erupted and was immediately followed by another.

'They're blowin' the vans,' shouted Parkinson into the night air as he started to boot the side door with all the force he could muster.

At the third attempt it splintered around the Yale lock and Parkinson rammed a huge shoulder into the door for good measure, relieved to hear it crack and then give way. He was in.

Looking over to his left at the small security office that also doubled as a reception, he saw Jackie Deans, his head slumped above the tartan donkey jacket that was like a second skin to him. Parkinson put his forearm up to his head to shield himself from the intensity of the blaze and billowing black smoke that was emanating from the exploded vans.

Another bang filled the air and, as Parkinson tried to take in the details of a picture he could barely comprehend, he noticed that the remaining vans had rags stuffed into their fuel tanks. It immediately dawned on Parkinson what that meant. He knew that he had precious little time to get Jackie out before the whole building blew around them.

He sprinted over to the guard and ripped away the piece of cloth that had been tied around his mouth, jolting him back into consciousness. Jackie started to splutter, his nostrils already stained black with the soot of the thick, poisonous fumes that were curling around them.

Parkinson quickly got to work untying Jackie hands from the rear of the chair. 'Who did it, Jackie boy? Did you get a butcher's?'

'Not a scooby,' spat Jackie before dissolving into another fit of coughing. 'They wiz masked up, but I reckon they were pros, knew exactly what they wiz about, Duncy.'

Parkinson set Jackie's feet free from the bottom of the chair and helped him to a standing position just as an almighty explosion ripped through the air as another of the vans caught alight. Deadly steel fragments hurtled through the depot in their direction.

'Hit the deck, Jackie,' shouted Parkinson and hauled the older man down with him onto the cold concrete floor.

Parkinson looked up to see a huge burning timber detach from the depot roof and smash through the top of one of the vans as the inferno started to rip through the building at a frightening pace. He knew that their window of escape was closing fast; he rolled over and shouted to Jackie, only to be met with silence.

Crawling back to his mate, Parkinson turned Jackie Deans over and saw with horror that a huge metallic splinter had harpooned the older man straight through the heart.

Parkinson howled into the night as a mixture of grief and rage enveloped him.

CHAPTER 9

Billy Davidson sat in the kitchen at the back of Lennox Hill Office and cursed as he lost another hand of poker to an increasingly gleeful Brian Jones. 'You fuckin on the pockle again, Jonesy?'

'What? In the back of Lennox Hill Office for a quid a hand, against two of my most valued colleagues? You cannot be serious,' replied the burly Jones before slamming his cards down on the splintered kitchen table and erupting into peals of laughter.

'I don't know how you do it, Jonesy, every time you look like yer busted, you pop up with a winning hand. There's no wonder that Pug over there prefers to study the *Daily Telegraph* rather than get fleeced by the likes of you, ye giant wassuck,' said Jimmy Sykes, who had been sent down from Divisional HQ to help maintain the four-man shift at Lennox Hill Office.

Behind his paper, Thoroughgood initially said nothing before his mounting frustration at the slow start to the night shift got the better of him and he dropped the sports pages onto his knees. 'Just wondering if we'll be taking a turn out anytime soon, gents?'

The words were barely out of his mouth before Davidson fired back a stinging rebuke. 'I don't remember any one of your senior constables giving you permission to speak, Thoroughgood, never mind question what your superiors are up to. The reality of your position, Probationer Pug, is that you can't walk the beat without one of us holdin' your hand, so you can tuck that petted lip away before I come over there and burst it wide open wi' my right mitt. Or better still, why don't I come over there and teach you how to wipe yer arse with that fuckin' bleedin' *Daily Torygraph* you've

33

always got yer ponsy little mug in... What would you prefer, uni boy?'

Thoroughgood's self-control was fraying dangerously at the seams, but with three sets of eyes scrutinising his every twitch, as the senior cops waited for the probationer to go into meltdown, he sucked in a deep breath and tried to compose himself before he replied. 'I'll take a turn at the bar and let you finish your hand and your piece breaks. The PR rack could do with a clean, so I guess now is as good a time as any.'

'Now that's more like it,' said Sykes. 'Know your place in this man's army, boy, and you might just make it through your probation. Respect is everything when you're a rookie, even for a fast-track graduate on accelerated promotion.'

'You're right, Constable Sykes, but for the record, again, I'm not on the AP scheme and nor did I ever apply to be on it. Enjoy your game, gents.' And with that, Thoroughgood pushed the swivel doors that led out of the kitchen and headed into the corridor that linked the building to the public bar and, teeth gritted, made his exit.

Two hours later, with the bar clock striking 5 a.m., Thoroughgood's anger and frustration were starting to get the better of him. 'What the fuck am I doing here?' he demanded of the chipped and cracked wooden front doors of Lennox Hill Police station.

From his left he heard the squeak of a footstep on the blue linoleum floor. Jimmy Sykes appeared, smiling thinly at the probationer. 'Life is just one big drag for a graduate of Glasgow university who's now having to slum it with the rank and file of Her Majesty's Police Service, is it no', Pug?'

Thoroughgood attempted to cover his anger as best he could. 'Just getting a bit stir-crazy, Sykesy.'

'Sykesy? Who gave you permission to call me that? You, a snotty-nosed probationer who thinks that a piece of paper from a brats' finishing school entitles him to familiarity with a group of men who put their lives on the line when you were still a twinkle in yer daddy's eye,' spat Sykes, his brown eyes bulging through his square, silver-rimmed spectacles.

'Sorry, Constable Sykes, it won't happen again,' said Thoroughgood, trying to play the straight bat.

'You're fuckin' right it won't, son. But in any case, it's time you hitched a ride out with me in Panda Bravo. I know it's been a slow night with barely any calls coming out over the PR from Division or AS or, for that matter, from Force HQ, but you never know – we might pick ourselves up a wee drunken breach or catch someone lurkin' where he shouldn't be and land us a Section 57. And then you'll have something worthwhile to mark up in that probationer's workbook of yours. What do you say, Thoroughgood?'

Surprised as he was, the rookie couldn't help his enthusiasm for some real coppering from showing through. 'That would be brilliant. Sykesy – er, sorry, Constable Sykes. I'll get my hat.'

'You do that, son, and old Sykesy, as you like to call me, will be outside in the jam sandwich waiting for you. Then we can get to know each other that bit better. You never know, maybe we have more in common than you think, young Thoroughgood.'

The probationer broke into a jog as he surged out of the bar, along the corridor and into the kitchen, where he grabbed his hat from a clothes hook inside the swing doors.

'There he is – Strathclyde Police's new secret weapon, Angus bleedin' Thoroughgood, the answer to all our fuckin' problems,' said Davidson, barely looking up from his hand of cards, a small glass of clear liquid next to his left elbow.

Across the opposite side of the table, Brian Jones attempted a semblance of some civility. 'Yer as well going oot wi' Sykesy and takin' a wee turn round the Hill, it's just one o' those nights that's as dead as a dodo. Sykesy has a good nose on him and he's sniffed out plenty of neds on the prowl just when you least, or where you least, for that matter, expect it, so you never know what you might turn up.'

'Yeah, hope so,' replied Thoroughgood, his eyes glinting with hunger for a bit of meaningful police work.

'Well, once you've done all that and dropped the sergeant's

package off at HQ, I'd imagine you'll get an early shoot. I'll give the gaffer a call in half an hour or so and say we've no problem with that,' said Jones, smiling benignly.

'Good stuff, that would be brilliant, Jonesy,' replied Thoroughgood before he could stop himself once again repeating the cardinal mistake of overfamiliarity.

Before he could recover himself, Davidson scraped his chair back over the kitchen floor and slammed it into the sink behind him. Within seconds the senior cop had grabbed Thoroughgood by his shirt and rammed him up against a kitchen wall.

'Who the fuck gave you permission to get familiar with your senior man? Listen to me good, you snotty-nosed probationer fuck. You're no' one of us and no way will you ever be one of us, so don't even try and get all cosy by using our chosen names. No-fuckin'-body on the shift wants you here and the sooner you realise that and get tae fuck the better we will all be.' For a moment Davidson's pulsing grey eyes held Thoroughgood's emerald gaze, but as the seconds drew on the rookie was determined he was not going to look away.

With a mixture of nicotine and something more toxic seeping over him from Davidson's stinking breath, through his rotten teeth, the probationer finally snapped.

Thoroughgood grabbed the senior cop's balls with his right hand and squeezed as strongly as he could. A look of shock and total surprise at the temerity of the rookie's actions swept over Davidson's face. His eyes looked like they were about to pop out his head and Thoroughgood noticed a vein running down the side of his neck starting to pulse through the skin.

The agonised Davidson let out a deep scream of pain.

'Fuck you,' spat Thoroughgood and rammed the senior cop back, still gripping his testicles tight with his right hand but bringing his left elbow up and pressing it against Davidson's windpipe to ensure that he was no longer vulnerable to the headbutt that was a speciality manoeuvre of the army veteran's.

Picking up momentum, Thoroughgood increased his pressure and Davidson toppled back and onto the kitchen table. As the senior cop landed, his cards and the glass of clear liquid flew into the air, along with the other glasses and cards that had previously belonged to Jones and Sykes. The table tipped up at the opposite side as the moment seemed to stretch on, almost in slow motion. Jones did his best to vault clear of the developing rammy.

Releasing his grip on the now prostrate Davidson's testicles, Thoroughgood pulled his right hand back, balled his fist and prepared to slam it down into the senior cop's jaw with everything he had in the punch, but as he cocked his right mitt he felt his arm grabbed from behind.

'Oh no you don't, sonny boy,' rapped Sykes, holding Thoroughgood back.

Breathing heavily, Davidson cupped his testicles tenderly with both hands, wincing as trickles of moisture ran down his cheeks. He tried to regain his feet as he saw his tormentor now left completely vulnerable to a counter-attack.

'Big fuckin' mistake, Thoroughgood, and now you're gonnae pay for it,' he snapped gulping in a huge gasp of air. 'Jonesy, unlock the back door and we'll finish this in the back yard. You want to be part of the shift, you sponging student bastard? Now is the time to prove you belong in it. Get the fuck outside for a square go, Thoroughgood. Now.'

Jones took a step towards the kitchen back door and planted his feet squarely, crossing his arms across his chest. To Thoroughgood's amazement, he said, 'No way, Billy boy, this isn't the way.'

Davidson looked like he was about to blow a gasket and once more his eyes seemed to strain against their sockets with a determination to burst out of his face.

'What you mean, Jonesy? There's no way I'm gonnae take that off a fuckin' rookie and especially no' a grass. Get the fuckin' key in the lock, open the door and let me gie that piece of student shit the bleachin' he has been needin' ever since he joined this fuckin' shift,' ranted Davidson, spittle firing out his mouth as the last semblance of his self-control threatened to go into meltdown.

But Jones's eyes had lifted beyond his fellow senior cop's and towards the front of the kitchen where Sykes continued to restrain Thoroughgood.

'What the fuck is goin' on? I'm sittin' out there in the panda like a feckin' lemon left twiddling my thumbs and meanwhile all hell is breaking loose back here.'

Jones provided the explanation. 'Just a small misunderstanding over the card table. Now, Sykesy, if you would be so good as to take the boy out on patrol with you then myself and Davidson here will tidy up the mess, won't we, Billy boy?' Jones took a step towards his fellow senior cop before clamping his two huge mitts on either one of Davidson's shoulders, whispering, 'Get a grip, Billy,' in his ear.

Davidson let out a grunt of affirmation, but turned towards Thoroughgood. 'Don't think this is finished, Thoroughgood, I'm marking your card right here, right now, in front of witnesses – you've got the mother of all beatings comin' yer way. No one grabs Billy Davidson's baws and gets away with it.'

'I'll be waitin' for you, you fat little fuck. Ex-Para? My fuckin' arse. If you can't see a schoolboy move like that one coming your way then I don't think I've got much to be scared of. You're all fuckin' talk, Davidson, and remember I know exactly where you keep your little insurance policy. There's people in this job know exactly what you're all about, Billy Davidson, and someday soon you're going to get exactly what you deserve. I just hope I'm there to see it.'

But as soon as the words escaped his mouth Thoroughgood knew that he had said way too much. The startled look that was shared between Jones and Davidson proved that their mental alarm bells were now ringing, but neither said a word. Instead, Thoroughgood felt Sykes's grip on him relaxing and he was given a soothing pat on the shoulder by the old cop.

'Look, son, you're always going to get flash points when you're in the job. It goes with the territory. Why don't we get going and let the dust settle a bit. No harm done – just a routine bust up between two colleagues letting off a bit of steam,' soothed Sykes.

'Aye, Sykesy is right, boys. Now why don't you both shake on it, put it behind you and then we can all move on. Remember, lads, there might come a day when one of you two is all that's between the other one and a right good kickin',' said Jones, playing the peacemaker.

'Jonesy's right,' said Sykes. 'Come on, Billy, you've been dishing it out to the boy since he got here, it's no surprise he snapped. Time you gave him your hand, after all, at least he's shown some balls – pardon the pun!'

The room was filled with Jones's booming laughter. After a brief hesitation, Davidson extended his right hand. Searching the senior cop's features, Thoroughgood knew that this was not the end of the matter by a long chalk. The worry that he had said too much about his suspicions about Davidson gnawed at the rookie.

At last Thoroughgood gripped Davidson's hand and squeezed with every ounce of strength he possessed in him. Davidson immediately pulled the probationer towards him until the two men were locked face to face, and as a stony silence drew on, he hissed, 'You're a dead man, Thoroughgood.'

Then both cops were pulled away from each other by Jones and Sykes, like two seconds hauling their prize fighters off just before the first bell sounds out.

Moments later Thoroughgood was sitting in the passenger seat of the marked police car and staring out through the front window.

'Look, Thoroughgood, you've picked the wrong man to fall out with in Billy Davidson and I don't think you need me to tell you that,' said Sykes.

The rookie looked at Sykes, who had a Benson & Hedges dangling from his mouth and was puffing out of the open driver's window. Thoroughgood had long since realised to his amusement that every senior cop he seemed to work with had a thirty-a-day habit and their reliance on nicotine meant the driver's window was always wound down, as their fags gave them a vital buffer against the stress of 'the job'.

'You think I don't know that? What option did I have? You

39

can only let someone intimidate you so far and Billy Davidson, ex-Para or not, is a fuckin' bully. Did you know he pulled a switchblade on me when I was out with him under the gas works?' asked Thoroughgood.

The way that Sykes's eyebrows shot up showed that he hadn't, and as he almost choked on the draw of his cigarette, Thoroughgood did not feel the need to wait for a reply.

'The man is a borderline psychopath with a serious drink problem, yet he seems to be untouchable. Why is that, Constable Sykes?'

'Look, when it's just the two of us feel free to call me Sykesy,' said the senior cop. 'And the answer is simple. A fair percentage of the shift are ex-army, me included. They have that whole band-of-brothers thing that comes with having been under fire in life-and-death situations together. So you can't be surprised that they're as tight as can be and distrustful of newcomers, especially ones that come from your background,' explained Sykes, taking another drag of his cigarette and blowing the smoke out of the window. 'But I've got a question for you, Thoroughgood. What the fuck did you mean when you said, "There's people in this job who know exactly what you're all about, Billy Davidson"?'

Thoroughgood cleared his throat nervously as he tried to give himself time to compose a believable answer. 'That was nothing but bullshit. Come on, you know that the way Davidson goes about his business is not exactly a secret and that Jimmy Rentoul lets him enjoy a long leash. Between him and big Jonesy they have Lennox Hill croaking under their Doc Martens.'

'You sure about that, Thoroughgood? Because I'll tell you something for nothing – Davidson, Jones and everyone else on this bleedin' shift think you're a plant for the brass and a remark like that will have been taken as confirmation that they were right all along about you.' He turned his pockmarked face back to Thoroughgood and shook his head. 'If you ask me, boy, you've just made your life a hell of a lot harder and the bottom line is, if I was you, I would be looking to find myself a new job and a way out as soon as I feckin' could, son, cos that target on your back just got a hundred times bleedin' bigger.'

'You think I don't know that,' snapped Thoroughgood and banged his forehead against the passenger window.

CHAPTER 10

Thoroughgood opened the door to his flat and headed straight for his Sony music system. He needed some musical accompaniment to help him absorb the events of the day. Christ, he needed a drink.

Selecting Tears for Fears from the cardboard Bell's Whisky box that housed his vinyl collection, he gently placed the album onto the turntable and let the needle hit the groove.

Unclipping his black polyester police tie he let the air percolate down the inside of his shirt, ripped off his Harrington jacket and threw it over the back of the faded brown settee.

Moments later, with his Doc Martens parked on top of the glass coffee table at the centre of the lounge-cum-dining-room, Thoroughgood, his eyes shut, gulped from a can of Oranjeboom and let the magical words and music of Messrs Roland Orzabal and Curt Smith fill the air.

He mimed the clever lyrics of 'The Prisoner' and couldn't help the thought occurring to him that was exactly what he was. 'What a fuckin' mess,' he shouted at the wall, and its hideous orange wallpaper.

Ruffling his left hand through his mullet of black hair he stared out of the room's only window but failed to see a thing, wondering what he should do next. He had just about had enough. Was it time to put his application for a teacher training course at Jordanhill College in the post? It would open up an escape route from the mad world he had entered, which was ironically the song now booming from his speakers.

Looking around the rented studio flat, with its three-quarter partition wall separating his bedroom from the lounge area and the tiny kitchen, he shook his head and felt tears well up in his eyes. Where had it all gone wrong? It didn't seem that long ago that he'd graduated from the University of Glasgow with his MA Honours in History, feeling like he had the world at his feet. Now he couldn't even afford accommodation with a proper bedroom.

Crown Gardens may be one of the most sought-after addresses in the west end, but what was the point in paying over the odds for a postcode when the accommodation attached to it was so pathetic, Thoroughgood wondered, before trying to force his brain to concentrate on the matter in hand.

Anger surged through his mind as he recalled how he had turned down a place on the graduate fast-track induction scheme with Merseyside Police after a two-day stint with them had revealed just what kind of mayhem young academics, promoted without any real police experience to senior positions, could create.

It had been after his spell on the Mersey that Thoroughgood had elected to start at the bottom with Strathclyde. For that, he had been ostracised by a shift who were determined to humiliate him, break him and make the point that Zulu Land was no place for a graduate who was little more than 'a grass for the brass'.

But while he could cope with that, it was the uncovering of the rotten core at the centre of the shift that was leaving Thoroughgood with the feeling that he had bitten off more than he could chew. The voice inside his head was telling him it was time to chuck it all in and become a teacher instead.

Removing a Café Crème from its tin, he opened the lounge window, clicked the lighter and lit the small cigar, before inhaling and blowing the smoke out into the back garden.

Schoolteacher, bank clerk, candlestick-maker... What was he going to do with the rest of his life? If he quit the police now, they'd have won and he might as well be everything Davidson said he was.

His wallowing was interrupted by a sharp rap on the door and the shouting of a heavily accented European voice. 'Mr Thoroughgood, I have brought your cereal.'

'Fuck,' cursed Thoroughgood, taking a last drag on the Café Crème, blowing the smoke out the window and flicking the remains of the miniature cigar in the same direction. He grabbed the air freshener from the kitchen and sprayed it around the lounge, wafting it with both hands, like a madman convinced he could fly, to try and mask the rich cigar aroma.

The voice belonged to Bill Kaye, his septuagenarian Lithuanian landlord, who supplied his tenants with cereal as part of some tax-dodging scam that Thoroughgood couldn't be bothered to take the time to work out. He liked the old boy but the one thing Kaye abhorred was anyone smoking in the nine flats within the three-story building he had purchased back in the sixties for a song that he never stopped singing about.

Thoroughgood opened the door and smiled wanly. 'How are you, Mr Kaye? What's on the breakfast menu for tomorrow?'

'My dear Angus, cornflakes will be good for you, yes?' asked Kaye. He may have been in his seventies but he still cut an imposing figure that hinted at a military career somewhere in the dim and distant past, and one which Thoroughgood had no doubt he would be regaled with soon enough.

Despite his hair thinning on top the landlord still opted to tint his receding locks a dark brown, that, combined with his thick horn-rimmed spectacles, gave him a slightly incongruous appearance, but one that masked a warm sense of humour that mixed well with the homespun philosophy 'Old Bill', as the landlord liked to refer to himself, loved to deliver to his youthful lodger.

'Breakfast is most important meal of the day, young man. It sets you up for the rest of the day. I made sure every day before I went on shift at the Rogano, I enjoyed a good, how you say, ah, hearty, that's it, breakfast, to keep my strength up. You know being maître d' at the Rogano was very demanding but it also had its rewards as you see from this fine building that is all property of Old Bill Kaye.'

Here we go, thought Thoroughgood, another reading from the life according to Old Bill. But Kaye surprised Thoroughgood by changing tack and, pulling his horn-rimmed specs off, he jabbed them in Thoroughgood's direction.

'What is wrong, Angus? There is saying that problem shared is problem solved. I can see you have the weight of many problems on your shoulders. For young man that is not good.'

Kaye brushed past Thoroughgood and entered the flat, tilting his nose up in the air and sniffing in an exaggerated fashion. 'Still enjoying Café Crème, Angus?'

'How do you know they're Café Crèmes?' asked Thoroughgood resignedly.

'Because, my dear Angus, it is Old Bill Kaye who has to clear them off the back lawn you flick them out on every time I drop in,' said the landlord, and laughed long and loud. 'Now sit down, boy, and tell me your problems and I will see what I can do to help you.'

Before Thoroughgood could move, Kaye whipped out a packet of King Edward Invincible cigars and with a wide yellow grin he laughed once again. 'You will be joining me, yes?'

Thoroughgood didn't know whether to laugh or cry, but feeling a sense of relief at the prospect of unburdening himself, he sat down and did as he was bid.

Kaye pointed at the hi-fi and raised an eyebrow. Taking the hint, Thoroughgood turned off the music. As he parked himself in the fraying easy chair opposite Kaye, he found a clipped King Edward being tossed through the air to him. He caught the cigar neatly in his right hand and watched, amazed, as the landlord puffed furiously on his own Invincible. At last satisfied that it had caught alight, Kaye leant back in his chair and took a long draw. 'It surprise you that I like King Ted, Angus?' he asked from behind a smoke-wreathed grin.

Thoroughgood couldn't help himself. 'You can say that again,' he replied and they both burst into laughter.

Kaye pointed his cigar Thoroughgood's way and said, 'You know, Angus, you and I are not too different. I was once, and you are now, a stranger in a stranger's land, where you feel no one loves you and everyone wants to stick the knife in your back, am I right?'

Thoroughgood spluttered on the cigar he was attempting to

inhale but was now choking on, such was his surprise at Kaye's perception of his unhappy position.

'Do not worry, Angus, I am not here to tell you that God will save you. You are, I think, just as I was, a loner, and when you are a loner nothing is easy. But that is when you must believe in yourself above all else.'

Gobsmacked by the sudden unforeseen direction Kaye was now guiding the conversation in, Thoroughgood attempted to regain his composure and admitted the truth. 'You're right. I should be studying private archives in France on the Hundred Years' War, not being surrounded by a pack of wolves claiming to be police officers who're worse than the people they are supposed to be protecting the public from. I don't know what I'm doing, why I'm doing it and what the fucking point is in it.'

Kaye pushed his horn-rims back onto the bridge of his nose and sniffed. 'In life, my young friend, I have always found there are two choices, the one you make for yourself or the one that others force upon you. But remember, no matter how bad it is for you, the choice is still yours to make.'

A frown crept across Thoroughgood's pale features and he shook his head in resignation before finally replying. 'The shift I've been attached to are rotten to the core, corrupt, and most of them seem to be ex-army. They all think I'm a "grass for the brass". I've already had a senior cop pull a knife on me and I'm thinking it's time I found something else.'

Kaye smiled mischievously. 'Ah, the application for teacher training post, no?' He pointed his cigar towards the dining table. 'Yes, I did see it on way in. So you can run Angus, but is that the right choice? Because it is not the only one.'

Thoroughgood felt his teeth grit but as they did so he felt a new resolve radiate through his being. 'No, it is not the only choice and… you're right, nor would it be the right one. Thank you, Mr Kaye,' he said, puffing out cigar smoke from a mouth that now broke into a smile.

CHAPTER 11

The chimes of the ice cream van rang out their call to business as the vehicle crawled along the street, waiting for customers to emerge from their tenements.

As the black wrought-iron gates of the Botanic Gardens came into sight at the bottom of Queen Margaret Drive, Frankie guided the converted Ford Transit, with its brilliant gold roof and immaculate sky-blue bodywork emblazoned with the words 'Mojito's Ices', into its resting point at the kerb.

It was his ship and he was the skipper sailing the old girl into port – and in every port Frankie had a girl waiting for him, from Lennox Hill, Springburn and Royston, where the feminine charms were of a more abrasive nature but ultimately no less rewarding, to the more refined welcome of the ladies of the west end, where he'd had a recent, memorable success with a fresher female English lit student.

The great thing about working for Bobby 'Mojito' Dawson was that the sounds of his vans playing their chimes to the tune of 'When the Saints Go Marching In,' were not just confined to shitty schemes in the city's drug-ridden no man's lands, where most of the custom for the illicit delights concealed under the service counter could be found.

The other big advantage of his employment arrangement was that Frankie was Dawson's younger brother and that was something that had all types of advantages.

Frankie had sold out his entire supply of tenner bags of heroin and done so without any sign of the attempts at sabotage and petty intimidation that had seen two of Mojito's vans have their windows smashed and one incinerated by a petrol bomb. The younger Dawson smiled to himself, safe in the knowledge that the carnage his elder brother had wreaked in the last forty-eight hours would have made sure that the McGuigans had gotten the message once and for all.

'Amateurs are probably still brickin' it. Aye, they'll think twice about messing with Mojito,' muttered Frankie to himself, smiling into his mirror. He knew that he would be well rewarded by his 'boss' when he returned to the depot, less than a mile away in Maryhill, with two grand in his safe box.

The only thing gnawing away at Frankie was the incident with the cop the other night. The arrangement they had with the rozzers in Lennox Hill had proven a hugely beneficial one to both parties and had guaranteed that there had been no encroachment on their trade in the area by the McGuigan clan, who were trying to reclaim the action from Mojito's merry men.

In fact, Frankie had to admit to himself it was a pity that, so far, his big brother had been unable to come to a similar agreement with the cop shops at Maryhill and Partick, but he had no doubt that Mojito would get that sorted soon enough.

As he recalled the face full of rotten teeth and the stale whisky breath that had doused him when the cop had grabbed him and demanded his take, Frankie couldn't help venting his anger aloud. 'Aye, ye bastard, wait till Bobby hears about that, then you'll know which side your bread's buttered on.'

But now Frankie was relishing the most rewarding part of his night's work.

His Wrangler jacket collar turned up and his right arm hanging lazily out of the open window, Frankie blew smoke from the Consulate menthol cigarette dangling out his mouth. As two teenage girls crossed Queen Margaret Drive just in front of him, Frankie winked wolfishly at them and they dissolved into a fit of self-conscious giggles.

Jamming the Consulate into the side of his mouth, Frankie pulled his 'Boogie' stretch jeans tight round his waist and smoothed out the slight wrinkles that tended to gather in the denim if you sat stationary in them for too long. Pushing his sleeves up, Frankie enjoyed a quick squint in the cabin mirror, took a deep breath and prepared to deliver his charm offensive to the assembling queue of customers.

The howling gale and heavy rain of the previous night had been replaced by another warm evening and that meant custom was sure to be good. Frankie couldn't help himself voicing his anticipation at what lay ahead as he whipped out his steel comb from the back pocket of his jeans. He quickly ripped it though an unruly knot in his dark, wavy hair, which had drawn admiring comparisons with Donny Osmond the American singing superstar.

'Aye, Frankie boy, it's nice tae see ye, tae see ye nice, all right, son? Ladeez you are in for a treat the night.' Frankie couldn't help winking into the mirror as he swivelled his snake hips. Killing the chimes he quickly hit the play button on his tape recorder and the voice of 'Diamond' Dave Lee Roth immediately filled the air with his raucous version of 'California Girls'.

Dawson headed for the service hatch with a smile of anticipation across his chiselled features. Within moments a queue of mainly female customers was forming outside the van, and as he quickly served a couple of old-age pensioners their 99s, Frankie's attention was already beginning to home in on a buxom middle-aged blonde who was the double of Krystle Carrington from *Dynasty*, her dark brown eyes pools of inviting promise.

As she reached the front of the queue Frankie leant forward onto the service counter, his hands dangling out over the edge. 'Hi, darlin', what can I interest you in,' drawled the ice cream man, his opening gambit dripping with sexual innuendo.

The blonde was far from put off and smiled widely, exposing slightly yellowed, nicotine-stained teeth. 'I dunno, honey, what you got on offer?' she asked in a low, husky voice that suggested that she was indeed a smoker, which was something Frankie had always found attractive in a woman... particularly an older one.

While the size of her shoulder pads caused the ice cream man to stifle his laughter, the sight of her ample assets, which were now just an inch from his counter, suggested to Frankie that there might

R.J.Mitchell

be something more on offer than just fifty pence for a 99 cone.

As the strains of Lee Roth's outrageous version of 'Just a Gigolo' filled his van, Dawson pulled the Consulate out his mouth and, without looking, flicked it nonchalantly into the bin. 'I think I know just what will satisfy you, sweetheart... How about a double scoop nougat?'

The blonde flashed a mischievous smile and her tongue escaped from the side of her mouth and slithered along the underside of her top lip. 'That would be perfect, honeybunch.'

Dawson did his best to keep his desire under control and quickly scooped the perfect white vanilla on top of the nougat before placing a wafer on it and wrapping his van speciality in transparent greaseproof paper. As he looked up to hand it over to the blonde he noticed that she was quickly scrawling something down in a small black diary. She placed her pen in her mouth, ripped a bit of paper from the booklet and shoved it onto the counter.

'For Pete's sake, son, will you get a bleedin' move on, my wee girl is gasping for a cone,' shouted an impatient man from the rear of the line of customers.

As she placed the paper on the counter, she brushed the back of Frankie's hand with her slim fingers. The sensation sent a slight tremble through his body.

Their eyes locked and the blonde whispered, 'Call me any time, ice cream man.'

Dawson leant forward so that their faces were only inches apart. 'You can count on it, darlin'. Why don't you have that one on the house... As a taster?'

'I don't mind if I do,' she said, and with a sly grin she swivelled so that the cream cardigan that had been resting uneasily on her outsize shoulder pads looked like it was about to take off. As she sashayed away, Frankie took a deep breath and tried to focus on his string of impatient customers.

Fifteen minutes later, a fresh Consulate dangling out the side of his mouth, Frankie cruised down Byres Road, pulling in just outside Finlay's Bar, which happened to be just round the corner from the trainee nurses' residence, the inhabitants of which were next, Dawson hoped, to be treated to his silver tongue and vanilla scoops.

Frankie turned off the van's chimes but the momentary silence was replaced by the painful wail of rubber screeching on tarmac. As he entered the service hatch Dawson saw that a purple Austin Princess had just followed him round the corner and into the side street... at speed.

As the vehicle slammed to a halt, a male jumped out of the passenger side and Frankie's usual studied air of detachment was replaced by sheer panic. The male had a stocking mask over his head and in his hands was a sawn-off shotgun.

Five yards from the hatch the man lowered the sawn-off and aimed it straight at Frankie. 'Here's a message for Mojito,' he snarled, and pulled the trigger.

The explosion was the last thing the ice cream man heard as the shot flung him against the van's rear wall and dropped him, crumpled, to the floor.

Frankie's blood ran down the wall and into the previously pristine vanilla, transforming it into a unique brand of raspberry ripple.

CHAPTER 12

The blue Suzuki 750 drew to a stop on the cobbles at the rear of the nightclub. The rider jumped off and ripped his helmet from his head, cuffing away the tears that would not stop falling from his eyes.

From the shadows of the lane a grating voice spoke. 'Mr Dawson, I've some info that maybees will help you square yer brother Frankie. If yous can spare me a second… and a few quid, like?'

Dawson, initially startled, looked up and bored his black eyes into the darkness. 'Who the fuck are you?'

The male continued to conceal his identity in the night; it was a decision that sapped Dawson's patience and he waded into the black and clamped two gauntleted hands on the shadowy figure, pulling him out into the flashing nightclub lights that brightened the edge of the lane running along the side of Tutankhamun's.

Recognition swept across Mojito's chiselled features. 'I thought I told you never to come near me again, you junkie scum.'

'After whit they did to young Frankie I thought you'd want any info that could help ye avenge him, boss.'

'I'm warning you – if you're wasting my time you won't walk away from here,' said Dawson, trying to subdue the raw grief and raging anger that were tearing him apart.

'It's minted, Mojito, you'll be happy ye gave me the time o' day o'er this wan,' said the male and smiled through a gap-toothed grin.

Moments later Dawson was sitting at his grandiose mahogany

desk, the room dark, trying to process the information he had just been fed.

His grief was such that he could not concentrate. The beat of the music, pulsing through the floor beneath his feet, vibrating through the soles of his bespoke leather shoes, threatened to drive him to distraction.

'Blue Monday' by New Order... Again.

He lowered his bald head into his hands and rubbed his fingers over the drum-tight skin, trying to massage away a pain he knew would never leave him. While his eyes brimmed full of tears his self-control remained intact; he would not let the vortex of emotion that had sucked him in break into an outpouring of grief.

His agony was laced with guilt, for he had ignored the early warnings, from the smashed windows of one of his vans in Royston Hill to the petrol bombing of another vehicle down Alexandra Parade, which had left the driver lucky to book an overnight stay in the Royal with only badly burned hands from his attempts to douse the fire with a wet dish towel rather than use the fire extinguisher situated in the vehicle cabin. Then there had been the break-in at his Maryhill icehouse a month ago, during which gallons of his ice cream had been ruined.

All of this had prompted Dawson to escalate the stakes, only for the McGuigans to hit him where he was so glaringly weak by taking out his kid brother.

'Christ, how could I have been so fuckin' stupid, it was obvious, so bleedin' obvious,' Mojito said out loud. He should have known that the escalation in violence between the McGuigans and his own people over the lucrative drugs trade that was peddled from the vehicles of their rival ice cream vans would end in death. And now his younger brother had paid with his life for the mixture of pride and arrogance that had failed to countenance such a personal attack. The guilt he knew he had to deal with, but right now what mattered to Dawson most was revenge.

The office was lit only by the light of the street shining through the window and glinting curiously off Dawson's bald head. He had not bothered to remove the charcoal covert coat he had worn to his brother's funeral. He had left the wake in full flow, just three hours earlier, at the city's finest five-star hotel. So many images had been replaying themselves endlessly on a constant loop in his head since he had been given the news that Frankie had been blasted into oblivion on the end of a sawn-off shotgun, wielded by a coward hiding behind a stocking mask.

He couldn't stop picturing the terror of Frankie's final moments as he stared down the barrels of certain death. The one certainty was that Frankie's murder was not the end but the beginning of what was now a war.

Words he had spoken as Frankie's oak casket was lowered into the ground rang back through his skull. He rammed his fingers in his ears to try and blot them out but they would not stop.

'Brother, I promise you that you will be avenged. For your murder the McGuigans will pay with their lives, their misery will be total and their world shattered. I give you my word, little brother, there will be no hiding place for these scum of the earth, no place they run that Bobby Dawson will not find them. And when I do, my revenge, my brother's revenge, will send a message through this city that no one will ever forget. On our ma and da's souls, Frankie, I vow to avenge you.'

Then the other sights and sounds of the funeral began to fill his mind's eye.

The tears and endless sobbing of Lucy, the middle of the three Dawson siblings; the freeze frame of her stumbling to her knees at their brother's graveside, just feet away from him as he made his vow, staring accusingly at him through red-rimmed, mascara-stained eyes as she was helped to her feet and led away by the minister.

But Lucy's eyes were not the only ones that radiated accusation.

Dawson could read their minds. If Frankie had not been peddling the tenner bags of smack from his ice cream vans then none of this would have happened. Why had he allowed his carefree young brother to become involved in this deadly trade?

Yet he had met every one of their stares and forced them down defiantly. Then Frankie's casket had come to rest at the bottom of the grave and he had scattered the soil on top of it, marking the finality of his brother's death: 'ashes to ashes, dust to dust'.

'Sweet Jesus, what have I done,' said Dawson into the darkness.

If the graveside had been bad then the wake was almost beyond endurance. Thankfully he had chosen the discreet environs of One Devonshire Gardens as the venue for Frankie's send-off and after pressing flesh, expressing gratitude for support and ensuring that Lucy had been taken care of by a barely civil aunt, Dawson had escaped to the solitude of the hotel's cigar shack, tucked away in the garden.

It had been there that his thoughts had started to drift towards the vengeance he intended to wreak on the McGuigans. It was a revenge in which he could see a mirroring of the troubles that had blighted Northern Ireland for decades, spilling out onto the streets of Glasgow.

But Dawson did not care, for he would have Frankie avenged and by doing so he would have the one thing that would help dull the endless pain of his murder... Total control of the city.

He checked his Rolex: 11.30 p.m. The first stage in his plan to avenge Frankie should be well underway. He allowed himself a small smile of satisfaction.

His moment of contemplation was interrupted by a light knock on the office door.

'Come in.'

The door opened and in she walked – a vision of intoxicating, exotic beauty, shimmering like a goddess, framed in the doorway by a background of brilliant light.

'Your mojito, just as you like it, Mr Dawson. Rum, mint, lime and soda, poured long and cold,' said the cocktail waitress, slightly drawing out the last four words in an alluring purr.

Dawson's grief seemed to drain out of his head at the sight of her.

The afro tresses of her hair, the smooth, light chocolate of her skin and those lips that pouted at him in a way that made Dawson ache to kiss them.

He smiled thinly as his eyes devoured her, savouring every step she took across the office floor towards his desk. The elegance of her legs, sheathed in fishnet stockings, her perfectly undulating body encased in a tight black leather, side-laced skirt and iced by a low-cut white blouse, the cocktail waitress uniform of Tutankhamun's, almost took his breath away.

Bobby Dawson knew that he must have her and have her soon.

Yet he was master of all he surveyed and he would not have his self-control shattered by an all too obvious desire.

'Do you know, Celine, the mojito sits alongside the daiquiri and the cuba libre in the holy trinity of Cuban cocktails?'

Her answer was a brilliant smile that lit up the gloom for him and as she bent low to put the drinks tray down and lay his mojito on the desk Dawson grabbed her wrist and locked his burning gaze on her silken brown eyes.

'You know, young lady, that you have an opportunity to make a bright future for yourself in my organisation... if you play your cards right,' said Dawson, pulling sharply on her wrists. She was forced to sit on the edge of his desk, her legs sliding down its side and brushing against Dawson.

Celine kept her composure, smiling serenely. Dawson was impressed.

'A girl will do what a girl has to do to make a life for herself, Mr Dawson,' she replied in the low, husky voice that had come to leave him tossing and turning in the middle of the night.

Dawson let the fingers of his left hand stroke her stockinged leg, smiled and said, 'Do a good job for me waitressing here at Tut's, keep me in the know and informed of what's going on out on the floor, and let me know what the mood is in my camp and I will make sure there are rewards for your loyalty, Celine.'

Again that serene, slightly icy smile broke out across her face but she inclined her head in a coquettish fashion that suggested to Dawson she liked what she was hearing.

Raising the back of her right hand to his lips, Dawson kissed it and then let it drop back down into her lap. With a smile he brought her audience to an end.

Celine read the signs and she eased herself up from the desk and walked towards the door. Before leaving, she turned around and said, 'I'm sorry for your loss, Mr Dawson.'

Raising the chilled mojito to his lips, Dawson shot her a piercing stare with his dark, hard eyes. She felt a shiver run through her body.

Then he raised his glass and toasted his dead brother: 'To Frankie.'

CHAPTER 13

Gerry McGuigan checked the rear-view mirror of his Jaguar and saw that it was filled with the image of a marked Ford Transit police van.

'What's up, Gerry?' asked his sidekick, Danny French.

'Fuckin' rozzers. Just as well we're no' tooled up or they'd be looking to take us down for a long stretch. Ah fuck, that's the blue light on, they're pullin' us,' said McGuigan in disgust.

'Bastards'll probably try and do us for a baldy tire or some shite like that. Back o' eleven at night, you'd think they'd have something better to do with their time, like jailin' some junkie housebreaker. Christ knows there are enough tannings getting done round about.'

'Aye, why on earth would they want to tug two respectable businessmen like you and me, Frenchie?' asked McGuigan with a laugh.

McGuigan steered the black Jag into the side of the road and let out a world-weary sigh as he waited for the cops to get out of their van and go through the usual game of cat and mouse by trying to wind him and Frenchie up into a breach of the peace.

He afforded himself a quick smile of satisfaction at the fact that he had decided to make the short journey from one of his family's boozers, the imaginatively named 'McGuigan's', to his sidekick's home without any weapons on board. He knew that at 11.15 p.m. the local police night shift were not long out on the streets and would be looking for something to keep them busy on a quiet midweek night.

His mind wandered to thoughts of the funeral of Frankie Dawson, which he knew had been earlier that day. Once again he savoured the whisky he had shared with Frenchie as they had toasted the demise of the younger Dawson brother – a job he felt his sidekick had done particularly efficiently and one his father was sure to reward him for when he got back from the Costa del Sol.

Gerry wondered how Dawson's wake was going and how Bobby 'Mojito' Dawson was coping with the grief of his death and the knowledge that his reign as king of the lucrative ice cream van drugs trade was all but over.

But McGuigan was brought back to the present when his driver's window was given a short, hard rap. He stared out through the glazing into a mouth full of rotten teeth.

From the other side of the Jag he heard Frenchie say, 'Fuck's sake, there's one at ma windae as well. How many of these fuckers does it take to do ye for a baldy tyre?'

McGuigan rolled down the window and met the rotten grin with a wince, recognising the smell of stale whisky. He smiled civilly at the polisman and played the game. 'Evening, officer, how can I help you?'

The smile on the cop's face got wider. 'It's me who is here to help you, Mr McGuigan. We have received information that you have some illegal goods within the boot of your vehicle. Would you be so good as to open it for me and my colleague?'

McGuigan felt a grin split his face. He would enjoy winning this little confrontation.

'Of course, officer, but I can assure you there is nothing illegitimate in my vehicle. It is a pity you have been let down so badly by your informant. But I'm always happy to oblige the strong arm of the law,' said McGuigan, making no effort to hide his sarcasm. As the cop stepped back, he opened the car door slowly and stepped out, hearing the sound of the passenger door springing open as Frenchie followed suit.

'Like I said, if you care to open the boot for me, Mr McGuigan, we can get this check done and you can be on your way,' said the cop cordially.

McGuigan reached the rear of the vehicle as Frenchie appeared with the other cop, who may have been getting on but was still a powerful looking bastard who McGuigan fancied would be a real handful in a square go. He inserted the key into the boot lock and it clicked open.

As it did so another sound thudded out and McGuigan looked up to see Frenchie being sent sprawling onto the road and what appeared to be a pickaxe handle held in the big cop's huge paw. A hand gripped his neck powerfully and the point of something cold and hard rammed into the small of his back.

'Stay very still, McGuigan, do what you're told and maybes I don't blow your brains out here and now,' said rotten teeth, pulling him back and away from the boot.

The brute in the other uniform dragged Frenchie over onto his gut, tied his hands together at the small of his back and slapped a hood over his head. Then he lifted the enforcer's body up like it was a rag doll, unceremoniously dumping him inside the empty boot. The semi-conscious Frenchie let out a groan as the door was slammed shut.

'Keep your hands together and get them into the small of your back,' said the voice from behind McGuigan, and for good measure he was given another short, sharp prod by the point of what he was now certain was a handgun.

Then the monster in the uniform whipped out handcuffs, grabbed his wrists, pushed up the sleeves of his camel coat and slotted on the steel bracelets, tightening them until Gerry felt the circulation fading in his wrists.

'For fuck's sake! What's this all about?' demanded McGuigan.

'You'll find out soon enough you piece of Fenian shit!' growled the voice from behind him and then McGuigan felt a dull thud on the back of his cranium and the lights went well and truly out.

CHAPTER 14

McGuigan regained consciousness as a hood, fitted onto him while he was out cold, was ripped off his head and a pail of icy water thrown over him. As he came to, on his knees, in a fog of darkness, his ears were met with the sound of music playing at full blast.

McGuigan's own musical tastes and knowledge were confined to the gravelly offerings of Rod Stewart but there was something familiar about the classical strings followed by the blaring horns that threatened to burst his eardrums.

A thud two feet to his left brutally snapped McGuigan's attention back to the here and now. Although the pitch darkness meant that he couldn't see exactly what had made the noise, the grunt that accompanied it cleared up the mystery. Frenchie had been relocated from the boot of the Jag to the freezing cold of the warehouse floor.

Blinking furiously to try and pick up any sight of his captors, McGuigan was frustrated by the darkness and tormented by the continuing wall of classical sound that he was desperately trying to identify.

Then the lights went on.

Where everything had been black it was now blazing, searing white. McGuigan was forced to snap his eyes shut as quickly as possible. With his hands still tied behind his back he had no way of shielding himself from the brilliant light that seemed to burn its way through his eyelids.

The music went on and on and slowly it dawned on McGuigan

where he had heard it before. It was from the film *Apocalypse Now*, the Vietnam War film he had seen at the Salon cinema, in Vinicombe Street, ten years ago. He recalled the powerful presence of Marlon Brando.

But why was the music now being unleashed on his eardrums at full blast – and by whom?

This had to be the work of Dawson.

As the symbols started to crash together, McGuigan recalled the apocalyptic scenes of the film with the US Army helicopters bombing a Vietnamese village. Then just as soon as it had sprung up the music died and into the light stepped Bobby 'Mojito' Dawson. He smashed his right hand off McGuigan's jaw, sending him skidding onto his back, cannoning across the cement floor.

Before McGuigan could regain his balance, or find any words of protest, Mojito's sharp voice filled the air. But his words were not addressed to McGuigan, who lay prostrate on his back desperately trying to struggle to his feet.

'Bring the murdering scum over here,' said Mojito.

McGuigan's eyes immediately snapped to the denim-clad heap that was Danny French. His mate was hauled to his feet by the two cops who had intercepted them, what now seemed an eternity ago. They dragged him over to where Mojito stood, a menacing dark figure bathed in a sea of burning white light.

'For Chrissakes, what the fuck are you doin', you mad man, lemme go,' screamed Frenchie.

He was ignored.

Instead the gangland enforcer was rammed down onto his knees in front of Dawson.

The cop with the blown fuse box of rotten teeth walked into the darkness and McGuigan saw that he had gone in the direction of a set of stairs that loomed out of the shadows, just out of reach of the burning white light.

McGuigan heard a strange mechanical whirring sound and his eyes clapped on a giant metal hook that was now swinging menacingly through the air. It came to a halt, threateningly still, about four feet above Frenchie's head.

Frenchie begged for his life. 'I swear I'm innocent, Mojito,' he sobbed, but the enforcer got no further before Dawson smashed the butt of a pistol into his jaw.

As Frenchie's face was knocked to the side and then rolled back around, he found the point of the barrel rammed against his forehead.

'Don't insult me by protesting your innocence, you piece of sewage. Didn't you think I'd find out it was you hiding underneath a stocking mask when you blew my brother away?'

In the background McGuigan had scrambled to his knees and was desperately trying to locate an exit strategy.

But Mojito had not missed his furtive glances and strode over to his enemy, grabbing him by his lapels and dragging him across the floor until he was positioned on his knees five feet away from Frenchie and directly opposite.

Then the music started to play again.

'Ah... Music to die for. Beethoven's "Ode to Joy", a slight variation on our classical theme from Wagner's "Ride of the Valkyries",' explained Mojito matter-of-factly.

As the whirring of the giant hook started again the massed voices of a choir sprang to life as "Ode to Joy" burst over them.

Slowly the hook descended towards Frenchie's back.

'No, no, stop it, what the hell are you going to do with me?' screamed Frenchie in desperation, trying to make his words heard above the classical music. It was pointless.

The big cop rammed the razor-sharp hook through the back of Frenchie's Berghaus and into his flesh as the captive let rip an agonised screech. The other cop signalled to rotten teeth to elevate Frenchie a couple of feet off the concrete, then lifted a jerry can of what McGuigan guessed was petrol and proceeded to douse Frenchie in it.

The music seemed to get louder and Frenchie's screams were drowned out as his body was soaked in the fuel. When the jerry can had been emptied, the whirring noise started again and the screaming Frenchie was hauled ten feet off the floor, struggling furiously to find a way off the hook.

Then came the sound of another liquid hitting the cold cement, as Frenchie's self-control, along with his bladder, burst.

He made one last desperate plea for mercy: 'For the love of Jesus... I beg you, please dinnae do this. Please. I've got six weans and a missus...'

From behind McGuigan, Dawson spoke two words: 'Fuck you.' The big cop walked forwards, pulled a Zippo lighter from his uniform pocket, clicked its flame alive and applied it to the wriggling, denim-clad, petrol-soaked legs of Danny French.

The flames shot furiously up his writhing body and even the full-blast Beethoven could not drown out the piteous screams that escaped the human inferno that had been Danny French.

CHAPTER 15

The flames devoured the gangland lieutenant until a charred hulk was all that was left of Danny French, hanging from the giant hook and smouldering as it swung gently in mid-air. A study in almost still death.

A coppery, metallic smell, combined with what reminded McGuigan of the whiff of charcoal from a summer barbecue, filled the air, as smoke wreathed the flambéed remains of Danny French.

Then the crisp notes of a piano started to fill the warehouse, adding a surreal quality to McGuigan's nightmare. Beethoven's 'Moonlight Sonata' provided a funereal musical accompaniment to his impending death scene.

He heard footsteps as Mojito walked round from behind to face him.

The two men had not been in close proximity for years and McGuigan had forgotten the strange dead expression that exuded from Dawson's eyes, orbs of hatred that he felt piercing his skull.

'So the monkey who pulled the trigger is no more but what of the organ grinder?' asked Dawson almost conversationally, in a tone that was barely audible over the piano.

McGuigan felt his jaw clench. He would not beg for his life. He knew there was no point and he was determined to meet his maker with as much dignity as he could muster. 'That's fuckin' rich comin' from you, soldier scum. Go to hell you twisted fucker,' he spat, with every ounce of contempt he could muster.

'I may well do, eventually, but you, my friend, will be there very shortly and a long time before me,' said Dawson, a sparkle flickering through his dark eyes, the glint from his single diamond earring shining out brilliantly. 'You have been an irritation to me for a while now, but while irritations can be overlooked and sometimes forgotten about, you made a fatal mistake by murdering my brother, one that your own death and that of your associate will not even begin to pay for. I want you to know… My revenge will be visited on every member of your family. I have something very special planned for your father, the dearly beloved Francis. Every worthless piece of shit associated with the McGuigan name will feel my wrath and you, my friend, will not be here to warn them or do anything to save them.'

'Why would you do that, Mojito? The decision to take out Frankie was mine and mine alone. Leave my family be.' It was as much a plea as McGuigan was prepared to make and one he knew was a waste of breath.

'I can't do that, because what happens to you and yours is going to send out a message about what happens when someone is stupid enough to challenge Bobby Dawson. You wanted to take the ice cream smack trade off me, you couldn't stay happy with your empire of petty crime. You wanted a war but you did not prepare for one. It was a schoolboy error,' said Mojito flatly.

The music changed again and this time a lone female voice filled the air as "Ave Maria" played out.

'I don't suppose you've ever heard of Maria Callas?' asked Dawson. Then he pulled out his revolver and placed the point of the barrel against McGuigan's forehead. 'The great thing about death is that we know it is coming but in most cases we just don't know when it will arrive.'

McGuigan couldn't stop his eyes from flickering up to focus on his tormentor's index finger, which was wrapped around the gun trigger. Slowly he saw it exert pressure. The trigger pulled backwards and he spat, 'Still a murderer!' Then he shut his eyes and prayed as Callas hit her notes with crisp perfection in the background.

Instead of a mind-blowing bang there was only a click.

McGuigan's eyes sprang open as he realised that Dawson was playing Russian roulette with him.

Dawson laughed out loud and long, then, before McGuigan could shut his eyes, he pulled the trigger again.

Click.

'Isn't this just a moment to die for?' asked Mojito, breaking into laughter.

'You sick fuck, you've had your fun, now just get on with it.'

'Quiet,' said Dawson. He cocked his head to the right, apparently waiting for the next piece of musical accompaniment.

'At last, "Requiem", by Mozart, how appropriate.' Dawson took a step forward, placed the end of the gun barrel to McGuigan's forehead and pulled the trigger, watching in delight as his rival's head exploded like an overripe pumpkin.

McGuigan's corpse toppled onto the cement at a bizarre angle. Dawson stood over him and emptied the remaining contents of the revolver into his body.

Then Mojito looked up into the faces of Davidson and Jones, who stood just a few yards away. 'I want both bodies replaced in the Jaguar and then parked up somewhere nice and public where the McGuigans will get the message.'

Then he fished out two large manila envelopes from the pocket of his coat and handed one to each of the cops.

'A good job well done, gentlemen, for which, as you will see, you are being well paid. But there will be more work for you both, because Francis McGuigan will not take this sitting down. His biggest problem is that I've only just started.'

Dawson's dark eyes bored into their features one after the other, then he pulled up the collar of his coat and walked away from them, out of the warehouse and into the night, leaving the two cops to complete their orders.

'Fuck me gently,' muttered Davidson.

CHAPTER 16

Thoroughgood walked out of Lennox Hill Station on his own, his mind a mess.

He had been detailed to partner up Davidson but his senior cop had been nowhere to be found, and with Jones also inexplicably missing and a flu epidemic at divisional HQ on Bayne Street, meaning a shortage of manpower, he had elected to walk the beat for the first time solo rather than stay within the safe confines of the station and listen to the inane banter of the relief bar officer old Johnny Boyle.

Rentoul had made it clear down the phone that he needed at least one two-man team out on the beat and, with Davidson off the radar, the section sergeant had left it up to Thoroughgood to decide whether to stay inside until HQ could spare a senior man to 'mollycoddle' him, as Rentoul put it, or go out on his own.

Thoroughgood knew there was no choice. Although probationers were not supposed to go solo until they were almost ready for their second-stage course at the Scottish Police College, if he stayed inside and waited for a senior man he would have the insult of being a coward added to all the other terms of endearment he had to endure from the shift.

Rentoul had him by the balls and he knew which response the sergeant had wanted. He took the bait willingly, determined to use the situation to his advantage. Gritting his teeth, he made his way over the footbridge and began to trudge down the pavement, keeping his head held high and his eyes on a constant sweep.

As he approached a corner, which led to a row of shops, he

could hear the sound of raised voices and prepared himself for his first encounter with the natives without the safety blanket of a senior man there to protect him.

Four teenagers, in a variety of coloured shell suits, awaited him. Quickly Thoroughgood's eyes took in the essentials of each one's appearance. They were all aged between fifteen and maybe nineteen; one of them, leaning against the shutters of the shop they were standing outside, was guzzling a bottle of Buckfast. The next, resplendent in a white shell suit, was puffing furiously on an outsize fag while the other two were engaged in rolling up smokes for themselves. Then the sweet spicy aroma of the hash hit Thoroughgood's nostrils.

The youth drinking from the Buckfast bottle almost choked on its contents as he eyeballed Thoroughgood first. He shouted out a warning – 'Pig' – and half of his mouthful of tonic wine escaped in a ruby-red spray over the teenager who had been puffing away on what Thoroughgood now realised was a giant spliff of dope.

But it was the large ball of brown resinous substance that the other two youths were engaged in breaking down into roll-ups that caught Thoroughgood's attention, just as their startled faces reacted to their mate's warning.

The one wearing a green Berghaus anorak and black beanie hat was first to react. He grabbed the large brown lump, half wrapped in a clear film, and took to his heels.

Thoroughgood knew exactly what needed to be done. He took one last glance at the remaining three males, pulled his police hat off, held it tight in his right hand, deposited their descriptions in his memory bank, then clicked through the gears to get his Doc Martins moving at top speed.

Berghaus was fast. He vaulted a fence with Thoroughgood in his wake. As he pursued the back of the green anorak into the rear courtyards of a row of tenements, Thoroughgood groaned as he saw that they all had their boundaries marked by wrought-iron fencing, a row of barriers that replicated an Olympic hurdles race. Berghaus was already taking them like Colin Jackson in his prime.

'Shit,' gasped Thoroughgood as his left Doc Martin glanced off a spike. He skidded as he hit the wet turf on the other side of the fence and fought to keep his balance, allowing Berghaus to pull away from him.

But Thoroughgood knew that any hope he had of gaining credibility with his shift depended on him catching the youth and, bolstered by the hours of training he had put in on the squash court, he remained quietly confident he would get his man.

The problem was that for his plan to take effect he needed to be able to broadcast location, direction of pursuit and suspect description to divisional control, so that he could let the whole division know that he was out alone and busy with it.

After two hundred yards of intermittent hurdles, Berghaus legged it into a tenement close, almost as if he knew the door would be open. Thoroughgood veered down the dip onto the cement path and charged into the damp, all-embracing dark of the doorway, not sure if there would be a blade of glinting steel waiting for him. The sound of the building's front door slamming shut alerted him to the fact that Berghaus had already made it out of the other side.

As he ran out onto the pavement Thoroughgood could already see the green jacket weaving around a parked car and heading for the street corner at the end of the tenements. The gap was fifty yards.

He sucked in a gulp of air and put the foot down.

Turned into a side lane, he remembered Davidson's mocking words of advice: 'Know where you are at all times.' Thoroughgood smiled inwardly as he clocked and logged the street sign – 'Archer's Court' – and the voice inside his head said, 'Fuck you, Davidson'.

Berghaus showed no sign of slowing. As he reached an outside set of stairs at the rear of single-storey set of whitewashed houses, the youth charged up them without breaking stride.

Thoroughgood, encased in his black woollen monkey suit, could feel the sweat running down his back and his white shirt starting to stick. But, determined to catch his quarry, he took the steps two at a time. Berghaus had come to a stop at the end of the second-floor footway, his escape route apparently run out.

His suspect cornered, Thoroughgood slapped the lid back on his damp hair, pulled out the brick-like PR from his radio holster, gulped some air and made his broadcast: 'Z325 requesting assistance, first floor Archer's Court, suspect person cornered. Code 13 applies.'

The divisional controller replied sharply. 'Z325 remain in situ, divisional car Zulu Mike One is en route. ETA five minutes, repeat, wait for back-up.'

Thoroughgood deliberately failed to respond and walked slowly along the second-floor corridor that looked down over another set of postage-stamp back gardens.

Stalking his quarry, Thoroughgood smiled. As he advanced to within twenty feet, the beanie hat failed to disguise the youth's face. Thoroughgood recognised the sunken features, pockmarked skin and hooked nose of the youth from the divisional intelligence bulletins he liked to study almost as much as the job section of the *Glasgow Herald*.

Pulling the PR to his lips once more Thoroughgood broadcast in triumph: 'Z325, I can confirm that the suspect in question is Cat Collins, the housebreaker. Confirm sheriff's warrant to apprehend in existence for Collins? ETA for Zulu Mike One?'

But the controller's reply was almost made inaudible by the sound of a closing siren. Zulu Mike One was almost at the locus.

'So, Collins, nice lump of hash you've got in the right hand Berghaus pocket, let's just be keeping it there and don't be thinking about tossing it anywhere, wee man,' said Thoroughgood amicably.

'New polisman, are ye no'? Just oot the wrapper, eh?' asked Collins, undaunted but breathing heavily.

Thoroughgood was now three yards from his quarry and he smiled in triumph. 'Long enough in the job to know I've got you bang to rights, pal.'

'You think so, copper?' asked Collins and flashed a wicked smile.

Then the housebreaker grabbed hold of the top of the wall

that spanned the length of the walkway, swinging himself over the edge and into the black.

Thoroughgood immediately took a step forward and saw that Collins had dropped fifteen feet down onto a flat roof. He must have known it would be there. Without giving it a thought the rookie followed suit.

Collins had stumbled on his landing but the grip on Thoroughgood's Doc Martins held true and he closed the gap between them with all the speed he could muster.

Just as he was about to grab the junkie, Thoroughgood's attention was caught by something pale and gleaming that Collins had ripped out from inside his Berghaus.

It was a hypodermic needle.

Collins gap-toothed smile shone out and he sucked in oxygen from behind the gleaming point of the needle. 'You want HIV, Hep B? Then come an' get me, filth.'

Thoroughgood did not waste any words and pulled out the wooden baton from the elongated pocket in his right trouser leg.

'Ace beats a king every time, kitty cat,' said Thoroughgood and smashed the baton down on Collins' wrist. The housebreaker dropped the syringe and screeched out in agony. Thoroughgood lunged at him, wrapping both arms around his midriff, and smashed Collins down on to the flat felt roof.

He piniioned the Cat's arms down by his sides, forcing his back into the damp felt. 'Like I said, Collins, I've got you bang to rights and if you don't want a sore face, you'll let me get the cuffs on you and get us both down from here in one piece.'

'Listen, copper, I don't want banged up in the Bar-L doing time on a sherriff's warrant an' cold turkey all in a oner,' gasped Collins.

His knee now in the ned's chest, Thoroughgood allowed himself a smile. 'What you got in mind, Collins?'

'I give you some info that you'd sell yer granny for, you let me go and maybe we have an understandin' that works both ways, rozzer?'

CHAPTER 17

Thoroughgood stared into the junkie's dead eyes then pushed his knee down powerfully into Collin's chest. 'Maybe I am just out the wrapper, bawheid, but it don't mean I have a zip up my fuckin' back,' he said and whipped out his handcuffs. 'The most prolific housebreaker in the whole of Zulu Land and you think I'm gonnae turn you loose on a bullshit line? No chance,' spat Thoroughgood contemptuously.

'Look, shit for brains, don't you know a once in a lifetime offer when ye fuckin' hear it?' gasped Collins.

The sound of the siren getting closer seemed to add new urgency to Collins' beseeching. 'Look I know you's a rookie but I cannae afford to do time in the big hoose cos if I do I'll never make it out with ma baws intact. I've got the mother of all turns for you, but you have to cut me free. If you do I'll spill to you only. For fuck's sake, that jam sandwich is just around the corner.'

Thoroughgood's emerald-green eyes remained trained on the housebreaker's desperate features. 'Spit it out then, Collins,' he demanded.

'Half your shift are on the take, rookie, and they're being taken care of by Mojito, the ice cream van king. Word is that he paid them to take oot Gerry McGuigan and one of his henchmen, I knows him only as Frenchie.'

The information tallied up with the evidence Thoroughgood had seen with his own eyes during Davidson's little parley with the ice cream van driver the other night, but he still couldn't bring himself to believe it.

'Where did a pathetic little junkie housebreaker like you come by information like that? You're takin' the piss.'

'Like fuck I am, rozzer. I got it from a fence who's in the know and things are gonnae turn nasty when old man McGuigan comes back from his hols over in Costa del Sol. Look, let me go and I'll find you with more info, you pass it up the tree and turn oot a fuckin' hero,' said Collins, the speed of his words betraying his increasing desperation.

The sound of two car doors slamming shut indicated that the cavalry had well and truly arrived. Thoroughgood remained undecided as he weighed up Collins' claims and their likely truth.

Yet the ned's desperation to avoid the Bar-L was starting to convince the rookie that he would part with the crown jewels to stay out of the 'big hoose' as HMP Barlinnie was known to all and sundry.

Grabbing Collins by the scruff of his neck he hauled him up to within an inch of his own face. 'Okay, Collins, I'm going to take a chance that what you're saying is the truth but I want more and I want it quickly.'

'I'll find you within forty-eight hours, boss. I swear it on my wee man's heart,' said Collins. Thoroughgood let go of the junkie and watched as he sprang to his feet and vaulted off the far end of the flat roof, vanishing into the dark of the night once again.

The word 'boss' echoed inside Thoroughgood's head. It was the first time in his fledgling cop career he had been addressed with the mark of respect afforded to the police by 'the neddery', as Davidson liked to call them.

The thought allowed a smile to creep across Thoroughgood's face as it occurred to him that he might be able to expose the veteran as the biggest ned of all.

Hunkering down, he picked up the hypo then a voice broke the still of the night.

'Z325 are you up there?'

CHAPTER 18

Thoroughgood peered over the edge of the roof and clapped eyes on two uniformed figures. One had silver hair streaking out from below a police hat and a two-tone moustache; his shrewd eyes seemed to bulge from their sockets, devouring every detail of Thoroughgood's features, including, the probationer realised, the syringe he was holding in his right hand.

'So you got second prize, eh, son?' asked silver hair.

The second man had surprisingly youthful features considering the three stripes that shone out on either one of his arms.

'All right, Constable Thoroughgood? I'm Sergeant Cormac Malcolm and this is Constable Dennis Numan. Why don't you get down off the roof and you can tell us what happened, young fella,' said Malcolm in a quiet conversational tone that oozed a casual authority.

Thoroughgood used a helpfully located drainpipe at the top end of the roof to shimmy down the twelve-foot drop to the ground. But as his Doc Martens hit concrete he felt a palm smash into his back and ram him up against the lock-up shutter.

The powerful grip burled him round and he found himself with Numan's startling grey eyes burning into his features. 'We been listening to your little adventure over the airwaves, Thoroughgood, and it's been a blast, son, a real blast,' said Numan, continuing to pinion Thoroughgood to the lock-up.

Then Malcolm appeared at the junior cop's shoulder. 'You're a brave boy, Thoroughgood, going after a nasty piece of work like Collins on your own. Give,' he demanded, gesturing to the rookie

75

to hand him the hypodermic needle.

Thoroughgood did as he was bid and Malcolm repaid him with a crooked grin, but it was Numan whose words broke the brief silence.

'I'm wondering how you managed to back your man up onto a roof, lock horns with him, take his weapon from him and then lose him? You got any answers, son?' asked Numan, his eyes sparkling with mischief.

Malcolm took up the verbal baton. 'Numan is right, anyone would think that you and Collins may have come to a wee understanding, Constable. Is that right Z325?'

'Sorry, Sergeant, don't know what you mean. He threw the needle at me and vaulted off the roof before I could arrest him. With respect, Sergeant,' replied Thoroughgood, applying the straight bat.

Suddenly Numan relaxed his grip and the senior cop took a step back before barking out a laugh. 'Is that right, sonny?'

'I think you should join us for a wee ride in the back of the Cavalier, Constable Thoroughgood. That's if you don't have any objections?' asked Sergeant Malcolm.

Thoroughgood soon found himself sitting in the back of the divisional fast-response car, a Cavalier Mark II SRi, with Malcolm opposite him and Numan leering wolfishly at him from the driver's seat.

It was Malcolm who did the talking. 'It's Angus, isn't it?'

'Yes, Sergeant,' replied Thoroughgood stiffly.

'You been having a pretty shitty time of it, Angus, I believe?' asked the sergeant.

Thoroughgood looked down at his hands, which he now noticed were locked together.

'Look, we're no' here to snare you in any kind of trap, son. Quite the opposite,' said Numan.

Thoroughgood couldn't help his gaze shifting immediately from his handwringing to Numan's disconcerting gaze and then back to Malcolm's inquisitive expression.

'Dennis is right. We're here to see if you'll let us help you and in turn let you help us clean up the shift that's making your life hell on earth,' said Malcolm.

The probationer took a sharp intake of breath, hoping against hope that a form of deliverance was at last beckoning.

Malcolm continued, 'The chief constable is about to announce a new internal investigations unit which will be run by Detective Chief Inspector Michael McGurk and will include both myself and Dennis here. Right now no one in Zulu Land knows jack shit about it but they will soon enough. The main priority is to start cleaning up our own mess and there's plenty of that across the board. We have a roving commission across the force area but we intend to start turning the screws close to home.'

Thoroughgood remained unconvinced that it wasn't a set-up, despite Malcolm's apparent sincerity and an air of almost evangelical zeal for the job in hand. 'Sorry, Sergeant Malcolm, but I'm not sure how I can help you.'

'Look, son, you don't have to be bleedin' Einstein to figure out that a graduate in Medieval History, who has acquired a bit of a smartarse reputation throughout his basic training course at Tulliallan, has a big mouth and even bigger question mark hanging over his judgement, hasn't just been allotted to Group Three, Z Division by accident,' said Numan with a machine-gun delivery.

Thoroughgood held the senior cop's gaze but remained silent.

'You're no' making this easy, Thoroughgood, and I guess that's no surprise. Listen, maybe you asked for the arse end of the deal when it came to your shift allocation but they fucked you good and proper when they dumped you with this mob of hairy-arsed bastards who think they run the north by their own rules and are untouchable,' summed up Numan.

With Thoroughgood clearly at a loss for words Malcolm said, 'What Dennis is saying is that we know your shift are bad to their bones and on the take. We suspect they are hooked up with some of the biggest bastards in the north of Glasgow and we want to do something about it. But to do that we need someone on the inside of their rotten barrel. We think you're best placed to be that someone, Angus.'

'Come on, son. As someone once said, "we've just made you an offer you can't refuse",' chipped in Numan a roguish glint in his eye.

'It was Marlon Brando in *The Godfather*,' muttered Thoroughgood, staring into his hands. Then he took a deep breath and went for it. After all, what did he have to lose? 'What do you want me to do, Sergeant?'

Before Malcolm could answer Numan burst out with, 'Thank fuck for that.'

The sergeant extended his hand, patted Thoroughgood on the shoulder and said, 'Nothing, Gus – if I can call you that. Just keep your eyes and ears open and absorb.'

'It'll be my pleasure, Sergeant,' replied Thoroughgood.

CHAPTER 19

He took a swig of the whisky and emptied the glass in one mouthful, knowing that no amount of the golden liquid would dull the pain that raged inside of him. Twelve p.m. was early to be hitting the firewater but he didn't care.

Francis McGuigan ached for revenge but burned with guilt.

If he had not been on holiday then Gerry would never have overstepped the mark and taken out young Frankie Dawson. He knew his eldest son was in a hurry to make his mark, emerge from his shadow and put his stamp on Glasgow's underworld but that had been madness and now Gerry had paid for it.

At sixty-four, Francis had planned for a gradual handover of power as he eased control of his criminal empire into the hands of his number-one son, but Gerry's naked ambition and obsession with grinding Dawson into dust had blown those hopes to pieces. Now Gerry himself was no more than 'ashes to ashes, dust to dust'.

With Gerry's funeral less than forty-eight hours past, McGuigan's grief was still raw, and it struck him that there was an eerie parallel to the angst he was going through and that which would certainly have been experienced by Dawson after the execution of his younger brother, Frankie.

McGuigan stared balefully into the empty crystal glass and admitted to himself that it was all part and parcel of the life he had chosen all those years back, when he had first found work on the wrong side of the tracks as a 'Peter Man' or safe blower. It had been lucrative work that had allowed him to fund a criminal fiefdom that had dominated Zulu Land and stretched its tentacles into the north of Glasgow almost unchallenged until Dawson had arrived on the scene.

His feet resting on his desk, his tie loosened from an opened collar, he ran fingers through his white mane and then sprung the pocket watch from his waistcoat. The engraved writing on the inside of the gold casing read, simply, 'Da'.

McGuigan recalled the day he had handed it to his old man and the joy and pride that had been reflected on his father's face. When Sean McGuigan had gone to meet his maker he had left it to his only son Francis, and he in turn had always hoped to bequeath it along with everything else to Gerry. But now that would never happen.

A question echoed in Francis's head: 'Who do I leave it to now?'

He had to deal with Dawson, but before he could act he needed information. He knew that Mojito would expect vicious retaliation and the key was to make sure that it came where and when he anticipated it least.

Eyeing the bottle of Whyte & Mackay he saw it was empty. 'Fuck it,' he cursed and sprang out of the office chair with surprising energy for a man of his advanced years. McGuigan Senior was still fit enough to put those half his age to shame.

He would have to head through to the front of the bar and take a bottle from the gantry. It wasn't as if the 'shop' would be busy, just the usual pensioners playing dominos and enjoying the traditional 'hauf and a hauf'.

Still, at least there were some compensations, thought McGuigan, as he recalled that Lisa, the blonde that big Duncy Parkinson had hired the other week, should be serving.

Sure enough, as he made his way into the bar, Francis McGuigan was met with a welcoming smile from the curvaceous young barmaid and he nodded to the reserve bottle of Whyte & Mackay sitting beneath the optic. He was sure she would help attract a few more punters through the door, when she was ready to serve at peak times on Friday and Saturday night.

Big Duncy had made a good choice, and knowing his right-hand man only too well, he suspected that Parkinson had probably given the new model a test drive into the bargain. Aye, thought McGuigan Senior, and if not already, it wouldn't be long until she was broken in. But for now the owner of McGuigan's was happy to enjoy the rear view provided by his newest employee.

'There you go, Mr McGuigan,' said Lisa as she handed him the bottle. 'Will that be all?'

'Aye, pet,' replied McGuigan, aware that Lisa's sparkling eyes were now checking him out and no doubt wondering if the old dog still had any life left in him. The thought amused him and McGuigan couldn't help giving her a mischievous smile that he hoped would provide the answer she sought.

Looking over at the knot of pensioners in the corner McGuigan raised a hand in acknowledgement. One of the domino team shouted out, 'How are ye, Francis? Death will be too kind for that Mojito bastard.'

'It will indeed, Jimmy, but I'm sure when it comes we will have a special send-off ready for Mojito that will help him atone for his sins before he enters eternal damnation,' replied McGuigan Senior, fingering his pocket watch once more in his agitation.

'Aye, we'll drink tae that, Francis, awright,' saluted another member of the domino team.

McGuigan produced a facial expression that was a cross between a grin and a grimace and turned to face Lisa. 'Listen, darlin', I'm expecting a visitor to come callin' at the back door, can you keep a look out for him for me, pet?'

'Nae bother, Mr McGuigan,' replied Lisa and smiled sweetly.

Then McGuigan took the bottle of whisky and headed back into the pub office, his impatience eating him up.

Feet relocated to the top of his desk once again, McGuigan scanned the racing pages of the *Daily Record*, but his mind's eye was otherwise engaged, replaying over and over again the brutal revenge he ached to take on Mojito Dawson.

He stared at the golden liquid in the half-full glass and decided not to have anymore. He needed a clear head, but most of all he needed information. Springing his old man's pocket watch open he resolved that if the tout didn't appear within ten minutes he would have big Duncy go round the houses until he had him flushed out.

Then there was a light knock on the office door and McGuigan said, 'Come in,' in a voice that he hoped would mask his frustration and increasing desperation.

The door opened to reveal Lisa: 'There's a...' She struggled to find the correct adjective before continuing. 'I have a man here who says you are expecting him, Mr McGuigan.'

McGuigan looked up from the newspaper and smiled. 'Then send him in pet.'

The junkie's jaundiced features were immediately broken by a gap-toothed grin which he flashed Lisa's way as he walked into the office. As an awkward silence started to stretch out, McGuigan at last put the male, wrapped in a green Berghaus anorak and starting to sweat profusely under his woollen beanie hat, out of his misery. 'Sit down and fuckin' talk.'

Collins did as he was bid while Francis McGuigan trained his hate-filled gaze on the housebreaker and petty criminal in a way that left no doubt that the information he was about to provide was his only life insurance policy.

CHAPTER 20

The heat seemed to suck the very air out of his lungs and Thoroughgood felt the sweat run down his back as his nylon shirt dampened. He afforded himself a wry grin as he gripped a leg of his lightweight Lancers, imagining what it would be like traipsing around Zulu Land in the standard-issue woollen trousers of the Strathclyde Police uniform.

'What the fuck you smilin' at, uni boy?' demanded Davidson through his blown fuse box of a mouth.

Thoroughgood inclined his head towards his senior cop and levelled his green gaze into Davidson's grey eyes. 'Just enjoying the sunshine,' he said amiably.

'Well, fuckin' well don't bother cause around the corner there will be another shitty job waitin' to spoil your day, you bloody whelp.'

Thoroughgood realised he was pushing things but at the same time the rookie knew that he had to use the moment to try and get something out of Davidson on the gangland feud that was now being called the ice cream wars by the press.

'What do you make of all that stuff with the McGuigans and Mojito Dawson? I mean, poor Frankie Dawson, the ice cream man got well and truly iced there. Makes you wonder what you could be walking round the corner into.'

Davidson rammed his index finger into the rookie's chest. 'That is nothing for an ink-still-wet-on-his-warrant-card rookie like you to worry about, Pug. Believe me, you've got enough to concern yourself with if you want to make it out the other side of your probation. Anyways, it's a matter for the CID so just fuckin' drop it and concentrate on learnin' the real job, shit for brains.'

Davidson's jaw locked tight while he searched Thoroughgood's features with a malevolent stare for any hint of an underlying motive in the probationer's enquiry.

Thoroughgood let out a sigh and shook his head, but before things went any further their PRs crackled into life. 'Z321 Constable Davidson and Z325 Constable Thoroughgood come in,' ordered Zulu control.

'Well fuckin' take the call will you, Thoroughgood,' ordered Davidson as he removed his police hat from its customary tipsy angle and wiped the glistening sweat away from his brow.

'Z325 Constable Thoroughgood, go ahead Zulu control.'

'Location, please, Z325?' asked control almost disinterestedly.

'Six beat just outside the old Foresthall Hospital, Zulu control,' replied Thoroughgood.

'Excellent, how fortunate. Attend, please, Code 26, suspicious death within the grounds of Foresthall Hospital. Reported by a dog walker who remains nearby the location.'

'Shite,' spat Davidson and stormed off in the direction of the derelict hospital's rusting front gates.

Within moments the sound of a dog barking excitedly guided the two cops to the location. As they made their way through some barely upright outhouses, a dense clump of bushes appeared and just in front of them stood a middle-aged female holding an Alsatian straining at its leash.

'Stop it, Treacle. Calm down, boy, everything's okay,' she said as soothingly as her shaky voice would allow her. The dog eyed the approaching black-and-white clad cops with a ferocious show of its teeth.

'Take your hat off, sponger,' muttered Davidson, before adding, 'For some reason muts hate our lids, don't know why but it seems to get them going, so off with it and keep it down by your side.'

'Done,' said Thoroughgood by way of a reply.

They pulled up five yards short of the female; her face was

covered in trickling, glistening tears while her body was wracked with huge sobs. Her excited canine continued to growl ominously.

Davidson turned on his version of old-school charm. 'Hello, darlin, what've you and Treacle got for us,' he asked, flashing his rotten teeth in a hideous grin.

'It was Treacle, he went into the bushes and wouldnae come out… I followed him in and that's when I found the body…' With that the woman disintegrated into more sobs.

'Come on, sweetheart, it's gonnae be fine, trust me. What's your name?'

'Alison Henshaw,' she said through another tortured heave.

'Well, Alison, everything is under control now the strong arm of the law is here, so don't concern yourself. My boy here will take a look.' Davidson turned to Thoroughgood and inclined his head in the direction of the foliage.

Thoroughgood felt his facial muscles tighten but at the same time he knew that this, for once, was nothing to do with the personal enmity between him and his senior cop. No, this was just the way it was for any rookie cop, you learned on the job.

'No problem,' said Thoroughgood. As he walked past the woman and her Alsatian, he kneeled down and offered Treacle the palm of his hand, which had, resting on it, a Pan Drop mint.

Treacle didn't need a second invitation and scoffed the white, sugar-coated sphere down in a second, licking his lips in appreciation of the unexpected treat. Thoroughgood patted the dog on its head. 'All right, boy, you take it easy and I'll go and see what all the trouble is about,' he said, noting that Davidson had put a reassuring arm around the female now identified as Alison Henshaw, an attractive brunette with impressive cascading tresses.

'Better get moving there, uni boy,' spat Davidson contemptuously over the slight but heaving shoulders of the distressed witness. Thoroughgood rose to his feet and headed towards the foliage, not sure what he was about to discover.

The woman's sobs faded as Thoroughgood waded further into the thickening long grass and, trying to avoid coming a cropper on the broken bits of stone and occasional slabs that reared up from inside the cover of the greenery, he peered into the undergrowth, which was shielding a copse of birches.

His eyes scanned the foliage for any signs of life or, more likely, death. Nothing stood out. Then, as his gaze shifted from the bottom to the top of the treeline, he observed what appeared to be a piece of rope tied and knotted to the top end of a silver branch that was now drooping, half snapped, towards the ground.

Averting his eyes slightly to try and save himself the full force of the brilliant glare that was breaking through the branches, Thoroughgood saw that the rope sloped across to a second tree about five feet away, at a height of around twelve feet.

Thoroughgood followed the line of the rope with his gaze and saw that it descended towards a third and smaller birch, which was situated equidistant between the two bigger trees. Hanging from the smaller tree, wreathed in sunlight and gently swaying, its back towards him, was a body.

Ten feet away from the swinging corpse, Thoroughgood smelled death for the first time and gagged on it.

CHAPTER 21

Thoroughgood moved forwards in small, precise steps, making his way clockwise around the corpse, the back of his right hand held firmly against his nose to avoid the growing stench of rotting flesh.

He could see that the departed was an elderly male. Looking directly into the corpse's face he saw that where the man's left eye had been there was now a writhing mass of putrid movement.

Involuntarily Thoroughgood let out a one-word cry – 'Maggots' – then gagged violently as his mouth filled with vomit.

There was worse to come.

He noticed that the deceased's tongue had apparently exploded out of his mouth; purple and grotesquely swollen, it looked like some cruel fiend had choked the old man on a gigantic sausage.

Unruly silver hair dropped down from underneath a green woollen hat, which was completely at odds with the sweltering heat of the day and the week that had just past. Thoroughgood suspected that the elderly man was unlikely to have been of sound mind when he popped his mortal coil.

As he looked around, a picture of what had gone on during the final minutes of the deceased's life began to develop. There was another, smaller broken tree which indicated that the man had been so desperate to take his own life that he'd had a couple of unsuccessful attempts before he finally got it right.

Thoroughgood was snapped from his hypothesising by Davidson's harsh Glaswegian voice somewhere behind him. 'You got an identity for our suicide yet, uni boy?'

'Not yet, I was just trying to establish how he went about it,' said Thoroughgood, his voice monotone.

Turning slowly, he saw a malevolent glint of sunshine ricochet off the grotesque golden tooth that stood out in a ridiculous contradiction to the rest of Davidson's rotten molars. The senior cop followed the beaten-down grass left by Thoroughgood's footsteps until he was standing next to the rookie and gazing up at the deceased.

As he did so Thoroughgood wondered at how the nauseating smell of rotting flesh seemed to have absolutely no effect on Davidson.

'Fuckin' obvious to me, student sponger, don't need a degree to come up with the answer for that one. Sad, lonely old git has had enough and ties himself to a tree before jumping off. By the looks and stink of him he's been here for a good while. Aye, he's well hung!' said Davidson, cackling at his own tasteless joke.

Thoroughgood couldn't help a frown from escaping across his face, but said nothing.

'Smell too much for you, Pug?' asked Davidson taking a threatening step closer to the probationer. 'Well, you can fuckin' well believe me, this is a picnic compared with Lockerbie, so forget about feeling sorry for yourself. Just you rifle his pockets for any identification and I'll radio into control with an update and tell them to get a shell team to the locus. Get on with it will you, Thoroughgood.'

The elderly male was wearing a frayed checked jacket with a black woollen cardigan drooping out from below it, and Thoroughgood reasoned to himself that there would be something in the jacket pockets that would provide identification.

Gently he slipped his right hand into the inside breast pocket of the jacket and instantly recoiled as his fingers brushed a mass of wet, slimy, wriggling life forms. He pulled his hand back out of the dead man's pocket as if it had been burned and to his horror saw that it was covered in writhing maggots.

'For fuck's sake!'

He pulled his baton out of his trouser pocket with his free left hand and frantically tried to flick, roll and knock them away, desperate to get the maggots off his recoiling flesh any way he could.

Standing three feet away Davidson watched, and laughed long and hard. 'Wait till the shift hear about this one,' he said.

His hand at last clear of the maggots, Thoroughgood bent over and vomited up what was left in his stomach.

CHAPTER 22

Perched on a stool at the end of the bar, Thoroughgood gulped down his lager and stared into the mirror on the wall opposite him. His mind replayed the hideous images from earlier that day, the vile smell from the putrid corpse remained as strong in his nostrils as it had at 11 a.m. that morning.

He'd tried to blot out the nightmarish images by continuing with his planned game of squash at the grandly titled Scottish Squash Rackets Club, in Malloch Street, Maryhill, which was the oldest squash club in Scotland. In reality, though, it was far less grand – a whitewashed, roughcast shed, known to its members as SSRC.

But while his mind had been briefly distracted from the ghoulish scenes of the morning during the heat of battle, once he had reached the bar, in desperate need of a cold beer, the grim visions and the ghastly stench had returned.

Thoroughgood was brought back to the present as a pint of golden liquid was slammed down on the bar in front of him by his opponent, a captain in the Territorial Army Parachute Regiment who was known to everyone at the club as 'Ballistic'. He was resplendent, as usual, in a bright yellow sleeveless T-shirt, which showed off his bulging biceps.

'Fuck's sake, young Thoroughgood, you've got a face on you as long as a wet weekend in Oban. Christ, laddie, if you join the cops you've got to take what comes with it. It's just a pity it didn't seem to put you off your squash. Mind, if I'd nicked that fourth set you'd have been toast in the fifth, puppydog.'

Thoroughgood had given the fitness fanatic, chemist and part-time soldier, who was built like a brick outhouse and had a character twice as large, a brief synopsis of the morning's events before their game had started and now he returned there once again.

'Christ, what type of tortured soul is so determined to top himself that he keeps on trying even after the first branches snap? The poor old sod must have hung himself and prepared to meet his maker, and then *crack* – he's given a reprieve, but still isn't interested in taking it. How sad is that?'

'Look,' said Ballistic, trying his best to talk Thoroughgood out of the bout of wallowing and self-pity he was desperate to immerse himself in, 'almost every suicide has a sad story behind it. I'm betting the old boy was all on his lonesome, a widower, and with no family or none anywhere near to take an interest in him. Maybe throw a bit of depression or mental infirmity into the bargain and Bob's yer uncle. That correct?'

Thoroughgood nodded his head in agreement as, not for the first time, Ballistic had surprised him with his intuition. 'Yeah, one daughter… She emigrated to Canada fifteen years back. How'd you work that all out?'

Ballistic's moustache seemed to bristle with satisfaction at his correct hypothesising. 'I've spent too much time with too many cops in too many bars not to have picked up a few things. I've also seen a hell of a lot with the Paras,' said Ballistic, as usual failing to prefix the Paras with TA.

'If you take my advice,' he continued, 'you'll get a couple of beers down your neck with me and then RV with your mates down the west end and hit Tutankhamun's and pull yourself a nice bit of totty, preferably of the student nurse variety. By tomorrow morning you will have moved on and put what happened earlier today all down to experience.' The TA captain paused to take a short slurp of his lager. 'And for crying out loud, laddie, make sure you never put your hands anywhere near a corpse unless they are firmly sheathed inside a pair of polythene gloves.'

Thoroughgood remained unconvinced and his only reply was

a non-committal grunt from over the rim of his disappearing pint.

Ballistic spotted that the pool table had become vacant and would not accept no for an answer. 'Rack 'em and stack 'em, laddie, and let me take a skydiver off you and give you something else to worry about. Christ, boy, you'd think you were the only polisman in the world to ever discover a suicide. Well, let me tell you, you're no'.'

As Thoroughgood filled the triangle with the pool balls, alternating the spots with the stripes, there was a shout from behind the bar.

'It's for you Gus, a Ross McNab wants a word,' called Agnes, one of the bar staff, waving a phone around in the air.

Before Thoroughgood could reply, a sound that resembled the interference and crackling on a walkie-talkie came from Ballistic's grinning mouth before he said, 'Incoming eh, Thoroughgood, maybe your luck is in?'

Thoroughgood took the heavy cream receiver and smiled at the verbal music now playing to his ears.

'It's me, Gussy boy, fancy a trip down to Tut's to see what we can pull? It's a bank holiday weekend and it will be heavin'.'

'What time?' asked Thoroughgood, Ballistic's pearls of wisdom fresh in his mind.

'Ten p.m. at the front door suit you?' asked McNab from the other end of the blower.

'See you then, big fella,' replied Thoroughgood, replacing the receiver on its holder, hearing the involuntary chime that most members of SSRC claimed was the ghost of the former club steward hiding in the machine.

'Excellent, so you're sorted? Now let me take some weight out of your pockets, laddie,' said Ballistic with palpable relish.

CHAPTER 23

The queue extended right around the corner and Thoroughgood, his chin burrowing down into the upturned collar of his Harrington jacket to stave off an increasingly chilly breeze, turned to McNab and said, 'We've been here for half an hour and it has barely moved, big fella, so, as Baldrick would say, "I think I've got a cunning plan".'

McNab, a couple of inches taller than his friend at six foot three, peered down at Thoroughgood, before asking sceptically, 'And as Blackadder would reply, "Which is?"'

Fishing inside his jacket, Thoroughgood removed his warrant card. 'It's time for the Lennox Hill CID to get on the job.'

At the mention of CID the group of cackling girls in front of the two off-duty rookies turned round and the nearest female, an amply proportioned brunette, who had been a bit too heavy handed with her pale blue eye shadow, enquired, 'Did I hear yous say you were CID?'

'Aye, we're looking for a waitress in a cocktail bar!' quipped McNab, using a line from The Human League anthem of a few years earlier.

'Very funny, yous polis are aw the same, think you know the bleedin' lot,' said the clearly well-refreshed female.

Thoroughgood quickly smiled at her and soothed, 'Forgive my colleague, young lady. We are indeed here on an urgent enquiry. Now, if you don't mind, we need to make our way to the door and find a member of staff.'

Thoroughgood turned to McNab. 'Come on, Detective

Constable McNab and leave the talking to me, you ugly big git.'

'Keep yer hair on,' was the only reply McNab made, but he was happy enough to follow in Thoroughgood's slipstream. As they made their way to the front of the queue McNab's appreciation of the scenery escaped – 'Christ, it's tottytastic' – and was met with a glare from Thoroughgood for his troubles. A couple of minutes later they made it to the front of the queue of bank holiday Friday punters, arriving in front of the mirrored doors at Tutankhamun's entrance.

There they were met by two stony-faced bouncers enveloped from top to bottom in forbidding black, arms crossed and feet planted firmly in front of them.

McNab didn't fancy their chances and whispered, 'You sure about this, Gussy boy?'

A quick glare from Thoroughgood gave McNab the answer he needed and then the rookie turned to face the bouncers and gave it his best shot. 'Ah, gentlemen, nice to meet you. We are Lennox Hill CID and we need your help.' To McNab's amazement Thoroughgood reached up and patted the shoulder of the first outsize gorilla, who sported a huge pink Mars bar running down his left cheek, before muttering in his ear conspiratorially. The simultaneous raising of the doorman's bushy eyebrows underlined that whatever Thoroughgood had come up with was making an immediate impact.

Then the rookie removed his hand and said, 'Now, sir, if you wouldn't mind leading us upstairs we can begin our search of your establishment.'

At the top of the stairs there was a landing with a large stuffed camel staring contemptuously down at all those who were desperate to sample the delights of Tutankhamun's. As they followed the doorman past this bizarre creature, McNab couldn't help himself. 'Wonder what our friend likes with his tea, one hump or two?' before patting the camel's back for good measure.

Thoroughgood winced at his friend's attempt at humour. 'Given that he is of the one-hump variety, our friend here is a dromedary, as opposed to his two-hump cousin, who is known as a bactrian,' and then Thoroughgood patted his mate on the cheek patronisingly.

At that the gorilla with the Mars bar turned round and seared them both with a lacerating stare. 'Are you two jokers for real or just taking the piss and lookin' for a free night out? You wouldnae be the first pair of cops that tried to pull a fast one.'

Thoroughgood immediately held up his hand. 'Indeed we are not, my good man. We have information that inside your establishment there are two car thieves from our patch named Jones and Rennie. Now should you elect to hamper the lawful investigation of two CID officers, who have already identified themselves to you, and obstruct the pursuit of two known criminals believed to be on your premises, then we will have no option but to make a full report to the licensing sergeant,' said Thoroughgood from behind his best poker face.

Thoroughgood could see that the doorman was still far from convinced. 'I can tell you he will take a very dim view of such an obstruction and no doubt summon the establishment's owner, who I believe is a Mr Bobby "Mojito" Dawson, for a discussion about the terms of your license and the conduct of the premises' staff. Do you understand what I am saying to you?' he demanded in an officious and overbearing manner that left McNab gaping in awe at his pal's Oscar-worthy performance.

At mention of Dawson's name the doorman's scepticism evaporated. 'Aw right, aw right, no need to go that far, I was just doin' my job. On yous go and tell Billy at the bar that big Harry says yous are tae have a couple o' beers on the hoose.' And with that the doorman, now known as big Harry, half turned and extended his palm in an open, inviting manner before forcing a smile over his jowly coupon.

Desperate to get in on the moment of triumph, McNab couldn't stop himself adding, 'Thanks, pal, we'll make sure the licensing sergeant hears about your cooperation,' before producing an impish wink.

They bumped and banged their way past the bank holiday revellers as the powerful beat of Blancmange's 'Living On

The Ceiling' reverberated in time with the flashing lights and shimmering sparkle of the glitter balls suspended from the ceiling. Arriving at the bar, Thoroughgood quickly came up with a set of instructions as how to best play their hand. He leant back on the bar, propping himself up on his elbows and trying to cultivate the world-weary, suspicious look that seemed to accompany every member of the CID he'd ever come in contact with like an extra layer of old clothing. McNab, standing beside him, was enthralled by a redhead wearing a tight, dark mini skirt and a black-and-white outsized striped shirt that was pulled tight at her waist by a bullet belt. 'Jeez, I wouldnae mind a piece o' that,' he mumbled.

But Thoroughgood was determined to continue to play his part. 'Look, we need to make a decent show of this. Dirty Harry is still at the door and giving us the once over, so let's split up and make our way around the dance floor like we are at least looking for a suspect. Now point at someone like you've spotted one of our men.'

McNab seemed to give a double take before he realised what was required and managed to drag his bulging eyes away from the gyrating redhead. 'You mean in a pincer movement, like old Michael Caine did in *Zulu*?' he asked, before seeming to thrust his pelvis and point his right index finger at the redhead, who responded by pirouetting around and giving him the benefit of her svelte rear view.

'How many shandies you had already, big man? I meant… Ah, never mind. Just get on with it and I'll get you at the other side of the dance floor.'

Acutely aware that the eyes of the newly christened Dirty Harry were still boring into his back, Thoroughgood made his way in a clockwise direction around the dance floor while, he hoped, McNab had torn himself away from the redhead and was going in the opposite direction to complete the 'pincer movement', as per the example of McNab's great Cockney movie hero. '*Zulu*,' mumbled Thoroughgood. 'Next he'll be claiming we need to *Get Carter*.'

Thoroughgood attempted to make his way through the mass

of dancers leaving the floor after Frankie Goes to Hollywood's 'Relax' finally finished, and as he teetered on the step up from the dance floor Thoroughgood realised that he was also far from sober. But he continued to stare in an over-exaggerated fashion at the rest of the dancers still on the floor and focused in on a male in his early twenties who was resplendent in a red grandfather shirt and navy waistcoat and looked like a Status Quo reject.

Thoroughgood could see no sign of McNab. 'Bollocks, that big arse will get us shot.'

'Did I hear you say something about getting shot, Detective?' asked a sultry female voice from behind.

Turning around, Thoroughgood found himself gawping at the vision in front of him: black and brown cascading ringlets of hair, golden, coffee-coloured skin that glowed alluringly in the pulsing of Tutankhamun's flashing lights, and liquid brown eyes that held his own with a keen intelligence.

It then dawned on Thoroughgood that he had not answered her question and that, given she wore a white silk blouse, side-slit black leather mini skirt and had two lagers on the tray she was holding, this femme fatale was clearly a member of staff.

'You did indeed, Miss…'

'You may call me Celine,' she said, in an almost regal fashion, as if she had bestowed some unique honour on him.

Trying to regain his badly ruffled composure, Thoroughgood pointed to the beers. 'These for myself and McNab – er, DC McNab, I presume?'

'How very perceptive, Detective…' This time it was Celine who let her words trail into a question.

'Thoroughgood, but you can call me Gus,' he replied, returning the compliment, all the time trying not to drown in those delicious chocolate pools of pure silk.

'Well, Gus, if you want to follow me to our VIP area we have two seats reserved for you and your missing colleague. Follow me,' she ordered in that understated, slightly throaty voice which was already starting to do strange things to his head.

'It will be my pleasure,' said Thoroughgood, entranced by the

R.J.Mitchell

stealth and gracefulness of her movement.

Eventually they reached a roped-off area three levels up from the dance floor and Celine ushered him to a red velvet booth with a reserved sign on it. After placing the beers on the table her eyes met Thoroughgood's and held his gaze for a moment he would remember for the rest of his life.

'Will that be all?' she asked and smiled mischievously, almost as if she could read his mind.

Thoroughgood, despite himself, was by now putty in her hands, and couldn't help himself from asking for her number.

Her reply threw Thoroughgood off balance once again. 'So I can help with your enquiries, Detective?' she said, with no obvious hint of mischief.

Before he could formulate a composed reply the words were once again out of his mouth. 'No, because I think you are the most beautiful creature I've ever seen.'

She smiled in an almost girlish fashion. 'Why, flattery will get you everywhere, Detective.' Then she leant down, her perfume intoxicating him as she scrawled out a set of digits on a McEwan's beer mat.

Celine slowly straightened up and through the white silk blouse he noticed a tattoo of a sun in splendour at the top of her right arm.

'I look forward to your call... Gus.'

'You can count on it... Celine,' he replied, watching in awe as she slinked away from the booth as Duran Duran's 'Rio' filled the air.

And somehow Thoroughgood knew that life would never be the same again.

CHAPTER 24

He stared at the form for the hundredth time, the pen between his finger and thumb flicking back and forward, betraying his agitation. Laid out on the table before him was the paperwork that would hopefully gain him a place at Jordanhill Teacher Training College, but he realised it represented much more than a change of career. By signing it Thoroughgood knew that he would be admitting defeat. That Davidson, Rentoul and Jones, the sergeants who had berated and mocked him at Tulliallan, would all have won.

If he resigned, the mocking chorus of 'I told you so' that would echo around various offices and outposts of Strathclyde Police would be deafening – and nowhere more so than in Zulu Land.

The phone conversation he had just had with his mother had brought that plain truth home to him with a vehement force and echoed the sage words of wisdom spun him by Old Bill Kaye, his landlord. But what Thoroughgood couldn't work out was the point in continuing in a job he failed to fit in any shape or form.

He massaged the temples of his forehead with the fingers of both hands as the voice in his head erupted. 'What about Collins? For fuck's sake grow some, Gussy boy.' Then there was Malcolm and Numan, and the hope that there may be some kind of support and opportunity there for redemption and payback.

Staring at the garish wallpaper, Level 42's 'Lessons in Love' filling the atmosphere of emptiness and despair that was all he ever seemed to feel when he was in the flat, Thoroughgood decided that he'd had enough and needed some air – and a beer.

Grabbing his Harrington, he headed for the main door and two minutes later he was crossing Crown Circus and heading into the rear car park of The Rock, already anticipating the first mouthful of Stella Artois that was coming his way.

It was then that his anticipation was broken by the sound of screeching tyres on tarmac. Turning around he saw a white Transit van, two step ladders strapped to its roof rack and hung with various strips of coloured rag that whip-cracked in the air as the vehicle pulled to an abrupt stop just yards away.

Thoroughood's gut instinct immediately saw him ball his fists in readiness for an impending confrontation with a local team of worthies he was unlikely to come out on top of. Then suddenly the dented, grimy rear doors swung open and the eyes of Dennis Numan met his own. 'Come on, son, in you get, we're a man down and you need an opportunity to prove yourself to us, don't you?'

Thoroughgood stuttered, caught totally by surprise.

Numan vaulted out of the Transit and landed two yards away from him. 'For fuck's sake, Thoroughgood, this is where your police career starts for good and we huvnae got time to pussyfoot about. This is it, get in this van and see where the ride takes you, or walk on by and let that shower of scum on your shift piss all over you, break you and leave any hope of a polis career you ever had end in ruins before it's even begun.'

Thoroughgood couldn't tear his gaze away from Numan, and the two men remained locked in a stand-off that seemed to drag out to a backdrop of pounding that Thoroughgood realised was his heart.

Then Numan spat on the pavement. 'A shite-bag then?' he said, and before Thoroughgood could answer he turned and headed for the rear door of the van, through which Thoroughgood could now see several other faces.

As Numan climbed back into the van it dawned on Thoroughgood that he was dressed like a tramp, with an old, wide-brimmed black hat on his head, a faded and moth-eaten brown raincoat pulled tight round his midriff by a piece of string, a pair of grubby Dunlops and what appeared to be black-and-orange striped Adidas tracksuit bottoms.

But the importance of the moment also hit him smack between the eyes. This was it: the gold-plated shot at redemption and a chance to prove he could cut the mustard – and he was bottling it.

'Fuck it,' shouted Thoroughgood, sprinting towards the back of the van. He swung himself up and in, pulling himself onto the wooden seat next to a black-haired individual with a bushy moustache that made him a perfect match for a Mexican cut-throat who'd wandered in off the set of *The Magnificent Seven*. The man, resplendent in shabby denims, said nothing, but the intensity of his dark stare unnerved Thoroughgood and left him having second thoughts over whether he had done the right thing by jumping into the vehicle.

'Well, thank fuck for that, boy!' said Numan, shattering the uneasy temporary silence, before he picked up a bulging black bin liner and threw it at Thoroughgood.

'Ever watched *Mr Benn*, son?' asked Numan.

'As in the kid's cartoon show? Black bowler hat and suit, lives on Festive Road?'

'Number 52 Festive Road, to be precise,' chipped in black moustache. 'From where he heads to the local fancy dress shop where he's met by a shopkeeper wearing a fez!'

'Yes,' said Numan, 'but a shopkeeper with a moustache as well as a fez, so you may as well play the part, Kenny.' And with that, Numan fished into another bin liner and lobbed a burgundy fez at black moustache, also known as Kenny, who plucked it from the air with his right hand and a 'ya beauty!'

'So, do you know what happens when Mr Benn meets our moustachioed, fez-wearing shopkeeper, Thoroughgood?' asked Numan.

'Doesn't he get invited to try on a costume and then ends up having some kind of adventure in it?' said Thoroughgood lamely.

'Close but not quite the cigar,' said Numan. 'Come on, Hardie, paint the picture for our young friend.'

Kenny Hardie bristled with delight and seemed to be

exercising his moustache and jaw at once, as both appeared to move in tandem in a clockwise direction. Folding his arms across his chest, his fez now precariously perched on his unruly thatch, he took up the verbal baton.

'After he is invited to try on a particular costume by the shopkeeper, Mr Benn is then ushered out a magic door at the back of the changing room, where he does indeed enjoy an adventure in a world that is appropriate to his particular costume, before the shopkeeper reappears to lead Mr Benn back to the changing room where his adventure ends and Mr Benn then returns to his normal life in Festive Road.'

Hardie paused to flash a smile that any self-respecting bandito would have been proud of before adding, 'But Mr Benn is always left with a souvenir to remember his adventure, that about the short and curlies of it?'

'Aye, but you better watch whit type of souvenir you get left with from this little adventure, young man!' said Numan and the van rocked with laughter. 'Anyways, it's time you practised your quick change routine, Thoroughgood.'

At that Thoroughgood started to pull out the items of clothing stuffed inside the bin liner and as he did so a look of complete befuddlement and total amazement spread over his features. For the bag contained a schoolboy's uniform comprising a blue blazer, blue school cap and, to Thoroughgood's disgust and total disbelief, grey shorts.

'Well, what you waitin' for, wee man?' Hardie demanded.

The realisation that he was expected to change into the uniform may have dawned but Thoroughgood felt his limbs freeze and his pride bristled. 'Not before I get an explanation,' he said, just as the van lurched to a stop.

'Tonight we are going to catch ourselves a magician, Gus, and you are going to be the bait in our cunning little trap,' said a matter-of-fact voice from the front of the van and Thoroughgood could see that the words had been spoken by Sergeant Cormac Malcom.

'Sorry,' replied Thoroughgood.

'Aye, you bloody well will be if you don't turn into Angus fuckin' Young ASAP,' said Numan, his impatience starting to erode his self-control.

The reference to AC/DC's lead guitarist, who was famed for taking the stage in a schoolboy uniform complete with shorts, put Thoroughgood at ease again and he couldn't help himself erupting into a fit of laughter as the moment of tension dissipated in a flash.

'Now listen up, Thoroughgood,' said Malcolm from the front of the van, before adding, 'Dennis, I'll let you do the briefing as we're behind the eight ball a bit.' Malcolm, who Thoroughgood noticed had a white towelling headband around his skull and was wearing what looked like some kind of black vest, turned round in the driver's seat and started to gun the engine.

'Right you are, gaffer,' said Numan and turned his eyes back towards Thoroughgood. 'Listen and absorb, but while you are doing so get into that bloody uniform pronto, because there isn't gonnae be time for a dress rehearsal, got it?'

Thoroughgood nodded his head and Numan brought him up to speed.

'We're heading for the Kelvingrove Park, where we're going to try and catch us a magician – Ronald Manson, to be precise – who is making a bit of a nuisance of himself. Oor Ronald likes to prey on rent boys, schoolboys and anything that is male, has a pulse and is preferably underage. So you, young Thoroughgood, are going to be our bait,' said Numan, scanning Thoroughgood's features for any sign of hesitation.

Thoroughgood could feel the adrenaline shooting through his veins as he slipped on the blue blazer and then slapped the peaked cap onto his dark head of mullet-styled hair, before he shimmied into the shorts.

'Very fetching,' said Hardie, before dissolving into a peal of laughter.

'Aye, you'll get oor Ronald's attention awright,' said Numan. 'Manson is playing the Pavilion and we have noticed a pattern develop where every time he is in Glasgow a string of nasty little incidents seem to happen up and down the Kelvin Way. His, how shall I say, tastes, are well known, but he confined them to rent boys until a fourteen year-old schoolboy from Kelvinside found himself being fondled by a peroxide-haired male sporting a blonde beard, which fits Manson's description down to a tee. The suspect also tried to perform a sex act on him. Trouble is that Daddy didn't want charges pressed and the whiff of a scandal that would have attached itself to his son's being within the west of Scotland's biggest gay pick-up joint. Even although Manson almost drowned the poor wee bastard in the Kelvingrove Pond.'

CHAPTER 25

The white Transit van, emblazoned with the words 'The Brush-Off: Painters and Decorators, No Job Too Small', pulled up outside the peeling green, wrought-iron gates of the Kelvingrove Park, a couple of hundred yards down the Kelvin Way. All of a sudden the rear doors opened and a slightly overlarge schoolboy jumped out of the vehicle before a brown leather satchel came flying out through the doors behind him.

'Pull that bloody cap down and get the satchel strapped onto your back, boy, and don't worry because there's no radio contact, we'll have your every footstep under observation,' reassured Numan.

Catching the brown leather schoolbag, Thoroughgood did as he was bid, feeling acutely self-conscious, but hoping the dim evening light would help him keep up the right type of appearances.

Then the van doors were pulled shut and the vehicle drove off, leaving Thoroughgood to make his way down the lane that led into the park, where his attention was immediately drawn to the Carlyle monument. It was a tribute to one of Victorian Scotland's greatest men of letters, Thomas Carlyle, sculpted out of three massive blocks of grey granite, with the great man's head, shoulders and arms emerging nobly from the coarsely cleft stone.

Thoroughgood hoped that his dawdling was of the sort that any curious schoolboy would get up to, and as he approached the Prince of Wales Bridge he spotted a stick lying under one of the granite balustrades propping up the remnants of a once elaborate cast-iron lamp bracket. Picking it up, he ran to one of the red sandstone and granite walls and dropped the stick over before jogging back to the other side of the bridge to watch it flow under, carried away by the murky green volume of the River Kelvin. It was an amusement he had been taught by his grandfather, but one that he hoped would convince any spying eyes of his innocence.

As he reached the edge of the bridge a by-now-familiar face appeared. Raising a can of Tennent's Super Brew, a denim-clad male with an unruly shock of black hair and a moustache that seemingly had a mind of its own mockingly saluted. 'Does yer mammy know you're out past yer beddy-byes, wee man?'

'Fuck off, you old jakey,' shouted Thoroughgood, flashing an upraised digit to underline his disgust while trying not to dissolve into laughter.

As he continued his progress towards the duck pond, Thoroughgood breathed a sigh of relief that he had not in fact been cast off to his fate, and began to wonder where Numan and Malcolm would be located within the park.

As he made his way along the footpath that flanked the River Kelvin, there was no sign of the tall, peroxide-blonde male. Thoroughgood spotted a discarded publicity flyer from Manson's current run at the Pavilion and picked it up. The description of the predator he was looking for perfectly matched the image of the magician.

Coming to the end of the footway, Thoroughgood became increasingly concerned about the dying of the light and the accompanying sense of vulnerability that was growing within him.

The park was dead and he recalled some of the rumours and stories that had surrounded it when he had been at Glasgow uni, staying in a third-floor tenement flat in nearby Argyle Street. The most popular fable was that a rent boy had been found with his testes severed and inserted into his mouth, not far from the locus he was presently making his way towards in a not-so-orderly fashion. So concerned had he been at the tales of debauchery that plagued the park and the adjoining Kelvin Way that he had taken the dicey measure of purchasing a lock knife, which he had unfolded with the blade inserted in a cork and secreted within an inside pocket of the biker jacket that was his *façon préférée de robe*. It was an insurance policy should he encounter any unwanted attention when he was taking a short cut through the Park from the GUU bar or his favoured Byres Road hostelry, Bonhams. Fortunately, he had never had to use it, but right now Thoroughgood wished he had his old safeguard nestled snugly within the inside pocket of the school blazer that was straining across his shoulders.

His reminiscing was brought to an abrupt end when a figure loomed out of the gloom just yards away. Sporting a white headband, black running vest and wearing the tightest imaginable pair of shiny green running shorts, Sergeant Cormac Malcolm jogged past within a yard of Thoroughgood and as he did so quipped, 'Nice night for it.' As Thoroughgood turned to watch the black vest and green shorts recede once more into the gloom, he wondered at the sergeant's ability to shut out the increasing chill, though he welcomed the presence of another police officer in close proximity to him.

Thoroughgood had to hand it to them, Malcolm and his men were inventive and imaginative in their choice of undercover clothing, a park jakey and now a lone jogger. Numan was still to make his appearance as what Thoroughgood could only describe as a poor man's version of Worzel Gummidge, the TV scarecrow.

As he made his way towards the duck pond, Thoroughgood saw the imposing form of the Stewart Memorial Fountain lit large in the background. Hewn from granite, sandstone, marble and bronze, the flamboyant French-Scottish Gothic structure commemorated the establishment of Glasgow's first permanent supply of fresh water from Loch Katrine, which had been made possible by Lord Provost Robert Stewart. The fountain incorporated abundant imagery of the Trossachs taken from Sir Walter Scott's narrative poem, 'The Lady of the Lake'. The lady herself, originally resplendent in gilt, was perched atop the central clustered column.

Thoroughgood studied the magnificent and ornate edifice with fascination and wondered at the fact that, during his student days, he had passed it almost every day for four years without stopping to give it a second's thought.

Chiding himself for losing concentration once again, Thoroughgood plodded on towards the duck pond, and as he did so he sensed for the first time that he was no longer alone. The sound of a footfall on the pathway behind him, which echoed out of step with his own, warned him that he indeed had company.

CHAPTER 26

Thoroughgood drew parallel with the duck pond, monitoring the out-of-time footstep that followed his own at an increasingly close distance. Though aware that he was the bait to entice Manson the sexual predator to bite off more than he could chew, he was, at the same time, alarmed at his own ability, or lack of it, to fight off any such attack.

At a loss as to what to do next he paused by the railings that surrounded the duck pond and attempted a furtive glance to his left to try and register the unknown presence that had stalked him through the park's Victorian magnificence for the last hundred yards.

The voice in his head helpfully chipped in: 'Christ, it's just like a scene from the Phantom Bloody Raspberry Blower.'

Thoroughgood's mind was snapped back to the here and now when a leather-gloved pair of hands reached out to grip the rusting fencing that encased the duck pond, just yards away. Then a thinly accented voice said, 'Such a beautiful place to enjoy an evening stroll, but you are out late for one so young, no?'

Thoroughgood raised his jaw slightly so that he could get a full glance at the male, but not enough to give his stalker a full view of the less than youthful features that would confirm he was more Trojan Horse than innocent schoolboy. The male wore a black fedora and was clad from top to bottom in dark clothing. Beneath the brim of the hat were the remnants of a peroxide beard that had now been sculpted into a goatee. Immediately Manson's sly features from the flyer he had scrutinised moments before flashed through Thoroughgood's mind and provided a photo-fit for the male who now stood just three yards from him.

The best the rookie could do for a reply was, 'It's on my way home from rugger practice, mister.'

'Nevertheless, it's a cold evening for a young lad to be out in shorts. My car isn't far – if you wish, I could take you home so much quicker. I am a magician, my young friend, and I can take you anywhere in the world you want to go, and make you experience things that will give you so much pleasure, make all your troubles disappear,' said Manson, his words dripping with salacious intent. He sidled along the railings, edging closer to Thoroughgood, who felt a chill flash down his spine and a wave of nausea wash over him.

'You're okay, mister, my mum says I should never go with strange people I don't know,' said Thoroughgood, worrying that he had over-egged the pudding and would scare the magician off.

But Manson appeared to take Thoroughgood's words as a mischievous taunt that invited even more of his vile attention and, as he spoke, Thoroughgood could hear the rising excitement quivering in his voice. 'Don't be so shy, my young friend, have you never heard of "Manson the Magnificent"?'

Thoroughgood played the game. 'Yes, Mr Manson, I saw your face on a flyer for the Pavilion, people say you're the most famous magician in the world and that you can raise the dead.'

'I can do whatever you want me to,' said Manson. 'What is your name, young man?'

'Angus…Young, Mr Manson,' answered Thoroughgood from under his dipped school cap, in a whisper he hoped would entice Manson's predatory tendencies towards breaking point.

The magician flashed a smile that oozed vile intent and then Thoroughgood's performance, as the tempting bait, snapped the leashes of Manson's limited restraint and the magician took a step closer. Seeing his prey had taken hold of the railings, Manson clamped a leather-encased mitt on Thoroughgood's left hand with a vice-like grip.

'Why don't we take a little walk over to the bandstand?' asked

Manson, his breath quickening in his state of mounting arousal. As the words left his mouth, the magician grabbed Thoroughgood's left buttock with his other hand and squeezed lewdly.

The magician stooped slightly and the garlic from his breath enveloped Thoroughgood, revolting him. The rookie, who had attempted to remain side-on to the predator, saw that Manson was dipping down towards him as he swooped to conquer another innocent victim with his obscene lips.

As he did so, Thoroughgood smashed his forehead straight into the magician's nose. Manson attempted to place his gloved hands to his frothing snout but before they got there the rookie's right hand slammed into his midriff and, as Manson the Magnificent dropped to his knees, Thoroughgood grabbed his head and smashed his jaw off his right knee and the predator keeled over onto the pathway, out cold.

'Now make that all disappear,' said Thoroughgood before taking a wobbly step backwards, his body shaking with the intensity of the disgust he felt for the magician.

But his gaze, which had remained on the fallen fiend, was now diverted by the rustling of some nearby bushes and from behind the foliage stepped a down and out who looked remarkably like a scarecrow.

Moments later, from either side of Thoroughgood, a jakey and an evening jogger appeared, and all four looked down at the inert form of Manson the Magnificent.

'Aye, I reckon somebody better call the Pavilion and tell them they'll need to book a new magician!' said Numan.

CHAPTER 27

Thoroughgood snuggled into the old woollen blanket and wriggled his body in an effort to get comfortable, but sleep, just as it had proven the night before, was elusive, such was the impact Celine had made on him.

What to do now? She had handed him her number and, so far, he had bottled calling her. 'Why? You a man or a moose?' asked the voice in his head, but the truth was that from the minute he had clapped eyes on her he couldn't stop thinking about those brown eyes and her exquisite golden skin and it had literally left him sleepless in Hyndland.

He shut his eyes again but just as he began to drift off a violent banging at the front door of Lennox Hill Police Office snapped him wide awake.

Once again finding himself bar officer on the Sunday early shift, Thoroughgood had taken the opportunity to make the most of the peace and quiet and, left to his own devices, with the rest of the shift out and about, he'd made up the prisoner's bed in the cell behind the uniform bar, locked up the office door and attempted to get his head down and make up for a night spent tossing and turning.

But now someone was at that front door and in a hurry to get in.

He jumped out of the bed, flicked the sleep from his eyes, buttoned up his shirt collar, snapped on his police tie and tried to smooth out the creases. Then he quickly made the bed up as best he could and after he had satisfied himself that it resembled a bunk of flawless quality that would have been fit to grace a dormitory from Tulliallan Castle, the Scottish Police College, he headed for the station entrance.

As the sound of the knocking grew louder and more forceful, an all-too-familiar voice added its weight to the din. 'Thoroughgood, where the fuck are you, boy? If I catch you sleeping on the job I'll have your guts for garters, you little arsewipe,' raged Sergeant Rentoul from outside.

As Thoroughgood tried to unlock the station doors and draw the bolt back he was aware that his hands were shaking at the prospect of meeting the shift gaffer, who had undoubtedly timed his visit to coincide with the absence of the rest of the station's senior men, confident of the chances of catching his favourite probationer trying to catch forty winks on the quietest shift of the week.

As the doors opened and the morning sunlight pierced the gloom inside the windowless office, Thoroughgood's right hand quickly shot up to protect his eyes from the brilliant light. As such he did not see Rentoul's calloused paw exploding towards him until he had him gripped by his shirt and rammed up against the wall opposite the uniform bar.

'You little weasel, think you can get away with anything when Jonesy and Davidson aren't about? Well I've got news for you, Thoroughgood, I'm gonnae put you on paper for this. It's total neglect and you will swing for it,' the sergeant raged, spittle flying from his mouth to splatter on the wall on either side of Thoroughgood.

'Sorry, Sergeant, but I was caught short and needed to take a dump,' replied Thoroughgood, playing innocent.

'Don't bullshit me, Thoroughgood, I bet you were in the prisoner's cell giving it heavy zeds.' Rentoul released his grip and charged into the holding room.

With nothing but silence coming from the cell, Thoroughgood began to breathe again, as it seemed that his immaculate bed-making, which had been so recently and painfully perfected on his basic training course at the Scottish Police College, had come in to good use.

Thoroughgood couldn't help the words slipping from his mouth: 'What do you reckon, Sergeant, a perfect fuckin' ten?'

By this time Rentoul had come back out of the cell, staring in utter disbelief at the probationer's temerity. 'What did you say, Thoroughgood?'

'Sorry, Sergeant, I said we could do with an alarm as loud as Big Ben!' said Thoroughgood, desperately trying to cover his tracks.

Rentoul wasn't buying any of it and, eyes narrowing, he advanced towards Thoroughgood and whipped out his baton, ramming it into the probationer's stomach and forcing him back against the passageway wall. 'I know your type, Thoroughgood, don't try and play the smartarse with me,' spat Rentoul. Then he flicked the point of the baton up just under Thoroughgood's chin, a malevolent spark in his eyes. 'What's to stop me pressing this a little bit harder against your windpipe?'

Gasping for breath, Thoroughgood stammered, 'I don't know what you mean, Sergeant. I meant no disrespect. It's a nightmare when you need to take a shit and the rest of the boys are out on the beat. I just couldn't hold it anymore, it was a Code 21 Brown, you might say, gaffer!' ended Thoroughgood, trying to inject some humour into a situation that was indeed scaring the shit out of him.

A slight smile played at the corners of Rentoul's thin mouth. 'Very good, Thoroughgood, but don't try and wriggle your way out of this one. What's to stop me paying the bog a visit and assessing the evidence?'

Thoroughgood lied for all he was worth. 'Be my guest, Sergeant,' he said, trying to hold Rentoul's piercing gaze with some measure of defiance.

The sergeant flicked the baton down from Thoroughgood's jaw and the rookie breathed a sigh of relief, but his ordeal was far from over. Rentoul walked back into the uniform bar and dropped like a stone into the station constable's swivel chair and waited for Thoroughgood to follow him.

Standing awkwardly at the other side of the reception desk, Thoroughgood attempted to build a bridge. 'Can I get you a coffee, Sergeant Rentoul?'

'Milk and three sugars, but while you're making it, Constable Thoroughgood, you can rest assured that I will be running my slide rule over every inch of this fuckin' uniform bar. Every folder better be up to date or you've had it. You understand, probationer?' he asked.

'Yes, Sergeant,' replied Thoroughgood and headed through the swing doors full of dread.

Moments later he returned with a steaming mug of coffee and placed it down in front of Rentoul, accompanied by a United chocolate biscuit, raided from the kitchen biscuit barrel. Rentoul took a slurp and slammed the mug down, causing coffee to spill over the sides of the drinking vessel and all over the previously pristine desk.

'You better get that cleaned up pronto, Thoroughgood, before your senior cops come back,' he said flatly.

Then as Thoroughgood attempted a mopping-up exercise with a paper towel he grabbed the probationer's wrist. 'Think you've cracked it after helping out those slimy bastards in the internal affairs unit to huckle that pervert Manson, don't you, Thoroughgood?'

The probationer smiled wanly but said nothing as Rentoul continued to hold his wrist in a vice-like grip.

'Well I've got news for you, arsehole, that fuckwit Malcolm and his attack dog Numan have no say on whether you make it through your probation. It'll be Jimmy Rentoul that calls that particular shot and I can tell you it will be a cold day in hell before I allow you to become a cop in this police force.'

Releasing his grip on Thoroughgood's arm he vaulted to his feet in a moment of rage and stalked out of the office, almost taking the front door off its hinges in the process.

CHAPTER 28

Lucy Dawson stared at the television as an episode of *Dallas* played out, but she did not see it. Instead, the vision that occupied her mind's eye on constant repeat was of her younger brother Frankie being pumped full of lead by some faceless thug hiding behind a stocking mask. Frankie, the younger brother whom she had loved with a ferocious maternal intensity ever since their own dear sweet mother, Senga, had gone to meet her maker when Lucy had been only sixteen.

As she swirled her Campari and soda around the bottom of the glass she remembered the good times they had had together as kids, when their mum and dad had both still been alive. They would go to the Kelvin Hall every New Year and slip down the giant slide. Frankie's face and his excited smile flashed back in front of her... so full of life.

Lucy sobbed and dabbed at her tear-stained eyes with her hankie. It was easy for Bobby Dawson to deal with their brother's death because at least he could do something to avenge it, something to turn his hate and torment on the people who had killed Frankie, but for Lucy there were only increasingly tear-soaked memories.

The gruesome murders of Gerry McGuigan and one of his henchmen were proof of Bobby's determination to make Frankie's murderers pay for his death with their own lives. Although her elder brother had not acknowledged that he was responsible for their horrific demise there was no doubt in Lucy's mind that that was the case.

Bobby had always tried to shield her from certain aspects of the family business he deemed as unsavoury, and the twin slayings of members of the rival crime clan were certainly that. Lucy dealt with them by focusing only on Frankie's death and the fact that his assassins had got what they deserved. After all, as the good book said, 'An eye for an eye, a tooth for a tooth.'

Although her younger brother had filled such a huge part of her life, now he was gone there were only so many visits to his graveside to lay fresh flowers that she could cope with. The question she kept asking herself over and over was whether it was time to make a fresh start away from all this hatred. It was the only way Lucy could see of escaping the memories of Frankie that tortured her very existence and left her sleepless and red-eyed. Was now finally the time to leave behind this lethal feud? It was not going to end until there was only one man left standing.

And Lucy knew now, beyond doubt, after the details of the revenge her elder brother had undoubtedly taken had emerged on *Reporting Scotland*, that Bobby 'Mojito' Dawson was determined to be that man.

But if she was to leave Glasgow where could she go? Wherever she went in Scotland, she was sure that the shadow of her elder brother and his notoriety would follow her. Maybe it was time for her to go and stay with Uncle Georgie out in Marbella?

Lucy pushed fingers through the tight curls of her blonde perm and looked at the reflection of her face in the glass coffee table. At twenty-nine, she was still in her prime and she took pride in her appearance; today she was immaculate in a bright red jumpsuit that was fitted to ensure her sharp curves teased from underneath it. Lucy had never been short of male admirers but she knew that the grief that seemed to stalk her every minute was starting to leave her once unblemished features increasingly strained and fatigued.

She stood up and walked over to the mirror above the phone, tracing her index finger around the first hint of a line at the side of her left eye. It was then that Lucy Dawson took a deep breath and resolved to take control of her life once more.

She smiled and watched the pleasing effect it had on her face in the glass pane. Would Frankie want her to spend the rest of her life in mourning for him, or get on with her own and find happiness far away from the goldfish bowl she lived in here in Glasgow?

But Lucy's moment of hope was broken by a pungent aroma, steadily saturating her potpourri-scented flat with its vile odour. For an instant Lucy's mind hit the panic button. Was there a fire somewhere outside or was it in the building? As she made her way into the hall she saw the smoke billowing from her main door and realised that the smell now filling her delicate nostrils was the ghastly scent of melted paint and scorched wood.

As the door began to disintegrate, the velvet curtain that hung behind it, which she used to provide an extra layer of privacy, sparked into flame and crashed onto the carpet. The hall erupted in a sheet of flame and Lucy turned and ran back into her lounge, grasping at the phone and trying not to drop it as blind fear swept over her.

But something was wrong, because at the other end there was only silence.

CHAPTER 29

The information from Collins had been spot on and after taking some time to watch the flat, confirming that the red BMW that sported the personalised plate belonging to Lucy Dawson, LUC 1, was resident in its designated parking bay, Duncy Parkinson had settled back in the front seat of a stolen Sierra and watched the first-floor window that Collins had confirmed was the west end des res of Dawson's sister.

The enforcer turned on the vehicle stereo and the sound of a bell began to chime out into the night. AC/DC's 'Hells Bells' – and now they were ringing for Lucy Dawson. He removed the Champs Elysées black silk stockings that he had specially selected for this moment. He was going to enjoy sending the Dawson bitch to hell with the scented silk trophy he had retained from a recent night of Parisian passion, one which had allowed Parkinson to combine business very much with pleasure.

Then, as darkness fell, Parkinson had the final confirmation he needed that his information was accurate when a permed blonde in a tight red jumpsuit drew the curtains. She was a perfect match for the description the snitch had provided. Now that any element of doubt had been removed, Parkinson mentally ran over his plans for Lucy as Angus Young's power chords let rip and 'You Shook Me All Night Long' sent adrenaline rocketing around his body.

Pulling the small mirror out of the glove compartment, he quickly poured two neat lines of white powder onto the glass from a small brown envelope, leant over and snorted the cocaine up his right nostril. He sat back in his driver's seat, shut his eyes and let the rush wash over him as he pictured the forthcoming moments.

He pulled the balaclava over his head, jumped out of the Sierra and strode across the road to the exclusive block of private flats. The security entry was easily overcome by one of the selection of keys that was part of Parkinson's stock-in-trade.

He made his way swiftly to the first-floor landing, inserted the Molotov cocktail into the letterbox and applied the flame from the Givenchy lighter he had been so pleasingly surprised with as a present for his services satisfyingly rendered in the French capital.

Parkinson watched the petrol-soaked rag in the Irn Bru bottle catch light; a roar and an explosion signalled the beginning of Lucy Dawson's end. With the front door disintegrating in front of him Parkinson knew it was time to do his work. The heat of the flames made him sweat under the balaclava that would protect him from the blaze, but nothing warmed Parkinson quite like the pleasure he was going to take from the lovely Lucy.

He ripped the silk stocking from the pocked of his camouflaged combat jacket and, with his size twelves, booted the remnants of the door off its hinges then charged through the flames like a giant demon set free from the depths of hell.

Lucy heard the crash of what was left of the door slamming onto the hall carpet and ran out of the lounge, wondering if she would be able to try and sprint through the gap it had left to safety. Instead she saw a hulking, balaclava-clad figure coming her way and, as she began to scream, his huge right paw shot out and backhanded her down onto the carpet in a crumpled heap.

Parkinson was immediately on top of her, straddling her and pinioning her flailing arms back against the soft cushioning of the carpet, his pulsing black eyes searing her with avaricious intent.

'Please, please, I don't know who you are, please let me go. If it's money you want, I'll give you the combination to the safe in the lounge,' she desperately panted.

Parkinson rammed both her wrists together, forcing them onto the carpet above her head with his monstrous right hand as he peeled the balaclava back with his left. He smelled her scent and felt the excitement in him threaten to go off the Richter scale.

'I don't want your fuckin' money, bitch. I'm here at the bidding of Francis McGuigan. He has asked me to make you pay for the sins of your murderin' bastard of a brother, Mojito. But before I make good on that promise I'll enjoy myself with you, Blondie – "One Way or Another",' he added, in a cruel mock tribute to the pop group of the same name.

Lucy's azure eyes filled with terrified tears, but the sight of them running down her tanned neck and into the plunging zipped cleavage of her jumpsuit broke the damn of Parkinson's self-restraint and he pressed his face onto hers, clamping his lips onto Lucy's just as she attempted to scream.

Then Parkinson relocated his mouth next to Lucy's left ear. 'Prepare for the ride of your life, bitch,' he whispered malevolently and ripped the zipper down across Lucy's heaving breasts.

But as he did so Parkinson's ears perked up as he heard the sound of a siren, growing stronger.

'Damnation,' he raged. Pulling himself off her he tossed Lucy Dawson onto her stomach like she was a child's plaything.

She had just enough time to make one last scream for help before Parkinson wrapped the black silk stocking around her neck and garrotted the life out of Lucy Dawson.

CHAPTER 30

Francis McGuigan sat in the lounge of his front room, staring into the glass of malt cradled in his right hand. Silence, broken only by the ticking of a garish gold clock placed in the middle of the mantelpiece and the occasional spark from the fire, filled the room.

His mind was full of conflicting emotions but right now it was the need to hear that Parkinson had done his job that was eating away at him. He stood up and stretched his stiffening bones, all too well aware that Father Time was also ticking away and that he was facing the greatest challenge yet to his family's domination of Lennox Hill without his beloved son and most trusted lieutenant, Gerry.

Above the fireplace sat the portrait of his da, Sean, fingering the gold pocket watch he had given him on his eightieth birthday. Once again he found himself talking to it. 'What now, Da? I'm too old for all of this. Why the fuck couldn't Gerry have stayed his hand… Ah, shite.' As he spoke, Francis McGuigan realised that his words were tinged with fear.

The noise of a diesel engine drew McGuigan to his front window and through the latticed glazing he saw a marked police Land Rover slow to a crawl on the road outside and then draw to a stop, the driver's side nearest to the kerb.

From behind the wheel, the cop driving the vehicle flashed a malicious smile that betrayed a mouthful of rotten teeth, before drawing back two fingers across his neck in a throat-slitting gesture and breaking into a laugh that McGuigan could almost hear from inside his lounge. Then the engine gunned back into life and the vehicle drew off.

'Fuckin' filth,' spat McGuigan, his mind trying to work out whether Parkinson was already being pursued for the murder of Lucy Dawson or if it was just another one of the wind-up drive-bys that the local cops liked to indulge in every so often.

Taking another sip of his malt, McGuigan pulled himself together. 'Don't be so feckin' silly, Francis. If they knew anything about Duncy they would boot the bleedin' door of its hinges. Get a grip, man.'

McGuigan cast another impatient glance at the clock and then counter-checked it by clicking open the pocket watch, the same one from his da's portrait, which now accompanied him wherever he went. 'Where the bejesus is he?' It was 2 a.m. He poured himself another dram of Glenfiddich, for he couldn't plan ahead until Parkinson had confirmed Lucy Dawson was no more.

Endless moments of torment and frustration passed before, as McGuigan felt fatigue start to envelop him, the lounge's mahogany-panelled door banged open and the hulking figure of Duncy Parkinson strode in.

'Lucy Dawson is done and dusted, Francis. Aye, and for my troubles I nearly ended up toast as well,' smiled Parkinson, his wide-eyed, almost innocent features in complete contradiction with the ruthless nature of his business and the relish with which he conducted it.

'That's great, Duncy, but did the emergency services get there in time to retrieve the body before it was burnt to a crisp?' demanded McGuigan, his irritation threatening his self-control.

'Judgin' by the sirens that started wailing while I was, er, on the job, so to speak, I wouldnae have much doubt about that boss,' smiled Parkinson before he flopped down onto a giant black leather settee.

'Let's hope you're right on that, Duncy, because I want Mojito to get the message that I will stop at nothing to finish this – and him,' said McGuigan and poured Parkinson a huge measure of whisky from an elegant crystal decanter that was at odds with the lurid pink wallpaper and outlandish purple drapes, selected by his wife Bridie, that framed the front room of the house the locals referred to as 'Southfork' in sarcastic tribute to the not-so-humble abode of the Ewing clan from Dallas.

Handing the glass to Parkinson, McGuigan once more took up residence in his fireside chair and stared into the flames.

But Parkinson's enthusiasm for the job he had just done on Lucy Dawson got the better of him and he whipped out the black silk stocking and sniffed it. 'Mmm, I can smell her scent, maybe a Chanel number fiver. Handy things, stockings.'

McGuigan glanced towards his number two over the rim of his whisky glass but he said nothing. Parkinson's laughter died in his throat.

Eventually the enforcer could handle the silence no more. 'So what next, Francis? As soon as it gets out that Lucy Dawson was strangled, Mojito is going to come looking for us.'

'He isn't going to be the only one looking for us, Duncy. I'd imagine CID will be wanting to give us a tug as well. You got a watertight alibi sorted?'

Parkinson smiled wolfishly. 'I'm on my way to meet her now, Francis. I think you met Lisa the other day at the bar,' he said, through another huge grin that seemed to set his sideburns moving up and down the side of his face of their own free will.

'Christ, Duncy, will you be careful. This is a war and from now on I want two boys doubled up here on the house and you makin' sure that you're no' takin' silly chances yersel,' warned McGuigan.

'Gotcha,' said Parkinson. 'But what aboot the Mojito wan? If you ask me, boss, we need to find him and take him out, cos as long as he's breathing we're no' gonnae be able to take it easy.'

CHAPTER 31

Thoroughgood perched on a wooden stool at the end of the bar in Bonhams and stared at the cartoon caricatures of Victorian and Edwardian gentleman in various states of sartorial elegance that adorned the cream walls. He wondered if these luxuriously whiskered dignitaries from the past had ever found themselves wedged firmly between the rock and the hard place he felt was his current location.

Looking into the bottom of his pint, he tried to make sense of where he was and, more importantly, where he was going. His involvement with Malcolm, Numan and the unit offered a glimpse of just how exciting 'the job' could be, and although the reality of where he, Z325 Constable Thoroughgood, was right now was straining his resolve to the limit, Thoroughgood knew that he had an opportunity to play a key part in bringing Davidson, Jones and Rentoul down, and in doing so there would perhaps be the chance for a secondment into the unit on a more permanent basis.

For, however embryonic his length of service, if he could prove himself useful enough at the particular line of work Numan and Malcolm specialised in, they would surely find a place for him, he argued with himself.

Draining his Stella, he raised a hand in an attempt to catch Anna's attention and was rewarded with a smile and her presence at the other side of the bar.

'Drinking on your own tonight, Gus? Don't they say that's the sign of an unhappy man?' said the bar manageress, running her fingers lightly through her long blonde tresses.

'But Anna, how could I ever be unhappy when I have a vision of loveliness like you to feast my eyes on?' replied Thoroughgood, aware that his eyes were indeed devouring the curves of her svelte body which were so enticingly amplified in a blue-and-white dress that he knew, as always, would stop well above the thigh.

'Very good, your patter is almost as bad as McNab's! Where's your big pal anyway?' she asked, and in so doing confirmed to Thoroughgood that his sidekick clearly occupied pole position in Anna's affections, while he was a good bit further back on the starting grid.

'Night shift, although knowing big bugger lugs he's probably pitched up at coffee hauf off the Alexandra Parade, boring some poor waitress senseless with his unique brand of humourless chat,' said Thoroughgood, trying but failing not to bitch.

As Anna laid his pint down he slipped a fiver across the bar. 'I didn't know you were interested, Anna, but if it's a help I think the feeling is mutual with the big fella!' he said with a wolfish wink. 'Anyways, could you look after my Stella, she is as close as I'm ever likely to get to female company these days,' he added, only half in jest.

'Detective Constable Thoroughgood, I'm sure you are being too modest by far,' said a slightly husky voice from behind him that had a hint of the Caribbean in it.

The words sent a shiver running down Thoroughgood's spine, while the reaction in Anna's face was a mixture of amusement and surprise that sent his spirits soaring in the hope that the words belonged to the girl he had so recently met who had been unlike any other female he had ever encountered.

As he turned around, his gaze was met by her brown pools of molten chocolate. Thoroughgood felt a light go on inside him.

'Hello, Celine, how are you?'

'I'm very well, Gus, but tell me – is your friend right, are you unhappy?' she asked, smiling.

Thoroughgood couldn't resist reaching for the cliché book when it came to his answer: 'I was... Until you walked in the room!'

From the other side of the bar came a round of applause and Anna said, 'Bravo! Even by your standards that was an exceptionally cheesy answer, Gus, or should I call you Detective Constable Thoroughgood?' Her heavy sarcasm hinted at the bogus nature of Thoroughgood's newfound exalted status.

Turning back to Anna, Thoroughgood quipped, 'Caught between two goddesses, it doesn't get any better than that, wait till I pinch myself and see if I've died and gone to heaven.' He duly did so and, laughing out loud, said, 'Nope, still alive and kicking!'

Then Thoroughgood turned back to Celine. 'Can I buy you that drink?'

But the answer to his question was supplied by a masculine voice. 'I think you'll find that's my job, my young friend,' said a middle-aged male dressed all in black, with a shaven bald head and a glinting diamond earring in his left lobe.

Thoroughgood's gaze darted from the male to Celine, and he thought for a second that there was a genuine hint of sadness in her eyes, as the rookie desperately sought confirmation that she was not with the male whose identity he knew instantly, and who exuded an understated menace.

He did not have long to wait for his answer and again it was not Celine who provided it. 'Bobby Dawson,' said Mojito, slipping a proprietary arm around the shoulder, deliciously coffee coloured, that Thoroughgood was so desperate to touch.

Thoroughgood looked anxiously for confirmation in Celine's face that she was not with the man who was rapidly becoming Glasgow's most notorious mobster and who was engaged in a lethal turf war that was dominating the front pages of every newspaper in Scotland.

For a second it was as though Dawson did not exist, as their eyes met and held once more, then she turned to Mojito and stroked long, lithe fingers over his left hand. 'Gus is a regular with us at Tutankhamun's, Bobby. Why don't you let me get the drinks in while you get us a table and I'll be right over with them?'

Her words crushed Thoroughgood.

But as Mojito widened his lips in a cold smile, his piercing black eyes darted from the cocktail waitress back to Thoroughgood as he assessed the threat level posed by the younger man and his intentions, romantic or not, for Celine.

'Aye, sounds like a plan, darlin'.' Dawson looked around and spotted a couple leaving a table for two located just by the entrance. 'Perfect timing. And I think you know what my preference is.'

'You know I do, Bobby!' she replied, with a sly laugh that implied an intimacy that made Thoroughgood feel nauseous.

He turned and stared into the mirror behind the bar gantry, trying to keep his emotions in check and also trying to reason why he was being so wound up by a girl he had only ever met once before and then so fleetingly.

While he acknowledged to himself that Celine's very presence was playing havoc with his self-control, he also realised that her apparent intimacy with Mojito may provide an opportunity… if it was superficial. But was it just his own desperate infatuation with this beautiful and exotic creature that was making him think that way?

'What's wrong, Gus?' she whispered from his left-hand side and he felt his body temperature rocket.

Before he could stop himself the words came out. 'Please tell me you're not involved with him?' he asked, almost pleading with her to deny his worst fears.

Celine applied a sidestep. 'That, Detective, depends on what you mean by "involved". Bobby Dawson is my boss and a man who is going through hell right now after the murder of both his sister and his kid brother. He needs company around him he can trust.'

'And can he trust you, Celine?' asked Thoroughgood, a little too forcefully.

She turned her gaze away from him and he felt like he'd been slapped.

'A Bacardi, ice and coke, and a Cuban mojito, please,' she asked Anna, whose eyes were devouring the drama that was being played out on the other side of the bar.

'For a *friend* of Bobby "Mojito" Dawson,' said Anna, 'anything.'

Anna's reply instantly prompted Thoroughgood to swivel minutely on his bar stool to check for the reaction her words had on Celine; he noticed a slight tightening of the skin around her mouth and lips.

'Anytime tonight, sweetie, would be good I'm sure,' said Celine and then she switched her gaze to Thoroughgood and asked curtly, 'Correct me if I'm wrong, but did I not write my number on a beer mat and hand it to you?'

Caught off guard and placed behind the eight ball by the directness of Celine's question, Thoroughgood cleared his throat. 'Yeah, but this whole business your boyfriend is wrapped up in has left us working round the clock...' He trailed off lamely, knew it and shrugged.

'But you still find time to come into Bonhams and chat up your little blonde bit of fluff behind the bar?' asked Celine.

'Do you mind?' snapped Anna.

'Appearances can be deceptive,' replied Thoroughgood looking solely at Celine.

'Exactly my point, Detective and one that, worryingly for a man in your profession, you seemed to have missed completely.' As she spoke, Celine seemed to smoulder in front of Thoroughgood.

Then she shoved a ten-pound pound note onto the bar counter, picked up the two glasses Anna had just laid down, and said, 'Keep the change, cutie, your wardrobe could probably do with any help it can get.'

As she turned away from the bar, Thoroughgood's left hand seemed to operate independently from the rest of him and relocated itself to her right wrist. Before he knew it, he was saying, 'Look, I'm sorry, can we start again?'

'I didn't know we had "started anything" in the first place,' she snapped, looking down at his hand. As he removed it, she walked off towards Mojito, with Thoroughgood mentally floundering in her wake... yet again.

As she sat down opposite Dawson, the crime lord scanned Celine's face, seeing the tension in her lovely features. 'I hope that boy wasn't giving you any trouble over there, Celine? He's a cop, isn't he? Big Harry told me we were paid a visit by two young "detectives" recently. Aye, one of the names he mentioned was Thoroughgood,' said Dawson, drawing the last word out sarcastically. 'That was just the other night. I don't think Harry was too convinced that they were who they said they were, or at Tut's on legitimate police business for that matter. So I take it that is where our young friend met you, or is there something else you want to tell me, Celine?' asked Dawson, letting his words trail of into a barely audible whisper.

Composing herself, Celine's face regained its usual serenity and she replied from behind a smile. 'I think someone has just got his wires a bit crossed, Bobby. But it's a misunderstanding that I hope is cleared up now. Can we just enjoy our drinks, please?'

But Mojito's foreboding features were taut, his eyes trained across the bar to where, Celine saw, Thoroughgood was holding his gaze with an all too contemptuous stare.

'I don't think the "detective" has got the message,' said Mojito and, before she could do anything to stop him, he rose from the table and strode across to where Thoroughgood remained perched motionless on his stool, staring into the mirror behind the gantry.

He saw Dawson's reflection in the glazing as the gangster stood just behind him, but Thoroughgood continued to sip his beer, apparently oblivious to his presence.

'What's your problem, pal?' asked Mojito, his voice laced with menace.

As he studied Dawson's drum-tight features in the mirror, Thoroughgood could see that the crime lord's self-control was being strained to its limit.

Smiling into the mirror, Thoroughgood played the wind-up. 'Just wondering what puts a beautiful girl like Celine on the arm of an old slaphead like you, Dawson? The money, the power or your magnetic personality?'

'Why don't you turn around and find out, arsehole.'

Finishing his mouthful of lager, Thoroughgood slowly placed his pint on the marble-topped bar and as he did so he saw Anna's worried presence materialising on the other side of the counter.

Bracing himself, he turned to face the gangster just as Mojito's right hand cracked off his jaw and smashed him back onto the bar, half sprawled over it. Then Dawson was on him like a rash, and grabbing the rookie by his Harrington he hauled him upright.

'Listen to me, you piece of shit. If I ever catch you looking in the same direction as Celine, never mind coming within a mile of her, I will personally make sure that your cop career is over and that you are in no fit state to try your hand at anything else, do you understand me?' demanded Dawson.

'How you gonnae do that, Dawson? Remember, I got 7,000 friends all wearing monkey suits to call on.'

Aware of the enraptured attention of everyone in the bar, Dawson refused to take the bait. He took a deep breath and then allowed a feral smile to slip across his face. 'I think you'll find, Detective Constable, if that is indeed what you are, that Bobby Dawson has friends in every walk of life in this city and you, my foolish young boy, have now made an enemy of every one of them. I can promise you one thing, Thoroughgood – hiding behind a uniform will not save you if you cross me again.'

Then Dawson pushed Thoroughgood away and, smiling sarcastically, began to smooth out his ruffled sleeves. The rookie tried to regulate his own breathing but couldn't help his left hand shooting up to his throbbing jaw.

'You can take that as your first and last warning, Thoroughgood,' said Mojito and walked away.

Looking past the gangster's black-suited back, Thoroughgood saw that Celine was now on her feet and as his eyes searched her face he found no sympathy. Instead he was met with an icy glare that left him in no doubt who had come off best in her eyes from his confrontation with Dawson.

As the gangster drew level with her she whispered something in his ear and, leaning forward, kissed Mojito on his cheek.

Before he could help himself the words slipped out of his

mouth: 'For crying out loud!'

Then as the gangster and his moll left Bonhams, Thoroughgood's attentions were pulled back to the here and now. Smiling from behind the bar, Anna said, 'I think you might be needing this, Gus,' and handed him an ice pack.

CHAPTER 32

'Where the fuck is he? Tell me how that miserable little maggot can have vanished off the street and you can't lay hands, never mind eyes, on him?' demanded Dawson.

The man at the other end of the line was in no mood to back down. 'Look, Mojito, Collins is as slippery as they come and he's wired to the moon, has fences and snitches tipping him the wink everywhere. That's why he's so hard to huckle. He's always one step ahead of us and he seems to have decided that he's better off touting to the McGuigans.'

'That's just as I suspected. I wouldnae put it past the little scumbag to have tipped them off with Lucy's address. Christ, how else would the McGuigans have come across it,' said Dawson, his voice starting to quiver with emotion.

'Don't worry, Bobby, I've got Davidson and Jonesy lookin' down every hole the little bastard has ever crawled into. Sooner or later he'll surface in need of something to feed his habit and that's when Collins gets careless and our boys will be ready and be there to pounce. If he's had anything to do with what happened to poor Lucy, I promise you we will deliver him to you.'

'Make sure you do, Jimmy. But I want you to take care of another little itch that's needing scratched for me,' said Dawson, but before he could continue the sound of a slight creak from the landing outside his office distracted him.

'Give us a minute, Jimmy,' said Mojito and, placing his hand over the receiver, he waited for a few seconds to see if there was anyone there.

Satisfied that his imagination was getting the better of him, Dawson swivelled his black leather chair round towards the small window behind him, partially illuminated by the orange sheen of a streetlight, and returned to his specialist subject. 'Do you know a detective called Thoroughgood?'

The explosion of laughter from the other end of the phone left Mojito bemused. Impatience and frustration getting the better of him, he snapped, 'What's the big fuckin' joke, Rentoul?'

At the other end of the blower a rough clearing of the throat took place before Rentoul was eventually ready to reply. 'Aye, yer havin' a laugh, Bobby! I know a Thoroughgood all right, a Gus Thoroughgood, but he's a rookie and no' close to being a DC in this life or the next. I'm making it my personal fuckin' mission to ensure that there isn't a cat's chance in hell that he makes the SID.'

'That's very interesting, Jimmy. You're sure there's no chance of there being more than one Thoroughgood in the force?'

'Early twenties, arrogant as hell, about six foot, jet black hair and green eyes that look like they belong to some picture on a wall that's watching you wherever you go?' asked Rentoul.

'I'd say you've got our man spot on, old friend,' said Dawson, a cruel smile slipping across his normally impassive features.

Now it was Rentoul's curiosity that got the better of him. 'Why you askin', Mojito?'

'Had a run-in with the cocksure bastard in a bar down Byres Road the other night, seems he's taken a shine to a young lady I have high hopes for. But he was also round at Tut's on the bank holiday weekend, claiming he was CID and looking to nab a couple of car thieves,' explained Dawson.

'Well, blow me senseless, I'd never have credited the little fucker with the baws for it. What you want done with him, Bobby?'

The silence from the other end of the phone indicated that Dawson was left in two minds over his favoured form of retribution, but as it started to draw out, a light knock on the office door startled the crime lord. 'Just a minute, Jimmy, got someone at the door.' For a second time, Dawson placed his left hand over the receiver and directed a shout at the door. 'Who is it?'

The answer from outside brought a smile to his cold features. 'It's Celine, I've brought you the licensing documents you asked for, Mr Dawson,' she said, taking care to remain respectful while within the earshot of any other members of Dawson's staff.

'In you come, darlin',' said Dawson, and she entered the room with the strains of Bon Jovi's 'You Give Love a Bad Name' temporarily drifting into the office from the bar below. As she reached his desk, Dawson gestured to her to put down the paperwork, smiled and, taking his hand back off the receiver, returned his attention to the phone. 'I think it's time you arranged a meeting, Jimmy. That will allow me to deliver a message to our rash young friend.'

'That won't be difficult. Let's say we could use that to kill two birds with one stone,' said Rentoul.

'Okay, Jimmy, let's just make sure things get sorted. Keep me in the loop and you will have my usual gratitude for your help. Buenos noches, amigo,' said Dawson and put the phone back on its holder.

Slowly his dark eyes looked up at Celine and, holding her gaze, Dawson said, 'It seems your young admirer from the other night is not all that he claims to be, Celine.' He felt his blood run hot at the sight of her stockinged legs, just inches away from him.

'What do you mean, Bobby?' she asked in her velvet tones.

'Apparently Detective Constable Gus Thoroughgood is actually Probationer Constable Thoroughgood. I'm sorry, Celine, but when I care about someone I like to do everything I can to take care of them. Looks like your earnest admirer has been spinning you a line.' Then, aware of the bitter irony of his words after the brutal slayings of his younger brother and sister, Dawson's eyes suddenly pooled with tears.

Trying desperately to gain control of his emotions, Dawson cuffed furiously at the tears, determined to extinguish any show of vulnerability in front of Celine.

She smiled soothingly at him and her right hand spontaneously shot out to touch his fingers in a show of warm-hearted support.

'Come on, Bobby, don't punish yourself. There was nothing you could have done to save Frankie and Lucy.'

Looking up into her face Dawson couldn't stop himself shaking his head viciously in the negative. 'That's where you are completely wrong, Celine. They are both gone and for as long as I live I will have to bear the burden of the guilt for their murders on my conscience, and it won't matter what I do, nothing is ever going to salve it,' said Dawson, his voice once again quivering with raw grief.

Jumping to his feet, the gangster grabbed the back of his chair and launched it at the mirror behind his desk; the glass smashed into a thousand tiny glittering shards. Then, his mind a maelstrom of conflicting emotion, Dawson stalked out of the room without looking back.

Standing on a sea of broken glass, Celine ran her hands though her tousled hair, aware that she had reached a crossroads.

CHAPTER 33

Try as he might, Thoroughgood couldn't get her out of his mind. Of all the people for Celine to be mixed up with, why did it have to be Mojito Dawson? He asked himself this question over and over again. Then in an attempt to get some peace he tried to reason that, after their brief encounter in Bonhams, it was something that was no longer his problem.

'Fuck it,' he said out loud as he swivelled the bar officer's chair around, staring absent-mindedly at the front door of Lennox Hill police station and waiting for it to open and provide him with a customer that would help break his bout of self-torture.

Nothing.

He'd long since switched to a glazed-eyed autopilot as he filed the paperwork that was generated by the cops trusted to pound the beat while he, a wet-behind-the-ears probationer, kicked his heels in a dingy office, caught in a 1960s time warp, with its every window steel-shuttered tight.

The role of bar officer, or station constable, was either filled by old timers counting down the final years of their service towards a fat pension they couldn't stop talking about, or rookies like him, who detested the mind-numbing minutiae of a job they saw as only fit for the old, while they should be out on the streets chasing housebreakers and jailing junkies.

He placed the last 'green' section of the triplicate white, pink and emerald crime report form in its chronological place and contemplated heading through to the tiny kitchen at the rear of the station for another coffee. But Thoroughgood couldn't help

R.J.Mitchell

his mind focusing in on the turf war now raging between the McGuigan clan and Mojito Dawson that had played out across the length and breadth of Zulu Land and was starting to make the area front page news in the papers. The latest bloody episode had been the murder of Lucy Dawson, whose body had been retrieved from her burning west end flat, which was ghoulishly reported on the front page of *The Sun*: 'Gangster's Sister Found Strangled in Blazing Flat'.

While it was clearly an escalating case of tit-for-tat in a classic gangland feud, now leading to lurid headlines implying that Strathclyde Police had lost control of the streets, Thoroughgood found himself drawn repeatedly to what he believed must have been the luring of Gerry McGuigan and Danny French into the trap, right in the heartland of their manor and without any signs of an apparent struggle, which ultimately led to their grizzly slayings.

Something didn't add up, but right now he didn't have a clue what were the missing parts of that particular sum. In any case it was a CID matter, which was now attracting the attention of the Serious Crime Squad, and not for the likes of a fresh-faced rookie like him to worry about. Thoroughgood sighed to himself, leaning back on the swivel chair with his Doc Martens up on the desk, and chewed the black biro that was nestled in the side of his mouth.

The bang caused by the station door smashing back against the wall was like a rifle shot and Thoroughgood almost fell off the chair as Jones and Davidson burst through it, clearly in the middle of a heated argument.

'What the fuck is Mojito gonnae want next, where does it end now?' demanded Jones of Davidson, his open palm flashing out in front of him, just as the latter noticed the startled Thoroughood, who had previously been almost dozing, trying to regain his position on the station constable's chair.

'You sleepin' on the job again, you snivelling student arsewipe?' spat Davidson, his finger jabbing in Thoroughgood's direction.

'These greens better be filed in correct order by the time I finish my piece break, boy,' barked Jones, his eyes bulging from their sockets.

Thoroughgood did his best to try and regain his composure. 'Whites, pinks and greens all filed. Lost property book updated following the handing in of a brown leather wallet containing £3.52 precisely. There is also a stray dog currently residing in the prisoner's cell and waiting for the dog man to arrive and impound,' reported Thoroughgood, desperately trying to avoid any smugness creeping into his delivery.

He failed miserably.

Davidson ripped his police hat off and fired it straight at Thoroughgood, who ducked just in time as the saucer-shaped missile smashed into the radio charger behind him and toppled a PR onto the light blue linoleum that ran the length and breadth of the office.

His attention drawn to the clattering radio, Thoroughgood failed to see Davidson launch himself at the bar, attempting to grab the probationer by his clip-on police tie. Arching his back like a limbo dancer on fire, Thoroughgood only just managed to avoid the senior cop's grasping hands, but not the verbal volley that was heading his way.

'Listen to me, you smug little son of a bitch, there'd better not be a report out of place. Now give me the daily briefing register, and if you have missed an extra attention request I will come round the other side of the uniform bar and personally give you the hiding you are begging for, uni boy,' bawled Davidson, veins bulging down his neck, his self-control almost completely gone.

Thoroughgood could feel his whole body shaking at the intensity of Davidson's latest verbal broadside but gritted his teeth and played his best poker face as he attempted to avoid letting it show.

Jones attempted to offer a more placatory approach. 'Listen, son, it's been another shitty first half of chasing shadows and jakeys, just give us time to get our scran and cool down and I'll take over behind the bar and you can take a turn out for the second half. Edmund Philip is due down from divisional HQ in time to take you out after the break, so don't sweat it son.' And with that the outsize senior cop headed through the swivel doors that led to the rear of the tiny station with Davidson in his wake, but not before the latter cast a feral smile at Thoroughgood that let the rookie know that sometime soon there would come a reckoning between them.

CHAPTER 34

The two dark figures, their shadows lengthening with the dawning of the day, had walked 500 yards from Lennox Hill office and already one of them was moaning.

Edmund Philip was another ex-army senior cop, but different from the rest of the shift in that he was an Essex boy who had relocated to Strathclyde Police from the Met after meeting a Glaswegian nurse on an overnight bedside vigil babysitting an armed robber.

While Philip's figure was ramrod straight, the toes of his boots burnished to an immaculate glaze and the creases of his uniform sharp enough to cut a finger on, the matter that filled the slot between his two ears was less so and he had become the butt of many jokes at the hands of his merciless colleagues, though he seemed to be able to meet the ridicule with a sanguine mentality.

At fifty-one, Philip was already world weary and of the opinion that he was long overdue a set of stripes and a sergeant's promotion. Underneath it all he was a decent man but one who had enjoyed 'the freebies' that went with the job a little too much and who, as a result, had his promotion hopes scotched by what was commonly known as 'bootin' the arse out of it', in terms of milking the extras afforded to beat officers by the few members of the community who were desperate to court the strong arm of the law.

Having already spent the first half of the night shift at divisional HQ, he was less than happy to be nurse-maiding a rookie around Lennox Hill at 5 a.m., when the breaking of dawn and the early morning rounds of postmen and milkmen meant that any self-respecting housebreaker would be long ago tucked up.

'It's a bloody pain in the arse, that's what it is. I don't see why a man of my service should have to come down here to make sure you don't piss yourself at the sight of a shadow. Ain't you on the job long enough to walk the beat on your own, Pug?' asked Philip in his Cockney accent.

'It's nothin' to do with me, Edmund. You got a beef, then take it up with the gaffer. What's wrong – can't keep up with a rookie anymore?' said Thoroughgood mischievously, before ducking to avoid a playful clip over the head.

'Cheeky pup! You're a graduate, ain't ya? You know what they're callin' you up at divisional HQ?' asked Philip, but didn't wait for Thoroughgood to reply. 'They're calling you "the grass for the brass".' Philip let out a mirthless chuckle. 'Imagine that, a graduate probationer touting to the bosses, I can't imagine why anyone would think that, can you Z325?'

Thoroughgood attempted to provide a reply but found himself talking to Philip's back as the senior cop turned almost at a right angle towards a nearby, partially smashed-up bus stop, plonking himself down on the parcel shelf of a seat inside it.

'Me bleedin' feet are loupin'. Had a couple of homers to do during the day and only caught three hours kip. Knackered,' moaned Philip after he'd parked his arse as best he could.

Thoroughgood, speechless, stood opposite his senior man, who then amazingly tipped the hat down over his eyes and closed them. Under the rim of his police hat Philip's eyes may have been shut, but his mouth was open. 'Well, son, you gonna elaborate? I came across a few smart-arse graduates down in the Met, graspin' treacherous bastards they was, who would sell their granny to get a leg up. That you, Z325?'

'No way,' replied Thoroughgood tersely.

'But for one reason or another you ain't the most popular with the shift, are you, my son? Usually from my experience there ain't no smoke without fire either, matey.'

'Just because I don't play poker at piece break and read the

Herald or the *Telegraph* doesn't make me a grass. What it does make me is different and you ex-servicemen have a problem with anything that isn't boxed off, can't have a label slapped on it and doesn't walk in straight lines shouting "left-right, left-right" at the same time. I'm my own man, not one of the boys and the shift don't like it, do they?'

'No, matey, they don't, but then they don't like me either cos I'm a cockney. Fair enough you is different, pup, but all I'm sayin' is that an occasional hand of poker in the canteen might help you, er...'

As Philip struggled for the correct word, Thoroughgood helpfully added, 'ingratiate myself'.

'Nice one,' said Philip.

But Thoroughgood thought he had an opening and he wasn't about to let Philip's desperation to get to the land of nod stop him from making the most of it.

'I was just wonderin' if you've ever heard Jones or Davidson mention Bobby Dawson in any shape or form? I mean they must have come across him and the McGuigans plenty over the years and what with all the shit hitting the fan between them I was wondering who they reckon will come out on top.'

The probationer was surprised by the opening of Philip's eyes and the look of suspicion that shot across his face. 'Nosey blighter, aint ya, Thoroughgood?' replied the senior cop. Then an index finger shot out in Thoroughgood's direction as he added, 'The bottom line is I dunno, Z325. Just like you, I'm an outsider and the bastards don't go confiding in me however many hands of poker I've played with 'em. But I reckons there is something between Davidson and Mojito all right and if I was a bettin' man I'd say it goes back to the Troubles, cos the one thing I do know, matey, is that they were both over there with the army, but that's all I knows. Anytime I've tried to dig a bit deeper, the rest of the shift have closed up shop. But take some advice from me, young Thoroughgood, and that is don't go pokin' that nose of yours about in Billy Davidson's business, cos he's a wrong'un,' concluded Philip.

Aware that a look of incredulity was slipping across his face at Philip's revelation, Thoroughgood then gave a wince he hoped would make it appear to his senior man that he would do as he was told. 'Absolutely. It's none of mine, Edmund. It was just that with them having been stationed in Zulu Land since the dawn of time, I thought they would be bound to have crossed swords with our local Mafioso,' said Thoroughgood before shrugging his shoulders to indicate that his interest in the business was at an end.

Philip shook his head. 'Just keep it tucked, matey boy, and that way you'll keep out of harm's way. Now we have all of that cleared up, why don't you join me for a spot of shut eye here in the bus stop? Fifteen minutes and I'll be right as rain and ready to complete the rest of the padlock pulling,' said Philip from under his hat.

Impatience boiling up within him, Thoroughgood had other ideas. 'If you don't mind, Edmund, I'm gonnae crack on. If I come across anything I'll give a blast on my whistle, but like you say, at this time of the mornin' with the posties and milkmen out and about, the neddery will be well tucked up.'

'Be my guest,' said Philip.

As he moved off, Thoroughgood could have sworn he'd already heard the sound of snoring come from the bus shelter.

CHAPTER 35

The conversation with Philip sent Thoroughgood's imagination firmly into overdrive. 'Christ almighty, Davidson and Mojito both in the army. How far back was that, were they in the same battalion or regiment? Was there some kind of bond tying them together or just a set of shared experiences that dated back to their spell in the Emerald Isle?' asked the voice in his head.

Next Thoroughgood found himself questioning if this was the information that Collins had promised him and more importantly wondering what had happened to the housebreaker since their little rooftop conversation.

Rubbing at his sleep-starved eyes, he took a deep breath and once more began checking the shutters and pulling the padlocks on the row of shops at the top of Braidendmuir Street. When he had satisfied himself that all was good, front and back, Thoroughgood contemplated whether to return to Philip or to push on for a coffee at the snack wagon that straddled the boundaries between Zulu Land and the east.

Deciding that giving Philip a wake-up call was the best option, he turned the corner on his way back round to the front of the shops and there, as if by magic, was Collins. Startled by the junkie's apparent metamorphosis out of thin air, Thoroughgood let out a curse. 'For fuck's sake, Collins, they don't call you the Cat for nothing. How long you been stalking me?'

'Been on yer tail since you left the cop shop, rookie. You's a difficult boy to get a holdae,' replied the junkie, keeping to the shadows.

But Thoroughgood was determined to force the issue and he clicked his Maglite on and swung its glare onto the housebreaker, illuminating his gap-toothed grin and blinding him with the vicious light.

'You told me you had the, what was it you called it, aye, "the mother of all turns" for me, claimed you'd be back in touch in less than forty-eight hours. But you lied about the latter, make sure you don't do the same re the former, Collins,' warned Thoroughgood.

'Do ye think I'd be oot ma scratcher and followin' yous aboot this midden if I was gonnae spin you a fanny, rozzer?' asked Collins, trying to shield his eyes from the brilliant beam of the Maglite, which Thoroughgood eventually dipped to the ground.

'Then you better start talkin' before my senior cop wonders where I've gone and starts lookin' for me,' said Thoroughgood, his impatience becoming obvious.

'First you've got tae understand that the only way I stays alive is by toutin' to both the Mojito wan and the McGuigan fuckers, plus supplyin' a bit o' gear here and there to the needy. It's the law o' the jungle. I'm at the bottom of the food chain an' information is what keeps me oot and aboot and no' banged up in the big hoose doin' a stretch, comprende, rozzer?'

'I get the message, Collins, but if you want it to stay that way then you need to start singing,' replied Thoroughgood.

'Bastards wiz all in the army together,' said the housebreaker.

Thoroughgood feigned surprise. 'Who was?'

'Dawson, Davidson, Jones and yer gaffer, Rentoul. All of 'em were with the Paras o'er in the Province. So they's right tight and they figured they could boot auld Francis McGuigan's baws for him and bury his boy Gerry nae bother, but they underestimated McGuigan.'

'Will you stop speaking in riddles and spit it out?' demanded Thoroughgood.

'How'd ye think Gerry McGuigan and friend Frenchie got wheeched off the street with no one sayin', hearin' or seein' a bleedin' sausage? Doesnae add up, does it?'

'So make it add up, Collins.'

'It wiz Davidson and Jones that huckled 'em and dragged McGuigan and Frenchie to Dawson's warehouse where the Mojito wan had his fun wi 'em before they wiz dumped, burnt toast, as payback for the murder o' Frankie Dawson,' said Collins before hawking and spitting a mouthful of phlegm into the dirt.

Thoroughgood tried to remain outwardly unimpressed. 'I'll tell you something for nothing, Collins, you've got a knack of stating the bleeding obvious. Now why don't you try telling me something you haven't read on the front page of the papers.'

'Nobody knows nothin' about Mojito and half yer shift goin' back to NI, does they, boss? That shite is somethin' you could dae a lot wi', if ye were smart enough,' taunted Collins.

Collins' revelation that Davidson was not the only one of the shift to have been in Northern Ireland with Dawson, and that Sergeant Jimmy Rentoul in particular was thick with them, was gold-plated, even more so since it had linked them all to serving with the Paras and Thoroughgood knew this was information he would have to get to Malcolm as soon as possible. If they had served together with the elite of the British Army then they had experienced God knows what together, and it was these experiences across the Irish Sea that must be maintaining their bonds to this day. A band of brothers held together and perhaps haunted by the ghosts of their past.

Despite all of that ricocheting around his head Thoroughgood was sure the junkie was holding back a lot more than he was letting on. 'I need more from you, Collins, if you're going to stay footloose and fancy-free. What you've told me is that you're touting to both Mojito and the McGuigans, so you are up to your arse in this whole ice cream war. You need a way out and I am the only one who can provide it for you. And for that to happen you need to stop dicking me about.'

Collins grimaced. 'Huv you no' heard the sayin', rozzer, that Rome wiznae built in a day? The Cat doesnae like to trust anyone because he gets made a few cheap promises – that's why I've got nine lives. For starters, I could be doin' wi' a score-bag to stop me gettin' strung oot,' said Collins, shooting out an upturned palm.

'Your having a fuckin' laugh, Collins, you want me to pay for your smack?' asked a dumbfounded Thoroughgood.

'This the way o' the street, rookie. If ye want tae be the boss man then you need to learn how it is fast. Now splash the cash and I'll come back to you wi' mair when I have it,' replied Collins with a wolfish grin slipping across his face.

Although it went against every grain of his being Thoroughgood fished out a twenty-pound note from his pocket and slapped it into the informant's outstretched palm. 'Make sure you come back to me, Collins, the information you have given me is going up the tree, as you called it. The people there will be wanting more where it came from and your future existence is gonnae depend on that,' said Z325 Constable Angus Thoroughgood, amazed at the sound and meaning of the words that were coming out of his mouth.

Collins smiled and clasped the note tight in a clenched fist. 'I'll find you when the time's right, boss,' he said, and with that he was gone.

CHAPTER 36

Thoroughgood waited for the lift to reach the fifth floor, his mouth dry and his nerves jangling. As the doors opened he was met by Numan's intense grey stare, but the outbreak of a smile across the white-haired cop's wolfish features broke the ice.

'Good to see you, son, welcome to force HQ, Pitt Street,' he said, resplendent in a shiny black zip-up blouson jacket with red stripes down either side, jeans and a pair of Dunlop Green Flash trainers, which was in sharp contrast to the sartorial inelegance of his previous appearance.

Reading his mind, Numan said, 'Aye, old Worzel has returned to the fancy dress shop… Until Mr Benn's next outing!'

Numan offered his hand for Thoroughgood to shake. 'Follow me and I'll show you to our cosy little abode. Bit of a mess right now as we're still settling in, stinks of paint everywhere, but the least we can do for you after ruining your day off to come in and see us is make you a brew.'

Turning a corner of the brown-tiled corridor that ran the length of the fifth floor, they reached a grey door that seemed to open as if by remote control upon their arrival, and there, waiting for them, was Sergeant Cormac Malcolm in faded jeans and a green sweatshirt.

'Come in, Angus. Tea or coffee? By the way, good job the other night, that bastard Manson has been remanded and is looking at a decent stretch. And it was good to give the old running gear an airing in the process. We find a bit of imagination works every time!' said the sergeant.

'Coffee, just with milk would be great,' replied Thoroughgood and before he could stop himself he added impishly, 'You must have been frozen in that old running vest, it was bad enough in a pair of schoolboy shorts!'

'That's no problem to a man who helped build the roads around Loch Lomond and had to wash in diesel in the process!' replied Malcolm with a grin.

Ten minutes later, with the initial pleasantries complete, Malcolm cut to the chase. 'Okay, Angus, what have you got for us?'

'Half of the shift are connected to Bobby Dawson by their spell in the army over in Northern Ireland,' said Thoroughgood, feeling very uncomfortable with his revelation and aware that his right leg was starting to dance of its own volition.

Numan let out a whistle, before getting up from his desk and slamming shut the door, which Thoroughgood noticed for the first time did not have any identification on it. Malcolm was half-perched on a window sill that framed the Glasgow skyline and seemed to leave the sergeant superimposed on the view like a clip of botched amateur film work, but his eyes sparkled at the titbit he had just been fed.

'Right you are, first I need you to elaborate on that and then validate where you got the information from. That good for you, Angus?' said the sergeant.

Thoroughgood smiled uncertainly, still uneasy with this whole process but nevertheless aware that he had come to the point of no return. 'One of the other cops on the shift – Edmund Philip, who is also ex-army – told me the other night that he'd found out at the card table that Billy Davidson and Dawson were both in the army at the same time and served in the province. Another senior cop, Jimmy Sykes, did the same after I'd had another run-in with Davidson in the back of Lennox Hill office. But Philip, in particular, told me that anytime he'd tried to dig a bit deeper the rest of the shift put the shutters up and, in any case, given he is a cockney transfer from the Met and so an outsider, he didn't want to push things. He reckons Davidson is a, what did he call him, a wrong'un.'

Numan was first to respond. 'Aye, he's that all right. Jesus, Bobby Dawson was in the army? Why the hell didn't we know that?'

'There is more,' added Thoroughgood, quickly gaining confidence from the effect of his initial information. 'A tout of mine has confirmed to me that Dawson, Davidson, Brian Jones and the Group Three shift sergeant, Jimmy Rentoul, were all not just in the army at the same time but in the Paras.'

'The Paras?' questioned Malcolm in disbelief, before he rediscovered his composure and added, 'Sorry, Angus, go on.'

'My tout reckons that the reason Gerry McGuigan and his henchman were taken out with no one squealing is that Davidson and Jones did it at Mojito, sorry Dawson's, behest, and that they have some kind of pact binding them together. If they were all in the Paras together then it's pretty easy to guess where that bond has come from,' said Thoroughgood.

Out of the blue from behind the now-lowering pages of the *Daily Record*, a dishevelled shock of black hair appeared. 'How are you finding Jimmy Rentoul, lad?' asked Hardie.

Thoroughgood grimaced. 'I've had a couple of run-ins with him and from those it's clear he is going to do everything he can to make sure I don't see my probation out. The first one came after Davidson pulled a blade on me under the gas works at Lennoxmill and the second one, well, er…' Thoroughgood's voice tailed off into an uncomfortable silence.

'Please don't be shy, Gus,' said Malcolm flatly. 'Remember, every detail you can give us about the shift is vital.'

The probationer grimaced but, shrugging his shoulders, continued. 'He caught me, well almost caught me, sleeping in the prisoner's cell in Lennox Hill Office on the Sunday early shift. Told me how highly he regards you all at IA and promised me it would be down to him whether I make it out of my probation and that anything I do with you would have nothing to do with it whatsoever.'

'Did he now?' said Malcolm, smiling in amusement. He rubbed

his chin ruefully for a moment before continuing. 'I don't want to go into all of this right now, Gus, but there is a bigger picture here that I am not at liberty to explain to you right now. That will be for after the ice cream wars. But the bottom line is that things are changing in Strathclyde Police, the old culture of screwing every hauf on the beat and sloping off for a bevvy any chance you get is on the way out. There is a new broom that is going to ensure the likes of Rentoul, Davidson and Jones are extinct sometime soon. But it all takes time, which is what this unit has been set up for – or at least it's part, a big part, of our remit. But obviously Rentoul's threats are all part of the same web of deceit and duplicity that has woven its way around Group Three shift in Z division and Jimmy Rentoul is the big fat spider who is spinning it.'

Thoroughgood couldn't help himself. 'You're not kiddin', Sergeant,'

Numan was first to run with the theory and he started to pace the room, negotiating his way around a half-open paint pot into the bargain. 'Rentoul, Davidson and Jones on the inside and Mojito on the other side of the tracks, all brothers in arms with levels of personal loyalty and trust that go way beyond the normal. Although we may have that in the cops, if these guys were in the Paras then God knows what they went through together. So maybe it isn't a surprise that these loyalties have stretched across the law, especially when there's clearly big money to be made through the ice cream drug trade. Basically they see you as a threat and now that you've proven yourself useful to us, you are an even bigger one to them. So you are going to have to expect every dirty trick and act of intimidation Jimmy Rentoul and his boys can throw at you. Do you think you can take it?'

'I'll do my best,' replied Thoroughgood, aware that he was clenching his teeth,

'Okay, that's good news, son. But, no disrespect, our priority is to find out when our band of brothers were in Northern Ireland and see if we can pin them down to the same unit. The Paras is a big outfit and we need to make sure that things haven't been exaggerated by your informant, Angus, but that will not be hard to do. Would I be right in saying the tout who has been singing to you is Collins the housebreaker?'

Thoroughgood saw no point in prevaricating. 'How did you know?' he asked.

'Simple really, you manage to take his dripping needle off him and disarm him, yet he escapes you? Doesn't add up son, there was obviously a spot of summary plea-bargaining going on up on that roof. Fair play to you – learning on the job, at the deep end, is the best way to run a tout and learn the pitfalls that come with it.'

'But the short and curlies of it is whether you trust Collins' info,' said Malcolm. 'Although I guess to a certain extent you have corroboration of it through Philip. But we'll check things out with the military and then take it from there. If you don't mind, young man, the next stage is going to be to bring Collins in and have a more formal chat with him. Do you think you can set that up for us without attracting any unwanted attention from your colleagues?'

Thoroughgood gave a grimace. 'It isn't going to be easy. Collins is the most elusive housebreaker in Zulu Land, which is where, as you will be aware, his nickname of 'the Cat' comes from. The other night he just materialised out of the gloom while I was checking property along from the office. The way things were left, he said he'd find me again for our next meet,' said Thoroughgood with a shrug of his shoulders.

'Look, son, there are ways and means to get to grips with touts who are just a wee bit too slippery for their own good,' said Numan, adding a wink for good measure before continuing. 'You leave all of that to me and I'll find a pressure point that will allow us to put the squeeze on the Cat and let him know who's boss. I'll come back to you on that one but we'll try and set up something away from your division.'

'Sure...' Thoroughgood found himself unsure just what to call Numan, but it was Malcolm who came to his rescue.

'DC is the title you are looking for, Angus, while I am now officially DS Malcolm. As of yesterday we have both become full card-carrying members of the CID. But I'm sure Detective Constable Numan won't mind if you call him Dennis!'

'Aye, I'd say you have earned that right, young Thoroughgood,' said Numan before once again offering his hand and applying a grip that was like a steel vice.

Clearing his throat nervously, Thoroughgood knew that he had come to the point when he had to reveal his encounter with Dawson.

'There's just one other thing, gentlemen. I'm afraid I had a bit of a run-in with Dawson the other night in a bar down Byres Road,' admitted Thoroughgood shamefacedly.

Malcolm immediately adopted a deadpan glare. 'Go on, Constable,' he said, the use of Thoroughgood's official designation leaving him in no doubt that his superior was far from amused.

'I'm afraid there was a girl involved. Her name is Celine Lynott and she works at Tutankhamun's. Dawson seems to be seeing her and he didn't take too kindly to me having a chat with her. The bottom line is that I got a sore face out of it,' shrugged Thoroughgood.

It was Numan who responded first. 'Hence the bruised cheekbone. Interesting,' he said, stroking his chin thoughtfully. 'Do you think this Celine could be of any use to us, Gus?'

'Not now,' answered Thoroughgood balefully.

'Okay,' said Malcolm. 'All I would ask of you, Angus, is that you keep doing what you have been doing and...' He fished out his warrant card holder, took a small business card from it and slapped it down on the desk top in front of Thoroughgood. 'If there is anything else of interest then contact us on this number ASAP. But be careful. Davidson is a bad bastard and if he gets a whiff you're being a bit too nosey he won't mess about. Before we wrap things up here I just want to say, Angus, that you have far and away exceeded my initial hopes. Good work indeed, Constable Thoroughgood,' congratulated Malcolm, leaning forwards to pat the rookie warmly on his left shoulder.

'Aye, you might just have a future in this man's army yet, son,' said Numan and almost for the first time since he had joined Strathclyde Police, Thoroughgood felt he may have done the right thing.

CHAPTER 37

The marked police Land Rover's engine strained as it attempted to scale the steep gradient of the B822, or the Crow Road as it was better known, snaking higher and higher up into the Campsie Hills as the early morning mists threatened to engulf it.

Centuries back the Crow Road had been a drove road over the Campsies and was frequently used by Rob Roy and the MacGregors, who extorted protection money from the Campsie lairds and farmers, before it was improved by wealthy coal merchants in the late eighteenth century to allow the transportation of the black stuff from the pits of the south to the new industries that depended on it in the Endrick Valley.

The driver's window was wound down to the bottom and Davidson's right elbow perched precariously on its sill as he billowed out a mouthful of cigarette smoke. In the passenger seat sat the outsize figure of Brian Jones, his white uniform shirt rolled up to his bulging biceps and his left hand endlessly fidgeting with the greased-back tresses of his slick, but receding, chestnut hair.

'I don't like this one bit, Billy boy,' said Jones for at least the fourth time. 'I mean, what the fuck is Mojito wantin' to talk to us up at the well for?'

'I'll tell you why, shit for brains, cos the CID and the Serious are watchin' his every move like hawks and waiting for him to strike back at the McGuigans, and the last thing he can afford is to be spotted in a cosy little parley with the two of us. For fuck's sake, Brian, he's had his younger brother rubbed out and now his sister's been bleached, what do you think everyone is going to be expecting Mojito's next move to be?'

But Jones remained unconvinced. 'I'm naw buyin' it, Billy. Jamie Wright's Well? Anyway, who the fuck was Jamie Wright?'

'I don't know and I don't care and will you just stop whining, Jonesy. It's five thirty in the morning and there isnae gonnae be no bugger about and that is the most important thing. Whatever Mojito has for us, he wants us to get it in private. The well is just above the car park off the Crow Road, so it isnae such a big deal. Look, you don't have to be Einstein to work out what he's gonnae want from us next.'

Jones was keen to prove that he was indeed no genius. 'So, smartarse, what's gonnae be our orders from Corporal Dawson?'

Davidson flashed his blown fuse box of a smile Jones's way and blew a mouthful of smoke directly into his face. 'You never were the smartest, Jonesy son, were you. Christ, if your brains were as big as your biceps you would have made Einstein look like a bleedin' simpleton,' he said, and barked out a harsh, rasping laugh.

But then Davidson's grin was gone and, his forearms perched either side of the Land Rover wheel, he said, 'Mojito is gonnae want us to take out Francis McGuigan once and for all, and for my money, he will be wantin' to know why we haven't managed to deliver his baws in a box already.'

'Shit,' said Jonesy, 'And how're we gonnae explain that one away, Billy boy?'

Taking his motorbike helmet off, Mojito leant against the well and looked beyond it, out and over the view of the pastel-coloured Campsie Glen. He found himself puzzled by the fact that it was known as Jamie Wright's Well, after the Campsie burn fisherman who had discovered the spring, yet engraved on it were verses by the poet James M. Slimmon which had clearly been dedicated to his immortal memory by his friends.

Repositioning himself to take in the verse carved on the granite slab above the source of the water, Dawson took temporary delight in the distraction it provided. He started to read the words taken from the first and third of ten verses of 'The Packman's Salutation to the Mountain Well', from Slimmon's book *The Dead Planet and Other Poems*.

Initially Dawson mumbled the words almost incoherently, such was the absurdity of the moment to a man whose natural inclination was that spontaneity must be avoided at all costs.

'Hail to your dimplin', wimplin' drop,
'Cleark, caller, caul',
'That bids the drouthy traveller stop
'An' tak' his fill.'

Enjoying the moment and feeling his spirits lifted by the clearing of the mist and the dawning of a glorious morning, his words became more forcefully pronounced.

'Hail to your heart-reviving tipple,
'Enticing slee wi' twinklin' ripple,
'Thou crystal milk frae Nature's nipple,
'Wee Mountain Well!'

Lost in the moment, Mojito found his overriding desire was to stoop down and cup up some of the beautiful, clear liquid that was pouring into the well from the hillside. Giving in to his inclination he did so and slaked his early morning thirst, aware that he was following Slimmon's words and sharing his elation at such a simple yet soulful moment as man and nature united high on a hillside at the day's break.

His spirit overcome with joy, the murders of his brother and sister momentarily ejected from his consciousness, Dawson chanted the final verse out loud, aware of the accompanying echo to his words and relishing it in simple delight.

'Born of the whirlin' wintry flake
'Of Arctic shower
'When charging storms the welkin rake
'And scrudge the bower,
'You joukit frae the furious blast
'And seepin' doon the mountain past
'Till here my craig you weet at last,
'Sine ower the stour.'

157

Dawson felt the euphoria that had momentarily consumed him drain from his being and he found himself turning his thoughts to the impending meeting with Jones and Davidson. His mind filled with images from their time spent together in the Province, and the bloody chaos of the day that had bound them together ever since, and which he supposed would do until death did them part.

Dawson recalled the words of his first section sergeant who, after his closest comrade had fallen to a sniper's bullet in the Shankhill Road, had comforted him with the heartless words that 'in life and especially soldiery, everyone is expendable'.

For Bobby Dawson had come to the edge of the precipice, dragged there by the grief caused by the murder of his nearest and dearest, the realisation that his own unquenchable thirst for power was what had ultimately caused their demise, and the insatiable appetite for revenge that now stalked his every moment.

CHAPTER 38

The sleek racing lines of the Suzuki 750, which was the only vehicle present in the car park that nestled near the summit of the Campsie Glen, was proof that Mojito was already awaiting Davidson and Jones.

'Here we go,' said the former grimly, flicking his fag out of the window as the Land Rover drew to a stop alongside the motorcycle.

'Aye, here we go all right, but if Mojito starts any of his shite then I think it's time we make the point to him that he needs us every bit as much as we need him if he wants McGuigan taken care of and his ice cream fuckin' empire preserved,' said Jones flexing his giant muscles as if to reassure himself that Dawson posed no threat.

'Corporal bleedin' Dawson might not see it that way but maybe you're right, Jonesy, maybe it's time we helped him understand the realities of our relationship and the fact that this is 1989 and not 1972 on the Bogside,' agreed Davidson, flashing his mate a feral smile.

As they reached the brow of the hillock at the top end of the car park they saw Mojito leaning against the granite monument that encased the well, he raised his hand in salute, although the attempted smile that accompanied it was more of a grimace. A moment later the three ex-soldiers, who had shared so much, been through so much, all for Queen and country, stood face-to-face.

'Nice of you to join me, gentlemen,' said Mojito. 'The three amigos minus one... Where's Jimmy Rentoul?'

159

'Up to his arse in paperwork. You get out the city all right without a tail… in your disguise?' asked Davidson, smirking.

But Dawson was in no mood to joke. 'Let's just cut the bullshit, boys. I've two questions I need answers to. First, why is Francis McGuigan still alive? Second, have you got your hands on that double-dealing, grassing arsewipe Collins?' he demanded, the anger in his voice making it quiver.

Davidson was first to try and provide an explanation. 'With regards to McGuigan, no, because he is surrounded by a small army which makes it bloody hard for two police officers in full uniform to take him out without giving the game away. As for Collins, he knows we're shakin' down every tree for him and that only makes it harder to get our paws on the toutin' little bastard, he's been avoidin' all his usual shitholes and shootin' galleries,' he said in a tone that was hard edged and anything but apologetic.

'Look, Mojito, God knows we both feel for you with Frankie and now Lucy gone, but Christ, there's only so much we can do without blowing everything. Francis McGuigan will get his but it's gonnae take time cos the bastard's jumpin' at every shadow right now. He knows you're comin' for him. But the one thing he isn't gonnae expect is that when he buys it he's gonnae buy it from the law. As for Collins, sooner or later he'll get himself so spaced out he'll slip up,' said Jones with surprising clarity for one more usually associated with brawn than brains.

'Jonesy's right, Mojito. We will get them, it's just about making sure we wait for the right opportunity,' added Davidson.

'But while you've been fuckin' about, my brother and sister have been murdered by these bog-trottin' scum. Don't you remember who got you through that day in 1972, and the shitstorm that followed when you were wetting yourselves like two weans?'

'Aye, we know we owe you for feckin' Bloody Sunday and its backlash, cos you've never let us forget it, Mojito,' said Davidson.

But Dawson was far from finished. 'Funny how things change. Seventeen years ago you couldnae wait to start shooting the innocent but when it out comes to rubbin' out a card-carrying member of the Provos who's been laughin' at Her Maj ever since he got out of Belfast, you're no' so fuckin' trigger happy,' spat Dawson, the rage mounting within him.

Jones had had enough and the hulking cop took a step towards Dawson, his huge right paw clenched in a fist. But Mojito backhanded the motorcycle helmet he was holding off the cop's jaw, forcing a howl of pain from Jones, who staggered backwards onto the hillside, clutching his jaw.

Davidson moved onto the front foot. 'Now wait a fuckin' minute, Mojito…' But his words were cut-off in mid-flow by the Colt that now pointed directly at his forehead.

'On your knees, Private Davidson,' said Dawson, recovering his composure.

Davidson's hands shot up in a gesture of desperate supplication. 'Jesus H Christ, Mojito. Come on, man, I know you've been through a lot but this isnae the way, this is exactly what McGuigan would want most.'

'You bastards forget how I hid your tracks and helped point the finger elsewhere? Yet when I need you to do your job you fuck up, just like on the Bogside seventeen years back.'

As Jones regained his feet, Dawson took a step backwards and relocated the Colt his way. 'Stay where you are, Private Jones,' he spat.

'Okay, okay, I'm standin' still, Mojito, just take it easy. We can get this sorted, there is a way, trust me,' said Jones as a bead of sweat fell off the end of his bulbous nose.

Mojito's left hand ran over his bald dome and he fingered the diamond earring on his left lobe, which glinted in the morning sun, but the Colt remained lethally poised in front of him.

Then Dawson looked Davidson's way and said, 'Get up, Billy boy,' and to Jones and Davidson's vast relief he re-holstered the handgun inside his leathers, flashed a mirthless smile and said, 'I suggest you get it sorted once and for fuckin' all, boys.'

Then Mojito walked past the shell-shocked cops, jumped onto his bike and roared off down the hillside.

CHAPTER 39

Rentoul took another sip from the wee goldie and placed it back on his desk. The transistor radio relayed the drama from the British Lions first Test of the 1989 tour against Australia, from all the way down under. His sideburns seemed to switch up and down the side of his jowly face, apparently of their own volition.

The sergeant's silver-rimmed spectacles sparkled in the glint of the early morning sunshine as he leant back on his chair, burying his arse into the cushion he had brought from home to provide relief from the painful piles that blighted his every waking moment. He leant forward against the desk and scratched a rear end which tormented him with a burning sensation that left him constantly visualising sticking his derrière in the first bucket of cold water he could get his hands on.

Another slug of the whisky helped dull the sizzling pain and he stared out the window at the increasingly brilliant early morning sky.

'Where the fuck are they?' spat Rentoul into the empty room, his impatience at Davidson and Jones's failure to return from their meeting with Dawson beginning to gnaw at him. He needed to speak to them and get their full debrief before the early-shift gaffers came on duty, sharp as always, at around 6.15 a.m.

Rentoul's eyes flicked to the wall clock, saw that it read 5.35 a.m., and relocated to the transistor, just as David Campese embarked on another mazy run through the Lions forwards and his frustration burst its dam. 'Fuckin' nail him, will ye, Calder!' erupted Rentoul as he beseeched the Lions and Scotland skipper

Finlay Calder to take out the Wallaby wing king.

Seconds later the velvet tones of the commentator confirmed that Calder had indeed obliged and Rentoul raised his glass in salute just as the door to his office opened and Jones and Davidson strolled in.

Rentoul looked up and almost choked on his whisky. 'About bleedin' time. You been on a picnic? I fuckin' hope you haven't been hammerin' the sauce, cos I need a full debrief before that sanctimonious twat Ally Brewer turns up for the early turn.' Sitting back in his chair, Rentoul folded his arms and said, 'Spill.'

Davidson's facial muscles tightened; he'd taken enough shit from Mojito and, although he wasn't about to admit it, having the Colt placed against his temple had badly rattled him. It had also brought home the message that, despite the bond that they all shared going back to their days knee-deep in the Troubles, Dawson was fast losing patience with them.

Caught between the devil and the deep blue sea, Davidson did as he was bid. 'Mojito's on the edge, gaffer. He wants McGuigan wiped off the face of the earth and if we don't oblige fuck knows what lengths he'll go to get the result he wants.'

Before Rentoul could reply Jones burst in, 'Fuck's sake, Billy boy, he fuckin' put the barrel of a Colt against your bonce and threatened to blow yer brains out… Or are you forgettin' that small detail? He's fuckin' lost it, Lucy's murder has tipped him over the cliff, never mind the Campsies. We've got tae dae something before this spills over and the punters start gettin' hurt, Jimmy.'

Rentoul's bushy eyebrows shot up and the seriousness of the situation was underlined as he reached out and switched off the rugby.

'I hate that fuckin' prick, Campese, and those smug Wallaby tossers,' raged Rentoul while his eyes continued to bore into the now silenced transmitter. Then slowly his dark features lifted in the direction of the two cops standing before him. 'It's just as well I've the answer to all our problems then, boys,' he said, as a smile spread slowly across his face.

'And what would that be?' asked Davidson, his pessimism plain for all too see.

'Francis McGuigan has an appointment at the Jail Square doon at the High Court on Thursday morning, and a case to answer for his alleged racketeering, money laundering and drug dealing. That slimy bastard Mo Celtrani, his brief, has been unable to get deferred any longer. According to my information there's every chance he'll be remanded. In any case, owing to a shortage of cops in the court branch an appeal has been put out to division for assistance.' Rentoul gave a harsh laugh before ploughing on. 'Anyways, I couldn't think of two better cops to volunteer than the pair of you, my two finest ex-army officers. Given all the shite flying about between McGuigan and Dawson, the court bosses are particularly pleased to have two former Paras on dock duty.' Rentoul poured another goldie from the bottle of Black & White whisky, took a large sip and let out a satisfied sigh.

'Of course,' he continued, 'if McGuigan goes down, you'll also be in charge of transporting the soon to be dearly departed Francis to the big hoose.' Rentoul leant back in his chair, hands clasped behind his head and a smile of triumph washing over his face.

'Nice one, gaffer,' said Jonesy.

But Davidson was less than impressed. 'With all due respect, Jimmy, this is far from watertight. You wouldnae put your hoose against Celtrani coming up with some kind of alibi and McGuigan walkin' free. In any case, what you got in mind if he does go down? If we're the escort we can hardly rub him out.'

'How long you known me, Billy boy? Twenty years, and when did I ever not have a Plan B?'

Davidson remained unconvinced. 'So what is it?'

Rentoul reached into the top drawer of his desk and slapped out a sheet of printed paper with a signature at the bottom. 'Sheriff's warrant to apprehend, signed by my good friend Sheriff Brunton at 0030 hours earlier this morning, over a large hauf of Talisker, after I made him aware of some new information pertaining to the suspected heinous crimes committed by Francis

McGuigan Senior in the last few days.'

'But how the fuck is this gonnae work, gaffer?' asked Jones.

'Christ, do I need to spell it oot for you, Jonesy? If McGuigan walks then the two of you will huckle him the minute he leaves the witness box and takes his long walk to freedom out into the marble foyer. It will look like a case of the uniform taking the lead, cutting through all the bullshit and doing CID's job for them.'

Rentoul paused to take another slug of his whisky before continuing. 'If he's sent down then he's in your custody anyway and you can slap the warrant on him and we still come up smelling like roses. We'll have the alibi of serving a warrant on him as proof we were doing our duty to the letter of the law. Either way, Dawson will have been tipped off and he can intercept where and when it suits him, make it look like an ambush, and that allows us to get off scot-free and lets him take care of auld McGuigan with a bit of the personal touch. And when it comes to Collins, make sure its ditto,' said Rentoul before he took two empty tumblers from another of his desk drawers, filled them with whisky and handed them to Jones and Davidson. 'Now let's drink to that, gentlemen.'

'Aye, tae one less Fenian bastard on the streets of Glasgae,' said Jonesy.

'Fuck the RA and amen to that,' chorused Davidson and they charged their glasses together.

CHAPTER 40

It wasn't hard to get a hold of her details, but to do so was an abuse of position and a contravention of the Data Protection Act 1984 that Thoroughgood's conscience was having difficulty processing. Facing him was the age-old dilemma confronting those that wear the uniform of the law but enjoy the privileges that go with it when their own personal interests will benefit from bending them.

Yet finally Thoroughgood had managed to square it with himself by mentally filing it under an enquiry that could lead to information that would locate a possible informant, and so a source of info that may help bring Dawson down. But the bottom line, he could not deny to himself, however hard he tried, was that his desire to track down Celine was starting to leave him sleepless during the night and listless after the sun came up. What would happen after he doorstepped her, thanks to the information provided by a combination of the Police National Computer and the electoral register, well, who knew how it would pan out, but it was a chance he now knew he had to take – for his own sanity.

Sitting in his white MG Metro, images of Celine from the first time he'd met her at Tutankhamun's and then in Bonhams, when she had scowled so contemptuously at him after his tangle with Dawson, tormented him. But what made him feel physically sick was the thought of her in the gangster's arms.

He tried to lose himself with a bit of help from Love and Money, James Grant's effortless voice and the melancholy lyrics of 'Strange Kind of Love' drawing to a close as he arrived outside her address. Looking up at the third-floor flat in Belmont Street,

Thoroughgood was relieved that at 11.30 p.m. the lights were still on, for it meant that tonight Celine was home and not on the floor at Tutankhamun's.

The words from The Human League song 'Don't You Want Me' began to torment him... again. 'You were working as a cocktail waitress in a cocktail bar, when I met you. I picked you out, I shook you up...' Well, what happened if Celine didn't want picked out and shook up?

But Thoroughgood realised it didn't matter. He knew he'd been looking for someone like her, someone who made him feel alive; the only problem was that now he'd found her she belonged to the most dangerous man in Glasgow.

He realised he'd been sitting there in the semi-darkness for almost fifteen minutes, partially illuminated by a stuttering street light and the increasing brilliance of a full moon and the realisation dawned on him that it was now or never.

Gritting his teeth he took a deep breath and then as a spontaneous afterthought he pulled the Love and Money cassette out of the tape player, placed it in its holder, shoved it into his Harrington and jumped out of the MG muttering *carpe diem* to himself and wincing at the triteness of his words.

Thoroughgood crossed the street, feeling increasingly short of breath, his heart hammering as if it was about to explode from his chest. The storm door of the close at 23 Belmont Street gave way with a forceful dunt and Thoroughgood couldn't help giving a shake of his head at the lack of security. It was cheap student accommodation; the landlord probably didn't give a shit as long as he was getting the rent.

Old cigarette butts and yesterday's newspapers lay on the cold concrete of the close's floor and he wondered to himself how Mojito Dawson could allow his girlfriend to live in a shithole like this. He brushed the peeling white paint on the handrail as he made his way up the steps, his pace quickening until he was taking them two at a time. Moments later he arrived on the top floor and looked out the landing window, trying to recover his breath and his composure. He unzipped the Harrington to let the cool night air filter down his shirt. He seemed to be suffering an out-of-body experience as his right hand reached out in front of him, as if it belonged to someone else, and closed in on the chipped wooden door with the words 'Miss C Lynott' on it.

But before his knuckles could make contact with it, the door opened and there she stood, achingly beautiful and completely still.

As the seconds ticked by, silence reigned before she snapped, 'What do *you* want?' with the emphasis placed firmly on the 'you'.

Placed firmly on the back foot Thoroughgood could only stutter, 'Hello... Would you mind if I came in?'

The unruly tresses of her relaxed Afro curls had gone and instead Celine's hair was scraped back tight and shining luxuriantly in a bun at the back of her regal features. It gave her sculpted face a severity that Thoroughgood found intimidating.

'I guess you'd better, after all, how long were you sitting out there in the boy-racer motor?' she asked, and her face remained granite cold.

Thoroughgood felt his cheeks burn with embarrassment while his emotions were being put in the blender by this early indication his hope may not be totally forlorn. He offered a tepid smile and said, 'I don't make a habit of this... honestly.'

'Really? And why should I believe a word you say, Detective Constable Thoroughgood?' asked Celine with dripping sarcasm. As she turned to lead him into her flat he saw that she was wearing denim shorts and a white sleeveless T-shirt and once again found himself mesmerised by her figure.

They made their way in silence into the kitchen/living room of the studio flat, which had a huge skylight through which the moon provided a dazzling and powerful light that sunbathed the room in the most magical brilliance.

But before he could say anything, Celine turned on him. 'Detective Constable... So when did you get the promotion?'

Put on the back foot, Thoroughgood stumbled badly. 'Er... What do you mean?'

'Tripped up by one of your lies, Probationary Constable

Thoroughgood? Didn't you think I would find out? Or didn't it matter as long as you thought it would help you get your way with me?'

Thoroughgood's right hand instinctively ran through his black hair, then, grimacing, he replied, 'Look, it wasn't like that at all, Celine. Please let me explain.'

'Explain with another lie? Because it seems like everything you say is built on a web of lies, just another smart-mouthed young cop who thinks he can bullshit his way into a girl's...' Her voice tailed off into silence.

Covering the three feet between them with one bound, Thoroughgood grabbed her shoulders and forced her to look him in the eye. 'Listen to me, Celine, and believe me, everything I say from here on in will be the truth. Please give me this one chance?'

Something about the imploring look that filled his green eyes persuaded her to do so, and she nodded her head slightly for him to begin.

'I'd just had one of the worst days of, as you rightly pointed out, my probation. Discovered my first dead body which had been half baked, half decomposed in the heat and was squirming with maggots. I couldn't get the picture or the smell of it out of my head, my nose, my eyes, it was there everywhere I looked,' he said, but as he took a breath to continue Thoroughgood found himself interrupted.

'You expect me to pity you, Constable?'

But Thoroughgood ignored her barb and carried on regardless, his gaze locked on hers, his senses assailed by her proximity and the overwhelming smell of her. 'So I went out for a beer with my pal and when we hit Tut's the place was queued out around the corner, so we bullshitted our way in past Dirty Harry, more like blind Harry, on the door, by claiming we were CID and in pursuit of some car thieves and then I met you...' Losing his momentum, Thoroughgood couldn't help himself. 'Fuck it,' he said, as he took hold of Celine and locked his lips on hers.

She did not resist but as the seconds of their embrace stretched they finally slipped apart, and after a brief pause to regain his composure, Thoroughgood continued. 'That was it, nothing fancy, nothing smart, just a way to get to the front of the queue and then when I met you what else could I do but continue with the story? And you believed it.'

'Yes, I guess I did,' Celine replied and pushed him playfully in the middle of his chest. He exaggerated a stumble backwards into the spotlight of the moon's pale brilliance.

As Thoroughgood regained his balance, Celine said, 'The skylight was one of the reasons I took the flat, it's something special in here when you get the chance to dance in the moonlight, Constable, or don't you do dancing?' Again she flashed that coquettish smile.

'Nope, cause I always get chocolate stains on my pants,' replied Thoroughgood with a smile, and as a look of complete mystification crossed her beautiful face he explained, 'Come on, you must know that "Dancing in the Moonlight" is a Thin Lizzy song? Is it coincidence you share the same surname as Phil Lynott, the lead singer?'

She answered with the name of another Lizzy anthem: 'I "Don't Believe A Word",' that implied she knew exactly what he meant, and as she spoke Thoroughgood could feel his self-control disintegrating under a desperate desire to wrap his arms around her and kiss those smouldering lips with everything he had in him once again. He resisted... just.

'Can I ask how you found out about my bogus status?' he asked.

Almost instantly he could feel a frost begin to descend. 'How do you think?'

'Mojito?'

Her lips pursed and her cheekbones seemed to become high definition in the moon's brilliance.

Once again Thoroughgood felt himself floundering. 'Look, about the other night, with your friend, I'm really sorry, it just got a bit out of hand.'

But once again Celine's answer set him off balance. 'A girl quite likes to have two men fighting over her! I bet your little blonde playmate behind the bar wasn't too happy,' she said laughing.

Thoroughgood shrugged. 'Er, well, I don't suppose you have a cold beer in the fridge?'

'No, I'm afraid not, Constable Thoroughgood, but I could do you a nice little taste of the Caribbean, man,' she said slipping into a mock Jamaican accent and chuckling to herself.

Moments later Thoroughgood sat on a white leather settee and raised his tumbler to Celine's. 'Thank you,' he said as their glasses chinked together and then he took a large draft of the rum and coke, gave an appreciative wince with a sigh to follow, and added, 'Not bad at all.'

Celine sat down at the other end of the settee, with an effortless elegance that he adored, and sipped from her drink. Then she looked up at Thoroughgood and pierced him with those brown eyes. 'So why are you here, Constable? Business or pleasure?'

Thoroughgood choked on his drink.

CHAPTER 41

He took a deep breath and met her gaze, held it firmly and said, 'I'm here to save you, Celine.'

He knew from the fire that immediately blazed in her eyes he was in danger of blowing it, but just as she seemed set to erupt she took another sip of her drink and, tilting her head to the left, said, 'I could ask from what, but what I really want to know is just what gives you the right to come into my flat and presume that you have the right to play any part in my life. We haven't known each other two minutes and you want to save me. I don't know the first thing about you. Sorry, that's wrong – I know that you lie.'

Thoroughgood knew the time had arrived to put all his cards on the table. 'Look, you must know that the type of life that Bobby Dawson leads only ever ends up one way. Trouble is that en route a hell of a lot of people get damaged and become casualties. Is that what you want, Celine?'

Before she could answer, Thoroughgood's left hand shot up. 'Hear me out, please. Look at his family: his younger brother blown away in the back of an ice cream van and his sister strangled and left to burn in her flat. I'm not saying that Mojito didn't love either of them, what I'm saying is that they died because of the life he has chosen for himself. I guess what I'm trying to say, Celine, is that I don't want that to happen to you.'

Thoroughgood took a deep breath. It was out: an admission, or as close as he could bring himself to making one, that he had fallen for her spectacularly.

'The life that he has chosen for himself? What type of life

172

would that be? That of a successful businessman who has some of the best clubs and pubs in this city in his control? How does that add up to what happened to Frankie and Lucy? Dear God, Thoroughgood how can you say that?' she demanded, and as she did so he noticed that her drink began to shake in her right hand.

For the first time Thoroughgood felt anger surge through him. The voice in his head shouted, 'For fuck's sake! Surely she can't have bought all that legit city businessman bullshit?'

If she had, Thoroughgood knew he needed to make sure Celine was finally made aware that the bad and the ugly, when it came to Mojito, far outweighed the good. It was a case of now or never in that respect.

'Come on, Celine, you must know about the gangland turf war they're calling the ice cream wars, being waged across the north of the city? Christ, it's front page news in every paper.'

'What do you think? That I go about with my head in the sand?' she shot back.

'Thank God for that, at least we have a starting point. Well the ice cream war is being waged between your friend Bobby and a crime family called the McGuigans and what it all boils down to is the lucrative drug trade that is being peddled from under the counters of both factions' ice cream vans – hence the sobriquet. It's become a case of tit for tat and dear, heartbroken Bobby kickstarted it all when he had a McGuigan's ice cream man's hands reduced to mash. Then another one gets fatally harpooned through the heart by a shard of metal from a van that exploded in a warehouse fire, which was almost certainly started by Mojito's men and left the McGuigans' fleet in meltdown. From there everything escalated and that is when Frankie and Lucy Dawson were killed. Come on, Celine, tell me you get all of that?'

She dropped her brown eyes and stared into her drink, and Thoroughgood realised straight away that she had indeed 'got all of that' but had chosen to blot it out; chosen to believe that Mojito was the man to give her everything she had ever dreamed of and more.

Now he was ruining that fiction.

Thoroughgood reached out a hand and placed it on her wrist; when she looked up at him her eyes were swimming in tears.

'I know this isn't what you want to hear, but I need to tell you everything about Mojito, the whole truth and nothing but the whole truth. Are you up for that?' he asked.

'What choice do I have?'

'Did you know that Dawson was in the army over in Northern Ireland? The Paras, to be precise, and that he may have been mixed up in the whole Bloody Sunday episode back in 1972?'

Her silence confirmed that she did not and Thoroughgood ploughed on. 'He was there in the company of several colleagues who went on to join Strathclyde Police, and who are now all cosily serving on the same shift in an area called Lennox Hill, in the very north of the city, which is where the shit started to fly when the ice cream wars broke out.'

Looking up, she suddenly said, 'Would one of these cops be called Jimmy?'

A frown shot across Thoroughgood's face. 'Why? What makes you ask that?'

'Because the other night I was delivering some licensing documents to Bobby's office and I heard him on the phone to someone called Jimmy. They were talking about someone claiming to be a CID officer so he could get into Tutankhamun's. Well, I guess that was you, Gus.'

Thoroughgood exhaled heavily. He knew exactly who Jimmy was and eventually, after swilling the rum and coke around in his mouth, he said, 'That would be my dear, doting section sergeant, Jimmy Rentoul.'

'Oh,' said Celine almost guiltily.

Thoroughgood took another drink and ploughed on. 'Interesting what you hear listening at doors, Celine. But I'm glad you were eary-wigging, cos it helps prove the point that these cops are working for Mojito and are part of the crimes he has perpetrated in recent weeks, including murder. The bottom line now is that the net is closing on him and I don't want you in it when it draws shut.'

Before she could answer the voice in his head said, 'Christ, there you go again.'

Celine met his gaze and held it. 'You don't want me there when the net draws shut, you don't want this or that to happen to me? It seems to me, Constable Thoroughgood, that you want an awful lot for me without telling me exactly why or what it is.'

Thoroughgood knew that he had reached the point where words were a waste of energy.

Leaning across, he pulled her close and kissed her again, and once more, to his utter amazement, she did not resist.

CHAPTER 42

Slowly, he felt her pull away from him and immediately Thoroughgood worried that he had overstepped the mark.

'I'm sorry, I couldn't help myself,' he said, but while he spoke he kept his sea-green gaze levelled on her, because he wanted Celine to know that he had no regrets about crossing the line.

She smiled artfully and asked, 'And?'

Taken aback by her candour he played for time. 'Can I get my breath back, please? Would there be any chance of another rum? Oh, and maybe you could stick on some music? Hope you don't mind but I brought some Love and Money with me,' said Thoroughgood fishing out the tape.

Celine laughed out loud and Thoroughgood felt a smile as wide as the Clyde flash across his face. 'What's the joke?'

'Is that what you reckon I need? A bit of Love and Money?' she asked and he saw the tension and sadness drain from her face.

'Nope, I'm hoping that you'll find I'm your "Halleluiah Man",' said Thoroughgood, pointing to a track on the cassette box.

Moments later Celine handed him his refill and, crossing her legs, she made herself comfortable on the couch in front of him. 'You still haven't answered my questions, Gus.'

Her use of his Christian name warmed Thoroughgood from the inside out and lit up his face, and he didn't care if she knew it.

Standing below the skylight he lifted his glass, let the brilliance of the moonbeams sparkle through it and then he let it all out. 'Where do I start?' he asked rhetorically, before taking a deep breath. 'The first time I saw you, I knew you were... different.'

'Come on, is that another one of your lines you think I'm going to buy?' she asked, but her eyes were smiling.

'No way. I felt the minute we met at Tutankhamun's there was something between us. But what about you, Celine? What about Dawson? Is there something between you and him?' Thoroughgood steeled himself for her answer and searched her face for any information it might betray.

'Bobby Dawson has been kind to me but I am under no illusions as to what I am to him, just another pretty girl to be seen on his arm. And in return for my presence, for want of a better word, I get the chance to climb the ladder within his organisation,' she said candidly.

Thoroughgood sat down next to her on the settee, taking her hands in his. 'But pretty soon there will be no organisation and no ladders to climb inside it. People like Bobby Dawson are all the same – they may think they're above the law but eventually they find out the hard way that they're just as vulnerable to it as the ordinary punter on the street. This is only going to end one way for Mojito. And when it all comes tumbling down it's going to be messy.'

'But what do you want me to do about that, Gus? Or is there more than one reason for your visit tonight?' she asked, and he could see the doubt flitting into her eyes.

'Okay, you want the honest truth?' As Celine's head nodded in the affirmative, Thoroughgood got to the nitty-gritty. 'The way I see it, you have two options. One, you walk away and try and make a fresh start elsewhere. Or two, you can try and help us from the inside with information that will help bring Dawson down and end this bloody ice cream war a damn sight quicker than it would have been possible to, and hopefully before any more people lose their lives.'

Suddenly Thoroughgood could see the indecision writ large on her beautiful face replaced by a stronger emotion and he realised that by presenting her with an ultimatum he had got it spectacularly wrong again.

'What?' she demanded.

'I'm sorry, Celine, but time is one thing we just don't have. Who knows what Mojito has planned next to avenge Lucy's murder. But the one thing you can bank on is that he will take revenge and, after what he did when Frankie was murdered, it is sure to be bloody and no doubt imminent.'

As she brought her eyes to bear they smouldered with rage. 'I don't believe you. I don't know the first thing about you and you expect me to give up everything and grass on the only man who has given me an opportunity to make something of myself? But then, that is the real reason you are here, Gus Thoroughgood. If the McGuigans are behind the murder of Frankie and Lucy Dawson then they deserve everything they've got coming to them. Just ask yourself this, Constable Thoroughgood, how would you feel if your brother and sister had been murdered?'

Thoroughgood, aware that he had overplayed his hand, had no answer. He shot his right hand up to his head and clamped down on his black mullet as he stared at the floor helplessly. Then, gritting his teeth, he forced his eyes up and held her scorching gaze. 'It's your choice, Celine. I'm sorry if...'

But before he could finish the sentence her Bacardi and Coke engulfed him and she spat two words his way: 'Get out.'

CHAPTER 43

Kneeling down in the derelict first-floor flat of a condemned tenement, Collins pressed his back into the wall, tightened the tourniquet and then started to bang his left foot with the ball of his fist as he furiously tried to bring up a vein.

As his smack habit had progressed he had used almost every other less conspicuous vein in his body and as each turned toxic his habit demanded he found a replacement for the drug he craved so badly.

Syringe in his teeth, he looked out through the smashed window at the bleak back garden that was now no more than a midden, and reflected that his life had similarly turned to shit. For Collins had not always been a junkie housebreaker, and at one point had even harboured a notion to join the army, only for the cruel force of peer pressure to steer him down a different path that had led to this desperately bleak moment in a derelict building, where he sat all alone, his high hopes and great expectations long since shattered and his day spent living like an animal from minute to minute, his continued existence dependant on his ability to feed his habit.

Shaking his head angrily, he attempted to obliterate his conscience and its relentless chiding. He opened his mouth and let the needle drop into his right hand and then punctured the vein. As he felt the cool surge of the heroin swell through his body, and as its numbing effects enveloped him, Collins let out a moan of satisfaction and rocked back against the wall, his eyes rolling upwards as oblivion shrouded him temporarily.

R.J.Mitchell

But the quality of the hit and the length of time Collins remained on each trip was decreasing, just as the strength and frequency of his self-administered abuse was spiralling in the opposite direction, and only moments later he started to regain his faculties.

It was then, almost immediately, that his mind started to focus on the next turn he needed to pull off, the stolen goods it would yield, and just how much cash he could squeeze to pay for his next score.

Again the voice of Collins' conscious boomed in his head. 'You need tae get aff it, Cat man, cos yer nine lives are almost up, pal.'

'Fuck aff,' shouted Collins at a crumbling wall, sleek with wet and daubed with the slogans of the 'Lennox Fleet' gang that had long ago departed the area. Then he staggered towards the door-less doorway and gripped the splintered stairwell bannister as he attempted to descend to the ground floor.

Collins was thinking of a night-time creeper job, on an OAP-occupied ground-floor flat, that he had been led to believe would be particularly lucrative. He cut through the close and checked right and left just in case there were any black monkey suits on the horizon, but the coast was clear.

The need to take a furtive glance ahead was something he did without thinking, and he took pride in the fact that he, 'the Cat', was always one padded step ahead of the law.

But the double-score bag he'd injected in the tenement meant he was not as alert as he should have been and as he turned onto the street he paid little attention to the white Transit van with the two long ladders strapped to its roof, sporting several dirty rags billowing in the breeze.

As he drew parallel with the back of the van a grey-haired man in a white boiler suit stepped out and, seeing the paint pot he carried in his right hand, Collins failed to give the male a second glance as he meandered on his way, his mind occupied with the layout of tonight's turn.

When it came, the blow to his stomach took Collins completely by surprise and looking down he saw that the object that had been rammed into his midriff was indeed the paint pot. Winded, he looked up in startled amazement.

The grey-haired male in the boiler suit, who had failed to register on his threat radar, smiled benignly. 'Okay, sonny? Hope you like my matt finish!' And then Numan grabbed his right hand and twisted it to the sky before ripping it round behind Collins and frogmarching him into the back of the van.

Standing at the vehicle doors was a fresh-faced individual wearing a Fila tracksuit zipped up to his neck. Opening the doors the male said, 'Taxi for Collins to the Bar-L.'

'Whit the fuck?' asked Collins, his breath returning as he was pitched forwards and onto the van floor face first.

From behind him Numan, in his gravelly tones, said, 'It might be an idea for you to shut up and let me ask the questions, Collins.' Then the housebreaker heard his tormentor jump into the van and the doors slam shut.

As the junkie looked up he saw the dark features of a male with a moustache that seemed to have a mind of its own, but before he could protest further he found his jaw recoiling from a blow he never saw coming. The next thing he knew, as he regained consciousness, his hands were shackled in steel bracelets and the chain linking the two handcuffs looped over a wooden beam that ran the length of the van's rear area.

That left Collins half hanging with his feet trailing on the vehicle floor and as he began to take in his surroundings he felt another powerful blow thud into his midriff and looked up to see the male with the moustache crouching opposite him.

'That's just for starters, Collins. It's time you spilled your guts and you'd better do it pronto, because we don't have time to, pardon the pun, hang around,' said the male who Collins noticed was resplendent in a white boiler suit.

'Dinnae know whit yer on aboot, pal. Who the fuck are yous anyway?' demanded Collins.

A piece of plastic flashed before his eyes and as Collins scrutinised it he saw that the photograph it contained was of the first male wearing a police uniform, back in the days when his head of hair had been black.

'Yous could be anyone, never mind the polis. That proves nothin',' spat Collins.

The housebreaker found his Berghaus grabbed roughly by the grey-haired male with the mad eyes that were now just millimetres away from his face. 'Aye, you're right, sonny, we could be anyone and it's just as well for you that we're no'. Constable Thoroughgood sends his regards, by the way, if that helps?' said Numan.

The realisation that he had been hauled in at Thoroughgood's behest simultaneously put Collins at ease but also sent him into a rage. 'That fuckin' rookie, I wid have come through for him, if he'd just been a bit mair patient.'

'But he was patient and you, my friend, were takin' the piss out of an inexperienced young cop, but that all stops right now. The games are over, Collins, no more fannying aboot. I want chapter and verse on what you know about Mojito Dawson and the McGuigans while we are on our way to the Bar-L,' said Numan.

CHAPTER 44

'You cannae be takin' me there in my condition, the big hoose is no place to go cold turkey,' said Collins with his usual sob story plea.

'Cold turkey is it? You're half stoned, Collins. When I slammed that paint pot into your guts you didnae know what day it was,' said Numan, his eyes relentlessly scanning the junkie's features. Then the DC shook his head and turned to the front of the van. 'Sergeant Malcolm, you can start her up, that's one for the Bar-L, good to go,' said Numan.

But Collins continued to play hardball. 'Look, boss, I get it, yous are cops awright, but I'm just a junkie housebreaker who keeps his head doon, does his bit o' smack and stays oot o' trouble where he can.' Collins smiled a gap-toothed grin as he attempted to assure Numan of his sincerity.

He was met with laughter.

Then a vice-like grip took hold of his jaw. 'Look, you little fuck, who d'you think you're dealing with here?' demanded Hardie. 'The Village Green fuckin' Preservation Society?'

'Ah, come on, pal, I dinnae ken whit that Thoroughgood has told yous but I know fuck all, I just play the game with him to stay oot o' the big hoose and avoid gettin' daubed up on that fuckin' sheriff's warrant that's oot for me. Anyways, whit would I want to be toutin' to the Mojito wan for when he has half the local polis on his payroll?'

'Look, I don't give a fuck about the sheriff's warrant, what I do care about is that we're in the middle of a turf war that is making the streets run red and that you are a double-dealin' little weasel who knows everything that is going on round here and is, despite your bullshit, toutin' to both the McGuigans and Mojito Dawson,' said Numan, just as he was forced to throw a hand up to the beam to regain his balance when the van took a lurch.

Malcolm bawled back through the panelled window that was left open between the rear of the van and the driver's cabin. 'Sorry, lads, that's us on the M8 now, about a mile from HMP Barlinnie. But there's still plenty of time for a bit of fun, Dennis!'

'Aye, roger that, gaffer,' responded Numan.

'The fuck wiz that all aboot?' demanded Collins.

'You'll find out soon enough, Collins,' scowled Hardie. 'Now what about your double-dealing with Dawson and the McGuigans?'

'Don't know whit you're talkin' aboot boss, sometimes the Cat bullshits a bit but I know fuck all about the McGuigans and Dawson other than what I've told the rookie, and anyone could pick that up off the street,' said Collins from behind a jaundiced poker face.

'Right, that's it. We don't have time to fuck about,' said Numan, and then he looked over at Hardie and jerked his head at the wooden beam from which Collins hung.

The housebreaker looked on in confusion as Numan moved past him and opened the van's rear doors, and then Collins could feel his body starting to slide towards the doorway and saw the flashing tarmacadam of the M8 motorway that was rushing past at an increasingly high rate of knots underneath the vehicle.

Snapping his gaze backwards, Collins saw that Hardie was pushing the beam along its runners and towards the van's opened doors, the draught from which was beginning to blast an increasingly powerful force through the vehicle.

As the handcuff chain that secured Collins to the beam began to slip ever closer to the doors the housebreaker became increasingly agitated. 'Fuck's sake, whit are yous doin?' he shouted at the top of his voice, trying to make himself heard over the gale that was howling through the rear of the vehicle from the flapping doors.

With two feet of the beam now hanging out the back of the van and suspended over the onrushing M8, Collins' cuff slipped further down until he slid parallel with the doors themselves and just as he appeared set to slither out of the van and onto the final few inches of suspended beam, Numan grabbed the cuffs and brought his departure to an abrupt stop.

'Now listen to me, smartarse, you've got one final chance to spill everything you know about this fuckin' ice cream war or I tell Kenny here to help you walk the plank all the way out onto the M8, and judging by that Stagecoach about a hundred yards back you're gonnae end up a pun o' mince sometime very soon if you don't play ball, wee man.'

At mention of the bus that was slowly closing the gap on the Transit, Collins' eyes looked set to pop out of his head, but still he refused to burst.

'I cannae dae it, just take me to the big hoose and I'll dae my time, for God's sake,' he pleaded.

'Fuck you,' spat Kenny Hardie, placing a hand against the small of Collins' back.

'Has the prisoner any last request before he meets his maker?' he demanded at the top of his voice to make sure he got the message across over the icy blasts.

Then slowly the cop began to increase the pressure on Collins' back until inch by inch he slipped inexorably towards the end of the plank. The junkie frantically tried to back-peddle but the hand in his back rammed into his spine. His scrabbling feet failed to gain any purchase and he screamed out loud, 'Jesus Christ, naw!' as he slipped along the beam and started to overhang the rear of the vehicle and hover above the M8 below him, with only Numan's right hand and its granite grip stopping the handcuff chain dropping off the end of the beam and consigning the junkie to his fate.

At this point the driver of the Stagecoach had closed the gap to such an extent that he could see exactly the nature of the drama being played out in the rear of the van and the huge vehicle's lights began to flash as its horn sounded out in brutal blasts.

It was the final straw for Collins and he voided his bowels just as words of desperate supplication burst from his mouth. 'Awright, I'll tell yous everythin', for fuck's sake please dinnae dae me,' he begged, staring into Numan's cold eyes.

For a moment the DC glared at him and then he glanced towards the handcuff chain in his right hand, and to Collins' horror the fingers of Numan's paw began to peel back one by one as he released his grip.

'For fuck's sake, naw!' screamed the housebreaker.

CHAPTER 45

'So I've to drop you at the Blackburn office, young Pug, to pick up some such package for Jimmy Rentoul and then we're off to Bayne Street. You sure you're all right with returning to the humdrum of shift life after your heroics with these cowboys at the unit?' asked Edmund Philip with a sideways glance, before taking a long drag on his fag and billowing the smoke out of the Panda's driver's window.

Thoroughgood smiled thinly and replied, 'It's no problem, Edmund. After all, that's what being a probationer is all about.' Then, paraphrasing Jimmy Rentoul's words, he added, 'Let's face it, nothing I do with the unit is going to get me through my probation. It'll be Jimmy Rentoul who decides whether I make cop or not, so what the sergeant wants the sergeant gets.'

Philip's blunt features turned to regard Thoroughgood once more and he said, 'Aye, I heard he got a bit more than he bargained for when he turned up at Lennox Hill Office on Sunday early shift. From what I've heard you had the prisoner's bed all nice and snug for the sergeant. Still, at least you'd managed to make it up before letting him in. Taking a dump, weren't you just, me old son?' The senior cop erupted into a fit of unrestrained mirth.

'Very good, Edmund. After all, a bus stop beats a prisoner's bed anytime,' replied Thoroughgood, determined not to let Philip have it all his own way.

The big cop's moustache twitched and his eyes narrowed and Thoroughgood wasn't sure if it was the smoke getting in them or something more worrying, but when he spoke the big man was keen to impart some helpful advice. 'That's as may be, young Pug, but I'm not the one trying to make it through his probation and needin' to get Jimmy Rentoul on his side, now, am I?'

'I know, I know, but it isn't easy, Edmund, when you've come from the cloisters of Glasgow university, where you've been within touching distance of a PhD spent studying the Hundred Years' War, *en France*, to being detailed to a shift full of...' Thoroughgood trailed off into silence, aware that he was digging himself an increasingly big hole.

The marked Ford Escort swung in through the opening gates of the rear car park at Blackburn office and ground to a halt, with Philip applying the handbrake gratingly against the ratchet. Then the burly ex-serviceman turned his full gaze on Thoroughgood. 'Look, Pug, I know you're having a tough time of it but don't tar us all with the same brush. I may be ex-army, but like I told you before, matey, I ain't one of them. I'm on this fuckin' shift but I ain't part of it, if you know what I mean. There's a way to get by while you're here and it won't be forever. But the only way you're going to get of this fuckin' chain gang and make it out of your probation is by playing the game – Rentoul's game. You catch my drift, Pug?'

But before Thoroughgood could answer a call came out over PR. 'Zulu Panda Charlie, Constable Philip, please return to Lennox Hill Office immediately,' said the female voice of the controller.

Philip was far from impressed. 'Zulu Panda Charlie, we've just arrived at Blackburn Office to pick up a despatch for Sergeant Rentoul. Will attend the Hill after we've got it.'

'Negative, Panda Charlie, Constable Thoroughgood to attend Blackburn Office to relieve the bar officer and you to attend Lennox Hill Office, at the sergeant's orders,' said the controller.

'Roger, Zulu Control,' replied Philip, shrugging his shoulders and turning back to Thoroughgood. 'Blimey, fuckin' typical, they don't know their left foot from their right. I better get going, Pug, but just remember what I said and you'll come out the other side okay. Now jog on, son.'

Thoroughgood smiled wanly at his senior man and said, 'I'll do my best, Edmund,' then he jumped out of the Panda and headed through the car park just as the rear doors to Blackburn Office swung open obligingly.

Making his way through to the uniform bar, Thoroughgood met Jimmy Sykes sitting with his feet up on the front desk.

'Hi, Sykesy, how you doin'? It's your lucky day, I'm here to relieve you and let you get a night shift flier!' said the probationer.

Sykes shifted uncomfortably in his chair and met Thoroughgood's words with an awkward smile, running his right hand through his greying, wavy hair and then unclipping his tie from around his neck, undoing the top button of his shirt and re-clipping the tie to the side of one of his breast pockets.

Then he looked up at Thoroughgood and said, 'First things first, Pug, there's a despatch waiting for you upstairs in the support unit muster room that's been left for the gaffer, so if you wouldnae mind bringin' it down, it would save my back, young 'un.'

Thoroughgood noticed that although Sykes had looked up at him he had failed to meet his eyes; there was something about him that was completely at odds with the friendly nature of their last encounter.

But Thoroughgood put it down to fatigue and replied, 'Sure thing, Sykesy, back in a minute and then you can get off to your baws!'

By this time Sykes was now penning what Thoroughgood could see was the *Evening Times* crossword and, although he failed to look up, the station constable said, 'Thanks, son,' and continued to work his way across and down.

Bounding up the steps, Thoroughgood climbed to the first floor and jogged along the blue linoleum-lined corridor towards the support services muster room.

Placing his right hand out in front of him he went to push open the swing doors to the room but before he could make contact they were snapped back and his momentum saw him half stumble into the darkness.

'Put him on the chair,' said a voice from the shadows that

Thoroughgood instantly recognised, but before he could open his mouth, he felt a powerful grip take hold of both of his arms and he was pinioned and then frogmarched forwards and slammed onto a leather seat, his wrists bound roughly behind him.

Then the lights snapped on and Thoroughgood was met with the sight of Jimmy Rentoul standing opposite him, flanked on either side by Davidson and Jones.

'Welcome to court, Thoroughgood, Zulu Group Three court. I am the judge and this is my jury and I can tell you now, boy, there will only be one verdict,' said Sergeant Jimmy Rentoul.

Shaken and stunned, Thoroughgood couldn't help himself articulating his disbelief. 'What... What do you mean?' he stammered.

A vicious hand shot out of the light and grabbed his jaw. 'I was right all along, from day one, Thoroughgood, you are a grass for the bleedin' brass, a plant, and now your little turn with the internal affair unit has proven that point. There's no way a fuckin' probationer with the ink still wet on his warrant card gets a secondment like that without someone pulling strings for him in the background, you whelp,' spat Davidson, his grey eyes shining with icy hatred.

'That's garbage Davidson, you've had it in for me from the very first day I arrived at the Hill. You made your mind up about me before I took my first step on the beat with you, so don't give me that shite,' raged Thoroughgood, his fear receding as a more powerful emotion took over.

'But now, Pug, we've found out that you have been touting on us to the IA and if our information is right you are about to join them as a temporary aide. Now how does that add up for a fresh-faced graduate just out of university with only a couple of months' service behind him?' asked Jones.

'But that isn't all we've found out, Thoroughgood,' said Rentoul, taking a step towards the probationer and hunkering down. 'Tell me, how have the IA managed to get Cat Collins signed up as a tout? No, don't bother, because this all goes back to that little run-in you had with him on the Hill. You had him, took a syringe off him and yet he still manages to make a break for it. And you're supposed to be a squash player of some repute, I believe?' Thoroughgood, his jaw set, kept his mouth shut.

But Rentoul was determined to pursue his quarry. 'Then, as if by magic, Collins starts asking questions in the wrong places. Nope, it don't add up and that, you arsewipe, is because you've been squealin' to the IA and settin' us up.'

Before Thoroughgood could protest, Rentoul stood up and backhanded him with a vicious swipe.

CHAPTER 46

His jaw stung from Rentoul's blow but Thoroughgood gritted his teeth and did his best not to show it, for he knew that his ordeal had only just begun.

With his back towards his captive, Rentoul, now sitting behind the support service inspector's giant desk with the toes of his immaculately bulled boots shining on top of it, unclipped his tie, popped the silver buttons of his tunic open and proceeded to stack up the damming evidence against the rookie.

'What other evidence do we have against the defendant, Constable?' he asked, turning to Davidson.

Thoroughgood couldn't help himself from exploding with rage. 'For fuck's sake, this is ridiculous. A kangaroo court in the back of a bleeding police office, for crying out loud, I'm one of you.'

'But that's just it, Thoroughgood, you'll never be one of us. What you are is a lying worm,' said Davidson.

'Now, now, Constable, let's stick to the evidence,' ordered Rentoul.

Davidson looked over towards his sergeant and flashed him a rotten smile. 'Sorry, gaffer. Firstly, there is being caught sleeping on the job and so plainly being in neglect of duty, second there is attempting to undermine shift morale by turning colleagues against each other and then there is associating with known criminals.'

Thoroughgood's face was a picture of complete befuddlement. 'What the fuck are you on about, Davidson? This is fantasy, pure fuckin' fiction. Christ, you're in the wrong job, you should be writing crime novels,' he spat defiantly.

The words were barely out of his mouth when a fist smashed

off his jaw. 'Speak when you are spoken to, grass,' said Jones, a malicious sneer creeping over his fleshy face.

'So you are denying associating with known criminals... Thoroughgood?' asked Rentoul, deliberately allowing a pause to draw out where he should have prefixed Thoroughgood's name with the title of constable.

Blood dripping from his burst face, Thoroughgood ran his tongue around the inside of his mouth to check for internal debris and was relieved to find none.

'I haven't got the slightest clue what you're on about,' he said flatly, acutely aware that whatever he said was only going to be turned against him.

'Celine Lynott? Tell me about her,' demanded Rentoul.

Thoroughgood locked his green eyes on the sergeant's face and couldn't help himself giving a slight shake of his head. 'Tell you what?'

'But there's plenty to tell about her isn't there? After all, you've been spending plenty of time with her, including cosy little visits to her flat, you jumped-up, student, sponging bastard,' said Davidson.

'The same Celine Lynott who has previous convictions for till dipping, fraud and contraventions of the Misuse of Drugs Act 1971. So you've been tupping a fuckin' junkie, eh?' asked Rentoul, laughing out loud.

'A junkie whore, to be precise, gaffer,' said Jones, adding his rumbling laughter to the building glee.

The realisation that they had been watching him off duty and collating everything he had been doing while on it, all to use against him, smacked Thoroughgood between the eyes far harder than the blows he had taken earlier.

The voice in Thoroughgood's head helpfully said, 'You're buggered now, mate.'

His eyes darted between each of his tormentors as he sought a clue as to what was coming his way next.

After a short while Rentoul held his hand up. 'That's enough mirth, gentlemen. The evidence is damming and it's time to let the accused speak up in his defence. Have you anything to say, Thoroughgood?'

'Do you really think you're going to get away with this? The IA are closing in on you and your shift. Shift – that's a laugh, it's more like a fuckin' penal colony. Whatever you've got planned for me, the end is coming for you and your minions, Rentoul. The IA know everything and they will take you down... All of you,' said Thoroughgood, but no sooner had he spoken than he regretted his bout of self-immolation.

Through his rashness and loose tongue he had just confirmed everything that Rentoul had levelled at him, sealed his own fate and tipped them off that they were indeed under investigation by the unit. Setting his jaw, Thoroughgood stared straight forward and hung his head in resignation.

'Straight from the horse's mouth, gaffer!' said Jones triumphantly. 'Guilty as fucking charged, I'd say.'

'Have we reached a unanimous verdict, Constable Davidson?' asked Rentoul.

'He's done out the park gaffer. Bang to rights,' sneered Davidson.

'Now that we have reached our verdict, it is time that you have a suitable punishment meted out. But there is plenty of time for that because we are not the only people you have annoyed, Thoroughgood.'

'What are you on about, Rentoul? Annoyed, tell me how I've annoyed you? By breathing the same air? You're a sick joke and more bent than any of the criminals you've locked up. So who was it that torched Danny French and blew Gerry McGuigan's brains out? Come on, if I'm done for, why don't you come clean,' said Thoroughgood, both playing for time and trying to glean every last bit of information he could... Just in case.

Suddenly Jones's bloated features appeared in front of his eyes and the huge cop said, 'Now that would be tellin', wouldn't it, pal?' and after flashing a vicious smile he smashed another hand off Thoroughgood's jaw and put the probationer's lights well and truly out.

CHAPTER 47

The smell of damp hung in the air and sent a bone-jarring chill through his body. Regaining consciousness, Thoroughgood felt the rough fabric that sheathed his head grazing against his skin and realised that he was pinned to a cold stone wall, the surface of which he could feel was wet.

His fingers, pinioned high above his head, were secured against the rough stone while his legs were spread apart with his feet set slightly forwards, which forced him to stand on his toes while his body weight pulled heavily on his aching fingers.

As silence reigned and Thoroughgood's discomfort grew into a silent agony, both his location and how long he'd been there remained things he could not comprehend. The memory of his interrogation by Rentoul, Davidson and Jones, and the kangaroo court they had sprung on him, seeped back to Thoroughgood and he began to replay the highlights.

One remark in particular kept bouncing around his head. 'We are not the only people you have annoyed,' Rentoul had said, and that could mean only one thing: Dawson wanted a piece of him.

The reality of that conclusion and where it pointed seemed to drain Thoroughgood of all hope and his mind began to work its way through the memories he had accrued during his ill-fated probationary period.

It seemed like only yesterday he'd been working as a barman in Cul De Sac, down in Ashton Lane, and then lording it behind the bar at Finlay's in Byres Road and enjoying the charms of the ladies who frequented Tennent's third-busiest Glasgow bar.

The strains of David Lee Roth singing 'California Girls' and 'Just a Gigolo', songs that he'd used to amuse and charm them, repeated themselves in his head as Thoroughgood drifted into a semi-conscious state.

The harsh fabric being ripped from his face brought him back to the here and now with a painful jolt and there, sitting three feet away from him, was Mojito.

As his eyes adjusted to the light of a flickering candle that spluttered on an embrasure behind the crime lord, Thoroughgood realised that his imprisonment was almost certainly within a building that was of the ancient variety.

Seated on a simple, three-legged stool, his hands steepled, Dawson, his diamond-studded lobe sparkling in the candlelight, stared ahead of him, silent, unmoving and oozing malevolence.

As the moments drew on, his dark eyes eventually lifted and focused on Thoroughgood's battered and cut features. 'So what now, Constable Thoroughgood?' he asked.

'You're the only one that can supply an answer to that question, Dawson,' replied Thoroughgood, holding his gaze defiantly but aware that the dripping cold was starting to rack his body with a series of tremors. His fingers burned with the stress being placed on them thanks to his painful position.

As Mojito glared at Thoroughgood, the glints of candlelight that played in his dark eyes seemed to give him a ghoulish quality that made the gangster even more sinister.

'Have you heard of the five techniques, Constable Thoroughgood?' asked Mojito, almost amicably.

'I don't have a clue what you're on about, Dawson. All I want to know is where the fuck we are and what sick game you're intending to play with me,' said the rookie, for the first time aware that the rush of running water was coming strongly from the rear of the building.

Dawson stood up and walked over to Thoroughgood until his face was only an inch away from the young cop. 'Regarding our location, there is no need for you to know, but suffice it to say it belongs to another world. As for the five techniques, they very much belong to the world you currently find yourself in,' he said, a vicious delight creeping across his previously stony face.

Running his hand over his shiny dome, he continued, 'The five techniques are the interrogation methods adopted during Operation Demetrius by the British Army back in the seventies over in the Province.'

Then Dawson slapped Thoroughgood playfully on his jaw, underlining the helplessness of his plight, gave a short harsh laugh, and said, 'Your current spread-eagled posture is a key part of it. Currently you're in a high-stress position, as your fingers will no doubt be telling you, such is the pain you will be enduring through them with your body weight almost totally on your digits,' explained Dawson matter-of-factly.

Mojito devoured Thoroughgood's battered features and the rookie was aware that his every weakness was being assessed, but as he opened his mouth to speak Thoroughgood found his jaw clamped in an iron grip.

'I've spared you the pleasure of having your head enveloped in a bag any longer, because, while I want to interrogate you, I prefer to absorb every last expression, enjoy every tormented wince and see what makes you tick, Thoroughgood. You are also fortunate that I didn't have the time or the inclination to subject you to continued noise prior to our chat, deprive you of sleep, food and drink, or reduce your diet to scraps. But I can see that Privates Jones and Davidson have conducted some of their own softening-up work on you,' he concluded, this time thumping his fist into Thoroughgood's midriff.

'Privates Jones and Davidson? You're off your nut, Dawson, we're not back in Northern Ireland now. Your two buddies and Jimmy Rentoul are police officers, not Paras. I think you've lost it, Dawson, your grief at the murder of your little brother and your sister have driven you over the edge. But why were they killed, Dawson? Because of you and that's what's eating away at you, driving you mad... You're a fantasist. The bottom line is that you are a homicidal, drug-dealing bastard who deserves everything that's coming to him.'

But before Thoroughgood could say another word Dawson's right hand brutally buried itself deep into his solar plexus.

'Shut the fuck up and listen to me. In case you haven't worked it out, Constable, the war with the IRA is still raging on. Fuck me gently, the Enniskillen Remembrance Day massacre was less than two years ago. They've just murdered eleven British soldiers at the Deal barracks in Kent. This war is not just confined to Ireland, Thoroughgood, it's being waged here in the UK and the McGuigans are up to their necks in it. They are part of the Provos' attempt to open up a new front in the west of Scotland, and Glasgow in particular. Everything they make from their ice cream vans is being used to help bankroll the IRA,' said Dawson with such intensity that a vein throbbed in his neck.

'Come on, Dawson, this isn't about the war against the Provos, this is about you muscling in on the same lucrative drug-dealing trade that the McGuigans are peddling from their vans – or what's left of them,' spat Thoroughgood.

'I just told you where the money from their dealing goes, Thoroughgood, but I'll bet that neither you nor the IA knew that before his tragic demise Gerry McGuigan was working as an IRA quartermaster?'

Wincing from the searing pain that was pulsing through his fingers, Thoroughgood strained onto the last millimetre of his toes in an effort to relieve his agony. 'No, I didn't, but what has that got to do with me, Dawson? As for the ice cream wars, for crying out loud, Dawson, you're dealing drugs from under the counter every bit as much as the McGuigans are, so where's that money all going?'

'Where it is most needed, Thoroughgood. Now I have a deal for you. Harry here,' said Dawson, gesturing to a shadowy figure who, stepping from the shadows, revealed himself to be the giant bouncer from Tutankhamun's, 'will replace the hood on your head and then cut you down. But before I give him the go ahead, I need assurances from you, Thoroughgood.'

'What would they be?' asked the rookie, feeling like he had

stumbled into some parallel universe.

'I need you to go back to your bosses at the IA and mention 14 Intelligence Unit to them. Tell them to back the hell off and let me finish my operation and the McGuigans with it. There is only one answer to this request and if you get it wrong I'm afraid you'll have become excess to requirements.'

'What choice do I have?'

'None.'

'Can you answer me one thing, Dawson?' asked Thoroughgood, acutely aware that the menacing figure of Harry was poised to pull the hood back over his head.

'That, Constable, depends,' said Dawson flatly.

'What do you intend on doing with Celine Lynott?'

'I wondered when you would get around to her. I had plans for Celine but I'm afraid you have jeopardised them with your pathetic doe-eyed interest, but she still retains a use for me. Celine, my dear Thoroughgood, is my insurance policy and one that will ensure that, despite the chance I'm taking in releasing you, you will do exactly what I have asked of you.'

'What have you done with her, you murderin' bastard?'

Dawson's right hand viciously cracked off Thoroughgood's jaw. The rookie's body sank downwards and almost pulled his fingers out their sockets.

The agonised Thoroughgood let out a screech.

'That is your second question, Thoroughgood. Suffice it to say your girlfriend is being well looked after. My advice to you would be to forget the day you ever clapped eyes on Celine Lynott... hard as that may be.' Dawson once again grabbed Thoroughgood by the jaw and brought his own feral features back to point-blank range. 'Now, ensure you relay everything I've told you to your handlers and make them aware that all of it is completely deniable,' said Dawson, then he turned towards the huge brooding presence of Harry, clicked his fingers and once again Thoroughgood found himself in darkness.

CHAPTER 48

It had been a whole lot easier to leave the Province than she had expected and her undetected arrival in Glasgow, and the pleasure she took from eluding the security services, painted her pale features in a visceral smile.

Staring out of the window, twenty storeys up, she took in the view stretching out across the city's skyline. Then she checked her watch and realised that she was overdue for her rendezvous.

Fifteen minutes later she approached the park bench, a hundred yards away from the ruined splendour of the Victorian greenhouses that had once dominated Springburn Park. Taking a seat, she checked her watch again. She was impatient, but she was also nervous at her prolonged presence at a location that could so easily be surveilled.

She was snapped from her bout of introspection by the throaty roar of a powerful motorcycle and her gaze soon came to rest on a blue-and-white streak surging along the road that ran parallel with the park's rusted fencing.

Moments later the leather-clad rider dismounted, parked his gleaming machine and opened the gates. Although the motorcyclist kept a jet-black helmet on she had no doubt it was him.

The place was run down, thought Dawson, as a brief childhood memory of summer holidays spent running barefoot in the park ricocheted around his mind. But these sepia-dimmed recollections ended as, lifting his visor, he clapped eyes on the pale goddess with the magnificent, long russet tresses that flew in the stirring breeze.

He had forgotten just how much of a cruel beauty she was. It had been the description he had first heard used to describe her in the aftermath of the day that still scorched his soul... even from a distance of seventeen years. Yet her fine, almost flawless, features seemed to have remained untouched by the twin ravages of time and tragedy that had assailed everyone else who had lived through Bloody Sunday and beyond.

As he walked towards her, she remained icily motionless on the bench, like some winter queen surveying her dominions. Dawson drank in every inch of her ethereal features. His dark eyes locked with hers, green flecked with gold, which seemed to sear him with their intensity.

It was then that he realised that the woman he knew only as Devorgilla truly was every inch the killer they said she had become, and Dawson found himself, almost involuntarily, taking a deep breath before he sat down next to this maiden of death. Placing his gauntleted hands on his leather-sheathed knees he made his opening play. 'It is tragic, the way this place has been allowed to go to rack and ruin, but I still love to come up here, when I have time, to think.'

'And what, when you have the time, do you like to think about, Mr Dawson?' asked the harsh Northern Irish voice, in a flat monotone that betrayed not the slightest hint of emotion or feeling.

'Revenge,' answered Dawson staring at the ruined magnificence of the gardens.

'Then you and I are not too different, Mr Dawson,' said Devorgilla. After a short pause she surprised him and continued, 'So that is why you wanted me in Glasgow. But how do you want me to take your revenge?'

Dawson was in no hurry to join the dots. The index finger of his right hand shot up to point at the splintered frames of the glasshouse that had once been the envy of Europe. 'This place was originally made up of an old ironstone pit and a quarry until the Glasgow Corporation acquired the land to turn it into Springburn

Park way back in 1892.'

Dawson pulled the gauntlet off his right hand and slipped it inside his leathers, removing an envelope as he did so. Then he made a panoramic sweep of the park around him, making sure, as far as he could, that they were not being watched. Satisfied, he pulled the other glove from his left hand and removed the great black helmet from his head.

Then he removed a sheet of paper from the envelope and smoothed it out meticulously, before training his eyes on the horizon. 'We are seated on what is virtually the crown of Balgrayhill, one of the highest areas in the north of Glasgow, around 364 feet above sea level.' Dawson swept his left hand in a grand gesture. 'As you see, we have impressive views of Ben Lomond, the Trossachs, the Kilpatrick, Campsie and Kilsyth Hills, and the hills of Argyllshire. In fact if the weather is kind and clear, like it is today, they say you can see the peak of Goatfell on the Isle of Arran, which I think is just about there,' said Dawson, pointing to a barely visible summit somewhere out in the wide, faded-blue horizon.

Then he turned round and faced Devorgilla full on for the first time since he had sat down on the bench next to her and handed her the sheet of paper. 'So we meet for the last time, Devorgilla. The information you need is on this sheet.'

Her gaze filleted him and after a short pause she said, in her biting tones, 'There are not many men who would sanction this, Mr Dawson,' waving the sheet of paper in the air to underline her point.

'Unfortunately mistakes have been made, jeopardising my operation and the funds I had hoped would percolate their way back to your organisation to help continue the fight against Sinn Féin and the IRA. I've been left with no other option than to enlist your services to extricate myself from this situation,' said Dawson, staring balefully into the distance. 'I know what the Provos did to your husband in Belfast and while you may find the mission hard to swallow, I expect you will be able to take satisfaction from it nonetheless. I want you to help me take revenge against them and their allies – the scum who murdered my brother Frankie and my sister Lucy, here in Glasgow. As you will see, I pay well for your services.' He handed over a bulging buff envelope.

She took hold of it but showed no interest in its contents.

'It may have been the RA who murdered Peter but it was the RUC and the Paras who let the bastards get away with it, Mr Dawson. So you tell me, who you think I should avenge him on?' she demanded, the gold flecks in her green eyes on fire.

Her intensity disconcerted Dawson and he took a moment to recover his composure as his own anger mounted within him. With a considerable effort he stayed calm before continuing. 'In Peter's line of work there was always going to be a… danger, that his cover would be blown, it went with the territory. But Gerry McGuigan paid for his part in Peter's murder in a way that I hope has eased your pain.'

Devorgilla turned away and Dawson thought he could see a glistening trail run down her cheek, but when she spoke her voice remained steady. 'You are imaginative, Mr Dawson, I will grant you that. I prefer a more methodical approach to my work,' she said dispassionately.

'Death… It all amounts to the same, Devorgilla, whether you are burnt to a cinder or shot through the head by a sniper's rifle. Few of us get to pick the where and when of it,' he said before trying a change of tack. 'So your accommodation is acceptable and fit for… purpose?'

'It is,' she replied.

An uncomfortable silence stretched out as Devorgilla stared ahead, as though Dawson didn't exist. The sensation was not one that he enjoyed, or was used to experiencing.

Then abruptly she spoke again. 'So tell me how the objectives of 14 Intelligence Company avoid blurring with those of your own, Mr Dawson?'

'Do you think that the IRA worry about objectives blurring when it comes to getting results? In this war the end justifies the means… whatever it is. In every major city in the UK right now there is a battle for supremacy going on between the IRA and its cells, and the security forces who are trying to thwart them and stop the repetition of atrocities like the Brighton hotel bombing that nearly wiped out half the British government,' said Dawson.

'I brought you over here to do what you do because sentiment has no place in this war… That is the only way we will beat the IRA, and when that day comes you will surely welcome it,' concluded Dawson.

Devorgilla swung her emerald gaze back on him. 'The guilty lay on both sides, Mr Dawson. But the McGuigans' links with the RA are well known to us. I will follow the instructions you have given me and I thank you for your generosity,' she said, feeling the weight of the envelope in her hand.

Then she stood up with all the feline grace and stealth of a panther. 'To quote from the Good Book: "The time is coming when all who are in the grave shall hear my voice and come out: those who have done right will rise to life; those who have done wrong will rise to hear their doom. I judge as I am bidden, my sentence is just, because my aim is not my own will, but the will of him who sent me."' Then the assassin smiled for the first time and added, 'You, Mr Dawson, are the man who sent me. God help you all.'

Then she turned away so sharply that her burnt orange locks seemed to hang, almost suspended in the air, before dropping back onto her slender shoulders.

Dawson stared, transfixed, fascinated and drooling as Devorgilla walked away.

CHAPTER 49

As he regained consciousness, the throbbing from Thoroughgood's head sent waves of nausea sweeping over him.

His hands remained tied in front of him while the rough hood still covered his head, but the sound of a vehicle engine and the cold metal that met his skin as he was tossed about made it clear he was being delivered, wherever Mojito wanted him, in the boot of a car.

After what seemed like an eternity the sound of breaks squealing coincided with his body thudding once again off cold metal like a human ping-pong ball. The vehicle was now stationary and the sound of a door opening and slamming shut was followed by footsteps coming his way; the spring of the boot opening was followed by daylight filtering through his coarse hood.

Two powerful hands grabbed him by the shoulders and half pulled, half dragged Thoroughgood out of his temporary quarters, and he found himself being rammed upright against the end of the vehicle. The hood was ripped off his battered, throbbing head and Harry's scarred features were shoved into Thoroughgood's face. The rookie had to swallow back down the vomit that found its way into his mouth, caused by the overpowering stink of nicotine that seeped from the bouncer.

The glinting steel of a vicious blade found its way under Thoroughgood's chin and Harry smiled malevolently. 'You know how fuckin' lucky you are to be alive, arsewipe?'

Thoroughgood's answer was a grimace.

'You heard what Mojito said, now make sure you deliver the

message,' said Harry in his guttural Glaswegian. 'If you want to save your skin, Thoroughgood, you'd be advised to keep your nose out of where it don't belong and stay well away from her.' Then the bouncer slit the rope that was binding Thoroughgood's wrists, grabbed him by his right shoulder and threw him onto the pavement at the side of the vehicle.

As the probationer tried to pick himself up, Harry applied his parting shot: 'Cause if you don't, the next time we meet, my blade will have different work to do, boy.'

Then the bouncer jumped into what Thoroughgood saw was a tan Ford Cortina Mark III, and screeched off down the road.

Slowly, Thoroughgood got to his feet and stumbled across the pavement towards the stairs that led to the gleaming, white front door of number three Crown Gardens. Taking hold of the black wrought-iron railings he started to haul himself onto the first step.

As he did so the front door opened and the waiflike figure of Miss Lynch, the spinster who stayed in the apartment next to Thoroughgood's, appeared at the top of the steps. As her hawk-like gaze rested on his blood-crusted face and ripped clothing, the disgust that registered on her face soon found its way into a more articulate reaction. 'Call yourself a policeman? Look at the state of you, no doubt involved in a drunken, off-duty rammy. You are a disgrace, Angus Thoroughgood, I'm going to speak to Mr Kaye about this, it is just not...'

As the spinster struggled to sum up her disgust, Thoroughgood couldn't stop himself from helping her out. 'Acceptable, is the word I think you are looking for, Miss Lynch.'

'You cheeky young toe rag, how dare you put words in my mouth. Mr Kaye will hear of this all right,' she said. And with that she pulled her pale blue headscarf tight over her immaculately coiffed pastel tresses and to his astonishment jabbed the metallic end of her navy blue umbrella into his midriff. 'Get out of my way. You disgust me. What is this country coming to, allowing yobs like you to become policemen?' And with her parting shot barely out of her mouth Miss Lynch bustled down the steps and past Thoroughgood without giving him another glance.

Moments later he was sitting in an armchair in his lounge, staring out of the window, unseeing, trying to make sense of the last twenty-four hours. As the clock on the mantelpiece ticked, his attention was snapped to the here and now and it dawned on him that he was due on shift in eighty minutes time. There was only one option. Thoroughgood reached for the phone.

He dialled the station number and when he got a ring tone quickly pinched his nose with his thumb and index finger and waited for a voice at the other end.

'Z Division HQ, Bayne Street, uniform bar, Station Constable Sykes, how can I help you?'

Thoroughgood cleared his throat, squeezed his nose and then called in sick in the most flu-ridden, nasal fashion he could muster: 'All right, Constable Sykes, it's Angus Thoroughgood.' Before he continued any further, he threw in a succession of coughs. 'I've come down with the flu, Jimmy. I'm really struggling and I need to see the doctor.'

The temporary silence at the end of the phone left Thoroughgood wondering if Sykes was buying his Oscar-winning attempt to sound at death's door, or was, more likely, weighing up the ramifications of his call against the events that had taken place in Springburn Police Office and which would have made their way around the entire shift, if not the sub-division, by now.

'Aye, you don't sound the best, young fella. Okay give me a minute and I'll get your details down and get the sick book filled in and let you get back to your bed.'

After Sykes finished recording Thoroughgood's registered number and the relevant details the veteran cop's voice dropped to a whisper. 'How are you really doin', son?'

But Thoroughgood, unsure if this was an attempt to get him to admit the real state of his welfare or a genuine enquiry over his health, refused to bite. Pinching his aching snout once again he answered in as self-sorry a tone as he could manage. 'I'll be fine, just need my bed and hopefully some antibiotics from the doc. If you can let the sergeant know I've gone sick that would be great.' And before Sykes could ask any other awkward questions

Thoroughgood put the receiver down.

Then he glanced at the application forms for Jordanhill Teacher Training College, which sat, taunting him, in the empty floral fruit bowl on the dining table.

'What choice do I have?' he asked himself, knowing that the answer was none. Maybe he could have survived Rentoul and his minions, who were determined to force him out of the job, but with Dawson in cahoots with them and making it clear he was a marked man and one whose future conduct would have a direct bearing on Celine's fate, it was time to admit defeat.

His police career was over and now the tears came.

CHAPTER 50

The credits rolled as *Red Heat* concluded, but Thoroughgood sat motionless in the dark, alone in the back row of the Salon Cinema, replaying the key scenes from the last few days.

He had chosen an afternoon at the pictures as the ideal distraction from his present plight, but now that the escapism provided by the action-comedy movie starring James Belushi and Arnold Schwarzenegger had come to an end, the reality of his situation hit him straight between the eyes.

What did his future hold? Teacher training or a nine-to-five job as a bank clerk?

He'd spent most of his university career gorging on a never-ending supply of psychological cop thrillers, desperate to pursue a career in the police after realising that his aspirations of lecturing in medieval history were never going to be realised. But now, only months after finally starting the job, it was over almost before it had begun.

As the Salon's giant screen went black, silence descended around him and left Thoroughgood studying the ornate *belle époque* plasterwork of the ceiling and reflecting on how magnificent the building must have been when it opened in its pomp back in 1913.

The Hillhead Picture Salon, to give the cinema its full title, had been famous for housing a full orchestra, and for serving tea and biscuits to its patrons during the afternoon. Until 1914 and the outbreak of the Great War, the orchestra had been conducted by a redoubtable German, Herr Iff.

But Thoroughgood was all alone, burrowing into a velvety red seat and hoping the lights would never go on in the magnificently elegant B-listed cinema, which had become his favourite place of escape when the shit hit the fan; something that, he smiled balefully in acknowledgement, it had now well and truly done.

When the gratingly harsh Glaswegian voice hissed out of the darkness, Thoroughgood almost jumped out of his seat, such had been his conviction that he was alone in the Salon.

'Where the fuck have ye been, Thoroughgood?' demanded a voice he knew instantly belonged to Collins, aware that the housebreaker was seated behind him, enveloped in the black.

Without turning his head Thoroughgood replied, 'What does it matter, Collins, you know where I am now.'

'You bastard, why'd you set these maniacs oan me? I thought we had an understandin', but you shafted me, rookie,' said Collins, his voice bristling with anger.

'What does it matter whether you tout to me or the IA, as long as you spill? You stayed out of the Bar-L, didn't you?' asked Thoroughgood, keeping his gaze trained on the curtains, faintly illuminated in the dim lighting, around the big screen.

'Bastards nearly threw me oot a van oan the M8 at seventy mile an oor. Animals. But then I hears you've been havin' yer own problems with these fuckin' ex-sodees on yer shift.'

Thoroughgood's patience snapped and turning round he stared into the darkness until he detected the outline of a shadowy figure, the smell of stale sweat seeping from him, seated slightly to the left of him in the row behind. 'Just how do you know what my problems are, Collins?'

In the darkness Thoroughgood was sure he could detect the remnants of a ruined, gap-toothed grin as the junkie spoke. 'Cos the wee crossin' lady down at the Hill Primary School does a turn for the big polisman Jones and after he's had his fun he likes to boast. Problem bein' that when she's naw helpin' the weans across the road, or ridin' big Jones, she likes to smoke a wee bitty blaw. In turn for her stash I like her to keep me posted on this an' that.'

Thoroughgood shook his head in disgust. 'Look, Collins, I

don't give a fuck what you've got to say – I've had enough of the whole shebang. The shift has won and pretty soon I'm going to be elsewhere, doing something where I don't have to worry about the people I'm working with trying to slit my throat or breaking my fuckin' legs.'

'So they've no just bust yer coupon, rookie, eh?' asked Collins in a mocking whisper.

'Aye, maybe they have, but if that is what being a cop is all about they can stick their fuckin' job,' said Thoroughgood.

'But what aboot yer wee bird, that Celine wan? I thought yous were friendly, like?' sneered Collins from the dark.

Thoroughgood's self-control snapped and he turned to grab the housebreaker by the throat. 'Fuck you, Collins, I'm out of here. I don't want anything to do with you, the cops, or Father fuckin' Christmas, for that matter,' he raged, pushing the junkie back into the darkness.

But as he began to rise from his seat, Collins gripped his left wrist. 'Wan wee problem wi that, boss.'

'I don't care what your problems are, Collins. All that matters to me is that I get out with my hide intact and my head not fucked up.'

'You wantin' Glasgow turnin' intae Belfast then? Cause this shite is gonnae go off the deep end, that's whit's behind this shootin' match,' said Collins with surprising conviction.

'Ah, come on, Collins, where are you getting that pish from – the fuckin' lollypop lady?' demanded Thoroughgood, but Dawson's words were now ringing in his ears.

'Maybes aye, maybes naw, but if yous think the ice cream war is aw aboot smack then you know fuck aw aboot the real score here, and that goes for yer IA mob too. Bottom line is that yous have got the McGuigans on wan hand wi' their links tae the RA and the late Gerry a former card-carrying Provo in charge of fundraising for them in Glasgow. Then oan the other side we got half the fuckin' Paras being led by that maniac Mojito, and noo business has got mixed up wi' the personal and Mojito has sent for reinforcements.'

Thoroughgood, now hanging on every word that Collins fed him, sat back down. 'What do you mean reinforcements, and what the fuck do you want me to do about it?'

But before the informant could answer the lights went on and a florid-faced usherette with a thatch of dyed blonde hair, in a voice that brooked no argument, said, 'Sorry to break up your cosy little get-together, but show's over boys, time you left the building.'

CHAPTER 51

Trudging outside, Thoroughgood shoved his hands into his Harrington jacket but kept his gaze firmly on Collins.

'So yous still wanna play at teachers or whitever else your gonnae dae next?' asked Collins, before adding contemptuously, 'Copper.'

'Depends on what you've got to tell me, Collins.'

'First you buy me some grub, rozzer. Where you takin' me for ma treat then?' asked Collins as a grin swept across his face.

Five minutes later they were sitting on the red leather seats at the back of the Glasgow University Union bar. Thoroughgood, staring at Collins, shook his head in disbelief at the scenario that was now unfolding, as the informant hoovered down a mouthful of Scotch pie and beans, seemingly oblivious to the disgusted glances of the student inhabitants in the bar, who appeared dumbfounded by the presence of someone who appeared no better than a down and out in the sanctity of their alma mater.

The informant swallowed the remainder of his pint of Tennent's Lager and lifted the empty glass in the air, tilting it one way and then another. 'Any chance o' another, pal?'

The rookie shook his head furiously in the negative. 'Reinforcements?' asked Thoroughgood, before adding, 'You've had your lunch, Collins, now what did you mean by that?'

'I mean that Mojito jumps on a Suzuki 750, pulls on his helmet and leathers, and thinks he's invisible, like fuck he is.'

But before he could continue another voice, and one slightly familiar to Thoroughgood, interrupted. 'For a policeman you keep interesting company, Angus Thoroughgood,' said an elderly, grey-haired man dressed in a burgundy and black-trimmed GUU porter's jacket, before wagging an admonishing finger in Thoroughgood's direction. 'I would fancy that your *guest* here hasn't been signed in at the foyer, young man?' asked the porter, emphasising the word guest, but with a smile nevertheless across his kindly features and behind a pair of thick black National Health spectacles.

'Ah, John, how are you?' asked Thoroughgood as he jumped to his feet and shook the porter's hand warmly.

'A lot better once they stop showing these bloody Freds. These goths from the Queen Margaret Union were round again flour-bombing us and trying to flood the beer bar. Two fire engines were needed to drain the place. What a mess with all that flour congealed and sticking to everything. All over a few cartoons, aye, what a bleedin' mess all right. Anyway how are you adapting to life as a cop?'

'It's different, John, very different, but I still haven't found anywhere that does a better Scotch pie than the GUU!' Thoroughgood smiled warmly and patted the old man on the back.

'Looks like you could both do with replenishment. Two Tennent's do?' asked the porter.

Before Thoroughgood could answer he was beaten to the verbal punch. 'Perfect, auld yin, I've an awfy thirst oan me,' said Collins, grinning his decayed smile.

The porter smiled wanly and scuttled off to the bar as Thoroughgood shook his head and propped himself up on the enamel table inside the bar which had, until only a few months previously, been his home from home for most of his four years as a Medieval History undergraduate.

'You've got some cheek on you, Collins, but it's time to cut out the riddles and get to the point.'

'Aye, but whit the feck did the auld yin mean about the Freds?'

'Nosey, aren't you? Soft-porn cartoons, referred to affectionately as the Freds in honour of Fred Quimby the producer of the Tom and—' But before Thoroughgood could finish Collins did so for him.

'*Tom and Jerry* cartoons. Aye, we had a TV in the hoose when I wiz a wean, even if it wiz black an' white,' said the tout sarcastically.

Then he raised his empty pint glass in mock salute, smiled and leant over towards Thoroughgood in conspiratorial fashion. 'I had a very interestin' afternoon watchin' Mojito and some red-haired bird up at Springburn Park the other day and they were mighty cosy. Maybe she's his new tart, Thoroughgood.'

'Be very careful, Collins, my patience isn't going to last much longer,' warned the rookie, but he couldn't help himself adding, 'So if you've spent so much time keeping tabs on Dawson, have you seen Celine in his company?'

'I've got better things to do with my time than keep an eye oot for yer bit o' fluff, but naw is the answer to that wan. I'd be thinkin' that if she's been an inconvenience to yer man then she'll be somewhere she cannae be a pain in the arse,' said Collins bleakly.

Thoroughgood's head dropped into his hands and he stared at the table as the constant cacophony of the bar's fruit machines rang out.

But the arrival of the second round and another huge mouthful of Tennent's seemed to make all the difference to Collins. 'Look, I don't know about yer bird but whit I do know is I saw Mojito hand redheid a piece o' paper and a broon envelope that looked like it was stuffed full o' doe. Now, can you tell me what the fuck that's aw aboot?' asked Collins before he turned his attention to the fresh pint of lager now sitting in front of him.

'It could be a hundred things, Collins. I think you're trying to make something out of nothing for your own good. Sorry, pal, but you're pissin' against the wind,' said Thoroughgood, and taking a large draught of lager he started to stand-up.

'Aye, but this redhead was fae Northern Ireland,' said Collins.

'How the fuck do you know that?' demanded Thoroughgood.

''Cause she took pity on a poor junky beggar freezin' his baws aff ootside the Balgrayhill flats,' replied Collins with a wink.

Once again Thoroughgood shook his head but this time there was a grudging admiration sweeping across his face in the form of a half-grin and he sat back down. 'So what now, Collins?'

Wiping the foam from the lager off his mouth with the back of his calloused paw, Collins smiled his decayed grin. 'So yer back in, rookie?'

A resigned nod from Thoroughgood was the only answer he got.

'Gid. Whit happens noo is that you and me stay in touch and yous keep that mob away from me and I'll be good as gold. I'll keep ma ear to the ground, see if I hear anything about yer wee friend and see whit else turns up. Cause the wan thing yous can bet on, rozzer, is that somebody will talk, sometime, and the Cat will hear aboot it. But it's gonnae cost. I want a grand, so yous better send that up the tree.'

Thoroughgood scanned the informant's ravaged features for any trace of insincerity but decided it was pointless to try and look for any signs of deviousness in a being who was probably rotten to the core.

Yet the rookie stuck his right hand out and, when Collins eyed it with incredulity, he said, 'Okay, Collins, we have a deal. I'll get your money and...' He fished into his Harrington pocket, pulled out a twenty-pound note and laid it on the table in front of the informant. 'There's something for your trouble.'

Collins smiled once again and shook Thoroughgood's hand with a clammy paw. 'Noo yer talkin' ma language,' said the informant before he swallowed the remainder of his pint, jumped to his feet and said, 'Like I always say, I'll find yous.' And with that, Collins walked out of the GUU bar, in his peculiar balls-of-the-feet manner that Thoroughgood found almost comical, as the air continued to ring with the never-ending sound of the fruit machines being played by the addicted students of the union.

Thoroughgood reached the top of Dowanhill without seeing anything of his surroundings, his mind preoccupied with his conversation with Collins, and the housebreaker-turned-informant's revelation about the 'Lady in Red', as the voice in his head now dubbed her.

Nevertheless, Collins' claims had, more or less, backed up those of Mojito. Thoroughgood knew that he couldn't walk away and had no option but to take his information to the IA as soon as he could.

He reached the summit of the hill and began to cross the road just as he saw the marked Escort sitting outside number three Crown Gardens, which was now beginning to pull out onto the main road.

Immediately Thoroughgood drew himself back, crouched down behind the garden wall of the house on the corner and waited for the jam sandwich to drive-off. The receding of its diesel engine duly confirming that his moment of concern was over, Thoroughgood sprinted over to number three, unlocked the building's main door and found a buff envelope with 'Z325 Constable Thoroughgood' scrawled in meticulous handwriting that was all too familiar to him.

Thoroughgood walked over to the huge, grey marble Victorian fireplace that had long since been blocked up after Bill Kaye had converted the former four-storey townhouse into an apartment building. Leaning on it he ripped open the envelope and quickly scanned the contents, reading out loud the key part. 'Constable Thoroughgood, I am concerned for your welfare. Could you please contact me at Lennox Hill Police Station, as soon as possible?'

At the bottom of the paper was Rentoul's signature.

'What a fuckin' joke,' snapped Thoroughgood.

CHAPTER 52

Lord Justice Peterson stared down his pince-nez at the packed court and, in his gently lisping tones, made his closing remarks. 'Francis McGuigan, we have accepted your lawyer, Mr Celtrani's, plea for bail and you are now free to leave this courtroom on the grounds that you meet all the stipulations of the bail requirements I have listed.'

Before the judge could proceed any further the High Court erupted into outrage with cries of 'No!' and 'Fix!' filling the air. Peterson scratched furiously under his white curly wig, smashed his hardwood gavel off its sounding pad and demanded quiet. 'Silence in court or I will have the offenders taken down for breach of the peace. Silence immediately, I say.'

As the sound of his gavel echoed out across the courtroom, Peterson pointed at the two officers flanking McGuigan in the dock. 'Take Mr McGuigan out of this courtroom immediately, constables.' As he attempted to make himself clear over the rammy that had erupted in the usually staid confines of the south court, Peterson reiterated his order for good measure: 'Immediately, constables, do you hear me?'

The smaller of the two cops, his uniform hat perched at a jaunty angle above a head of protruding straw hair, smiled, pulled his ceremonial white gloves tight over his hands and stood up immediately. As he did so, a mouthful of rotten teeth appeared and this vision made Lord Justice Peterson grab his pince-nez, momentarily forgetting the bedlam in his courtroom as he peered with ghoulish fascination at the officer's horrific molars.

On McGuigan's left, the bigger of the two constables, a man with biceps that strained the polyester of his police shirt to a tautness that defied belief, lifted his baton from its traditional position across his thighs, stood up and bowed to the judge before turning to McGuigan and whispering to him, 'Let's be havin' you, Frankie boy, looks like your free to go.'

McGuigan took time to savour another moment of triumph over the authorities. Turning towards the slightly stooped figure of Celtrani, he flashed a smug smile and followed it with a theatrical wink. Then his gaze swept the assembled audience up in the public balcony, who had come to see him jailed on a variety of charges that had seemed certain to bring about McGuigan's downfall, all the time knowing that he should be in the dock for the murder of Lucy Dawson.

For show, he precisely adjusted the cuffs of his tailor-made Jermyn Street shirt and tightened the knot of his Italian silk tie and greeted the outrage with a benign smile. The public had once again been left disappointed, thanks to the shrewd services of the second-generation Italian lawyer who had served his family ever since his father's long-gone days, and watched his own star rise in tandem with McGuigan's ascendancy to overlord of Lennox Hill and the north of Glasgow.

'You're guilty as sin, you murderin' scum,' shouted a Glaswegian voice from the public stalls, but as McGuigan sought to find a face to fit the catcall his eyes were drawn to the glint of a diamond earring, attached to the lobe of a balding head, high in the stalls above.

Mojito's hands remained steepled while his teeth were clamped firmly together as he locked eyes with the man who had had his sister murdered. Slowly he stood up, and shaping the fingers of his right hand into an imaginary handgun, pulled the trigger. He held McGuigan's startled gaze for a brief moment, and then, his face an impenetrable mask, turned and climbed the stairs to the balcony exit.

McGuigan found himself led out of the dock by the huge cop whose bulbous features seemed vaguely familiar to him, but so shocked was he by the appearance of Mojito in the public galleries that he stumbled free from the Saltmarket almost unseeing.

In the foyer outside the courtroom, the giant figure of Duncy Parkinson ambled over to McGuigan as he leant against a marble pillar and tried to collect his thoughts.

'All right, boss? Wee Celtrani is worth his weight in gold, is he naw?' Duncy gave McGuigan the benefit of a congratulatory pat on his shoulder. Before the crime boss could do anything other than nod to his enforcer, they were joined by the gowned figure of Celtrani himself, the heat caused by his white powdered wig squeezing a bead of sweat out on his brow.

'So, Francis, we live to fight another day, eh?' queried the brief, but met only by McGuigan's troubled gaze Celtrani was left bemused. 'For a man who has just dodged a sentence you're anything but happy. What's the problem, my friend?'

McGuigan tried to pull himself together; he pushed his shoulders back and did up the buttons of his sleek, grey, double-breasted suit, straightened his red-and-white striped club tie and took a deep breath. 'Aye, Virgilio, ordinarily I would be made up with a result like that and don't think I'm naw grateful, amigo. But the gloss wiz taken off it by seeing that murdering proddy scumbag Mojito Dawson in the bleachers upstairs. Bastard even had the cheek to pull the trigger on me,' said McGuigan, repeating Mojito's malevolent gesture.

Parkinson couldn't contain himself. 'Mojito wiz upstairs, boss? You're fuckin' kiddin' me on. Never saw the bastard otherwise I'd have followed him ootside and…'

But before Parkinson could finish his threat, Celtrani placed a calming hand on his shoulder and tried to soothe the big man's volcanic temper. 'Now, Duncy, we are in the foyer of the highest court in the land,' he said, gesticulating to the thronging mass of punters pouring down the stairs from the viewing gallery and the police officers stationed outside the ornate mahogany courtroom doors they had just come through. 'In the presence of so many witnesses and of course the law, it is best to use moderate language, my friend, otherwise we may all find ourselves back from where we have just come.'

Then the brief placed his wig back on and proffered a theatrical, gown-swishing bow. 'Anyway, Virgilio Celtrani must be elsewhere, gentlemen. I look forward to my usual remuneration, Francis.' Celtrani flashed an obsequious smile before adding, 'Mind you, I believe you may be needing my services once again in the not too distant future!'

Before McGuigan could provide a reply, another hand was placed on his silken-suited shoulder and, startled, he turned to see a mouthful of rotten teeth being flashed at him.

'Francis McGuigan, I have here a warrant for your immediate apprehension for the murder of Lucy Dawson,' said Constable Billy Davidson, who then turned to the hulking figure of big Jonesy. 'Constable Jones, cuff him,' ordered Davidson.

'Toffee,' said the big cop.

CHAPTER 53

McGuigan was too shocked to offer any resistance, let alone make any coherent protest. A wolfish grin broke across Jones's fleshy face as he slapped the steel bracelets onto McGuigan's wrists and clicked them extra tight to ensure maximum discomfort.

But Duncy Parkinson was not so compliant and he threw a giant hand out and grabbed the steel linkage between the bracelets. 'Frankie is goin' nowhere, rozzer, until we've seen the bleedin' warrant.'

Celtrani added his velvet tones to the chorus of dissent. 'This is most irregular, officer. May I examine the warrant to make sure the details are correct?' asked the brief, offering a benign smile.

Davidson cocked his head and squinted a cobalt stare from under the peak of his cap. 'You can do what you want with it, brief, cos it was signed by Sheriff Brunton earlier this morning.'

Then Davidson whipped his baton out its custom-made uniform trouser pocket and smashed it down on Parkinson's hand. 'Take yer paw off these cuffs, Parkinson, or so help me God you'll be comin' with us to the Hill as well.'

Parkinson let out a startled yelp – 'Bastard' – and his hand immediately removed itself from the cuffs, as if by its own volition.

By this stage the foyer was filling with an enraptured audience of public and officials who could not believe their own eyes at the sight of the unique court drama playing out before them. The sound of hundreds of footsteps slamming off the green-and-brown tiled floor of the courtroom foyer punctuated an exchange that was threatening to get out of hand.

But the arrival of more police officers from the north court doorway underlined the pointlessness of any resistance to Parkinson and McGuigan. The latter took a deep breath, produced a gritted grin and said, 'Let it go, Duncy. We know we can rely on Mr Celtrani to prove my innocence and I am sure it will not take too long to help these officers realise the error of their ways.'

Parkinson's mouth opened, but before he could say anything Davidson's baton flicked up against his windpipe. 'Button it, Parkinson, or you'll be done for obstruction and we're no' exactly short of witnesses, are we?'

Then, as his gaze swept the packed foyer, Davidson made the most of his opportunity to showboat. 'Francis McGuigan, you are now under arrest for the murder of Lucy Dawson. You are not obliged to say anything but anything you do say may be taken down and used in evidence against you. Do you have anything you wish to say?'

The silence that washed over the jam-packed foyer was instant but McGuigan's reply soon punctured the quiet. 'Prove it!' he demanded at the top of his voice.

With the words barely out his mouth, Jones almost pulled McGuigan off his feet as he dragged him towards the Saltmarket's front doors.

The thronging mass inside the courtroom foyer erupted into a chorus of cheers.

McGuigan was slammed into the mesh cage in the back of the police Land Rover and as he tried to regain his footing he heard the door crack shut behind him and turned to see Davidson's bristling presence on the opposite bench.

Grabbing the mesh with his fingers, McGuigan pulled himself upright, but as he did so the vehicle jolted into life and he lost his balance once again and was thrown back onto the metallic floor face first. Two scarred hands grabbed at the lapels of his tailor-made suit and hauled him onto the bench. As he regained his feet, McGuigan found Davidson's sneering face in his.

'Got ya,' said the cop.

McGuigan gritted his teeth and tried to regain his composure but his breathing was coming thick and fast and a flop of his silver mane fell over his right eye, but he spat back with defiance. 'You haven't got me by a long chalk, believe me. Before this has run its course I will have your guts for garters and your career will be ruined – and then my boys will come for your wife and weans, scum.'

Surprisingly, Davidson leant back against the Land Rover and smiled viciously. 'Why don't you shut the fuck up and let me tell you how yer beloved little gobshite Gerry met his maker.'

The rage in McGuigan burst its banks and he smashed his forehead into the bridge of Davidson's nose, just below the peak of his cap. Instantaneously the cop threw McGuigan off and he slammed back onto the van floor as Davidson rammed his knee into McGuigan's chest. 'He squealed like a bitch an' I bet he'll prove to be a chip off the old block soon enough,' said the cop, his bloodied nose and rotten teeth millimetres away from McGuigan's face, and his toxic breath washing over him.

Davidson grabbed McGuigan's jacket and smashed a short, sharp right hand into his face. 'Eat that,' he said, and then to McGuigan's surprise the cop let go of his suit, removed his knee from his chest and returned to the Land Rover bench, dabbing at his gored snout with a white hanky he pulled from his trouser pocket. After a moment, his running repairs completed satisfactorily, Davidson casually lit up a fag as if nothing had happened.

Breathing heavily, McGuigan hauled himself up onto his elbows, but before he could get any further he found the glazed shine of a black leather boot in his chest.

'How long did you think you could go on funding the fuckin' RA and we wouldnae find oot about it?' demanded Davidson, before blowing a mouthful of smoke into his captive's eyes.

'What in the name of sweet Jesus are you talking about?' demanded McGuigan, gasping for oxygen as the pressure of the black leather boot on his chest increased.

'Shut the fuck up, old man,' said Davidson, relishing the shockwave of surprise that had engulfed his prisoner's face.

'You're talking rubbish, man,' said McGuigan, with all the defiance he could muster from his prone position on the floor of the speeding Land Rover police van.

'We know all about yer boy, Gerry – or should I call him Quartermaster McGuigan? You wurnae doin' enough to raise funds for the cause back in the auld country and yer boy came blunderin' back and thought he would take the play away from Mojito just like that,' said Davidson, clicking his fingers to underline his point.

'You're haverin' man, this is the stuff of bloody madness,' said McGuigan in apparent disbelief.

'Am I? Well we'll know soon enough, old man.'

But before either of them could add to the conversation the police van suffered a jolting thud that sent Davidson flying off the bench, thrown onto his back just inside the vehicle's back doors.

'For fuck's sake, Jonesy,' he raged at the driver.

CHAPTER 54

'We've just been rammed by an artic, looks like the game's afoot,' shouted Jones towards the rear of the Land Rover. There was another loud bang and the Land Rover violently shunted to the right.

In the driver's cabin Jones was shouting. 'Oh, ye fucker! Awright, we've got the message.' Then the giant cop looked over his left shoulder and admitted, 'Suppose it's got tae look the part.'

'So don't piss yer pants, Jonesy, you know what's goin' on, big man. Come on, its naw as if it's yer own bleedin' motor!' said Davidson, alluding to Rentoul's plan. 'You got an eyeball on the driver?'

'Naw, cos the cabin windaes are conveniently blacked oot. But there's playing the game and playin' the bleedin' game and we got the blind tunnel comin' up in a quarter o' a mile. Ah shite, here he comes again.' There was another shuddering thud as the Land Rover jolted wildly once again.

'Awright, I know it's got tae look realistic but fuck this for a game of soldiers!' spat Jones, and applied the anchors to the Land Rover, bringing it to a sharp stop. Checking his mirrors he saw that the truck had done the same about fifty yards further back. 'I've got a bad feeling about this, Billy boy. I'm gonnae take me a butcher's and see who we've got behind the wheel of that fuckin' artic.'

'Ah, don't worry aboot it, big man. Why don't you just sit tight and let things play out like auld Jimmy planned.'

'Naw, enough is enough,' was Jones's terse reply, and then he jumped out of the vehicle. As he turned to make his way towards the truck he found something cold and cylindrical was sticking in his midriff.

'What the fuck?'

But before Constable Brian Jones had even completed the question, three muffled blasts penetrated the fleshy folds of his corpulent body and he slid down the side of the Land Rover, hitting the tarmac with a grunt.

'Jonesy, you okay?' shouted Davidson, but his question was met only with silence. Then he heard the sound of footsteps coming round towards the rear of the Land Rover.

Knowing something was far from right, Davidson pulled his flick knife from inside his tunic and barked a quick warning to McGuigan. 'Sit there, old man, and stay good as gold and you'll get out of this alive. Try and be smart and I'll carve you up like my Sunday roast.'

Seeing a figure at the rear of the vehicle's meshed rear windows, Davidson attempted to play possum. 'That you, big man?'

Davidson knew his choices were limited. A quick glance towards the Land Rover ignition showed that Jones had taken the vehicle keys with him.

Lifting his PR to his lips he quickly fired out a mayday call. 'Code 21, location Royston Road and Forge Street side of the Blind Tunnel, Germiston. Z321 Constable Davidson requiring urgent assistance, officer down, repeat, officer down.'

But before the controller could get a reply out, Davidson decided he was taking matters into his own hands and instead of waiting for death to come looking for him he decided he would go in search of it.

He quickly unlocked the doors from inside and with all of his might booted them open in an attempt to catch whoever was lurking outside by surprise. Gritting his teeth and brandishing his blade, Davidson spat out the motto of the Parachute Regiment – 'Utrinque Paratus' – and flashed a demonic smile McGuigan's way before he jumped out of the vehicle, thirsting for blood.

But as he hit the road outside and checked the area surrounding the Land Rover he was surprised to see that there was no one there. Silence reigned. Davidson's next thought was to check on

Jones. Starting round the driver's side of the vehicle he saw his pal bleeding out on the deck.

Davidson kneeled down beside his prostrate friend and heard increasingly shallow breaths coming from the big man's chest. Lowering his face until it was parallel with Jones, Davidson asked, 'Who did you, big man? Was it Mojito right enough?'

With a groan Jones turned to face his pal then, through gritted teeth, he said, 'Naw... A damn... bitch.' And with that his eyes rolled to the heavens and his final breath expired in a tortured gasp.

'Jesus H Christ! For fuck's sake, no' Jonesy,' wept Davidson, but the man who had had his back in uniforms of green and black was no more, and Davidson wanted bloody revenge.

Shutting Jones's eyes, Davidson jumped to his feet and made his way back to the rear of the van.

'Where are you you heartless bastard?' he called, but as he did so a new sound broke the deadly silence.

For fifty yards away the artic engine had burst into life and now the vehicle was bursting forward at full throttle and bearing down on Davidson. Seeing death coming his way, the cop slotted his flick-knife blade between his teeth and turned to the Land Rover doors... just as they were slammed shut by McGuigan.

'For fuck's sake, McGuigan, let me in! Or do you want tae go the same way?' shouted Davidson through his mouthful of blade as his desperation mounted.

The cop pulled at the vehicle doors with all his might but McGuigan, given extra strength by his determination to see Davidson perish, held on for grim death and, as the powerful sound of the artic engine began to blot out everything else, Davidson turned to face his fate.

'Mother Mary!' he screamed.

A second later the huge vehicle smashed home, turning Davidson into the pulp filling in a two-vehicle sandwich.

Lying on his back inside the battered Land Rover, Francis McGuigan opened his eyes and a smile began to cross his face.

CHAPTER 55

'What a fuckin' mess, and I don't mean you by that, Thoroughgood, but to be fair, Dawson and his boys did you over nicely. I guess that's why you been lying low for a couple of days, eh?' asked Detective Constable Numan ruefully before taking another sip of coffee from a battered white mug.

Sitting on the windowsill at the back of the fifth floor IA office, Thoroughgood had spent the last twenty minutes bringing the unit up to speed on his audience with Dawson, and now he swung his legs to and fro, doing his best to get the circulation back in full flow. He stretched the fingers of both of his hands, trying to loosen them up but only succeeding in snapping out a series of cracks that left his companions wincing.

Eventually, after another pain-wracked grimace, the probationer said, 'It could have been worse and I guess the fact that I'm here to tell the tale does add weight to everything Dawson told me about 14 Intelligence Unit. But it all points towards McGuigan and his team. Brian Jones left with more holes than a colander, Billy Davidson a pun o' mince and McGuigan out of custody and nowhere to be seen.'

'That is the obvious conclusion, but what if it is not the correct one. I don't know, but it just seems a bit too bloody obvious,' said Malcolm, stroking his chin, before returning both of his hands to the rear of his head as he leant back on his desk chair. 'Everything you have told us about 14 Intelligence Unit and Dawson's claims would seem to suggest that Jones and Davidson were taken out by professionals who have also sprung McGuigan. But which side of the great divide have these professionals come from? That is the question. Because the report we managed to get a squint at has left the Serious with nothing to go on.'

'Do you believe any of that cock and bull, boss? I mean, for fuck's sake, an undercover intelligence op right here in Glasgow without the knowledge of the authorities and creating carnage in the process? It's feckin' madness,' said Hardie.

The bang of Numan's coffee mug hitting the laminate table brought its intended silence. 'Madness or no, it's playing its way out on our streets. What if Dawson has gone rogue? Maybe he was in this 14 Intelligence Unit over in Northern Ireland and has come back over here under deep cover and lost the plot? I've heard of the Special Reconnaissance Unit but 14 Intelligence Unit? You said Dawson told you that everything was deniable, Thoroughgood – but deniable to who, I wonder?'

'More importantly, who has given Dawson the sanction to deny anything? It isn't the type of line you'd come away with if it was bullshit,' chipped in DS Malcolm. 'But if, just for one minute, we take Dawson's claims as gospel, then we are going to have a devil of a time proving anything. You know how these things work, the establishment erect a wall of silence and everywhere you look the doors shut tight in your face. The question is, just how high does this go? Or are we talking about a 'rogue' operative, as you called him, Dennis?'

This time it was Hardie who picked up and ran with the metaphorical ball. 'All of which could well mean the ice cream war is nothing more than a smokescreen and a convenient press label that's masking exactly what is going on. What we're talking about here, bottom line, is an extension of the Troubles right into the heart of Glasgow.'

'Which surely underlines that Jones and Davidson were acting for, or in cahoots with, 14 Intelligence Unit and their old mucker Dawson, but what about Rentoul? Goes without saying he's up to his ears in it too,' stated Thoroughgood.

'Aye, if there's a Provo hit team minding McGuigan and having already taken out Jones and Davidson, Rentoul must be next, if they know he is part of the intelligence service's covert operations on the mainland,' said Malcolm.

'I just don't get it. It all seemed so grubby, a turf war between the local hoods and a team of bent coppers. I can't get my head round it all,' said Thoroughgood.

'Don't worry about it, son, that's our job. The main thing is that Dawson allowed you to live long enough to relay the tale and that is why I think there is substance to his claims, however farfetched they seem on the surface,' said Numan.

'Indeed. Dennis has a point,' said Malcolm, leaning forward and planting his elbows on the desk. 'On the other hand, while you were otherwise engaged, young Thoroughgood, we had a powwow with your friend Collins the Tout and he came up with an interesting hypothesis, didn't he, Hardie?'

From behind his lush moustache, Hardie said, 'Aye, well, after myself and Dennis had a friendly word, Collins came out with a story that he'd heard Mojito was looking to set up McGuigan by using Davidson and Jones as his escort from prison and hijacking them en route from the Saltmarket. Only thing is, Dawson isn't likely to take his own men out and leave McGuigan free to walk off into the sunset.'

'What if Dawson was using Jones and Davidson, despite the fact they were the escort, as bait and then it all went pear shaped?' asked Thoroughgood.

'Aye, I guess that's one way you could look at it. But the fact is we don't know if McGuigan is still breathing or if Mojito has taken him off to have some private sport with him before treating him to a nasty end, just like he did with Gerry McGuigan. And it still doesn't explain why Mojito would rub out Jones and Davidson. Christ, what a fuck up,' said Numan.

'Which is exactly why we decided not to taxi Collins to HMP Barlinnie but instead provide him with a return fare to his neighbourhood, free to do what he does best and us safe in the knowledge that the type of fright he was given by Numan and Hardie will make him extra keen to remain on our good side... Wouldn't that be right, gents?' said Malcolm from behind a knowing grin.

'Oh, I'd say so, gaffer. The Cat was left in no doubt that he is well and truly on his ninth life,' said Numan.

'Exactly,' agreed Malcolm, who then turned his gaze towards Thoroughgood. 'From what I've heard the Serious Crime Squad investigation is a long way from getting the final scoop on the ice cream wars, pardon the pun. In particular, as we know, they are looking to find out what exactly happened to the Escort manned by Jones and Davidson, who was behind their murder, and now where McGuigan is holed up – and hopefully that is where Collins will show his worth.'

Thoroughgood knew the time had arrived for him to come clean over his little tête-à-tête with the Cat and cleared his throat nervously to gain their attention. 'I had a run-in with Collins yesterday and he told me about your little meeting with him. I don't think there's much doubt that he has got the message.'

'Aye, but what message was the treacherous wee bastard tryin' to give you, laddie?' asked Numan, his eyebrows raised.

'Er, well, he wants to deal with me and me alone, but he has promised he'll play it straight with us from now on, if you leave him alone and let me handle him,' said Thoroughgood nervously.

'Oh he did, did he? The little scrote thinks he can dictate to us, well we can soon put him right aboot that,' said Hardie.

But DS Malcolm held his hand up for silence. 'Look, as long as the blighter comes across it doesn't matter who he's singing too.' He turned to Malcolm and Hardie. 'I don't see Collins takin' the piss after his little jaunt along the M8, do you, boys?'

Before either Numan or Hardie could speak, Thoroughgood quickly interjected. 'Oh, he got the message, definitely. Collins is on side and wants to stay there, and he also gave me some fresh info that may be of help.'

'On you go then,' said Malcolm as Thoroughgood felt all eyes turn on him.

'Collins said he watched Dawson get cosy with a redhead up at Springburn Park and that he handed her an envelope that the Cat reckons was stuffed full of money,' he said in a rush.

'Ah, come on, Thoroughgood, how does he know that? Turned into the Six Million Dollar Man?' said Hardie.

'Okay, he can't confirm it but what he did confirm, for the price of a Scotch pie and beans, was that this redhead has a Northern Irish accent and is most probably holed up in the Balgrayhill flats,' revealed Thoroughgood.

'Sounds like Mojito has got himself a new tart,' said Numan, looking distinctly unimpressed.

'Collins was adamant that the meeting wasn't of a romantic nature,' said Thoroughgood.

'Interesting,' said Malcolm. 'Dennis, I want you after this redhead immediately. We need an ID ASAP and everything we can find out about her, then let's see which piece of the jigsaw puzzle she supplies. Aye, I wonder if our friend Mojito has brought in the gentle touch to help him get the job done. We're also going to need to set up surveillance on the Balgrayhill, anyone have any contacts up there?'

'Sure, gaffer, I know a couple of the concierge boys up the Balgray and it shouldnae be too difficult to get an empty flat to set up an OP from,' said Hardie.

'Okay, but what about Rentoul?' asked Numan, but before anyone could give an answer, the office door lashed open.

CHAPTER 56

'Just who the fuck do you think you are, Malcolm?' spat a small, grey-haired man out the side of a mouth from which a large cigarette dangled, and in a voice that sounded like he gargled with gravel.

For once the laidback, articulate DS was caught on the hop and, as Malcolm attempted to regain his composure, the bespectacled three-piece-suited pocket rocket of an individual marched straight up to him and rammed his index finger into Malcolm's chest. 'You and your unit are a fuckin' joke and you're underminin' my investigation. Now I want everything you've got on this so called bloody ice cream war and I want it on my desk in less than twenty-four hours. I know you and your rent-a-mob have been investigating Three Group in Zulu Land and now two members of the shift are dead and the rest of 'em are looking over their shoulders wonderin' if they're gonnae be next. So you damn well better spill, Malcolm, or I'll have you bust back to uniform and your minions with ye before you can say Bo fuckin' Diddley. Understand?' spat the red-faced male, a vein throbbing on his neck above the collar of his shirt.

But while Malcom remained silent, Numan took the floor: 'Well, well if it's no' Detective Chief Superintendent Johnny Johnstone. Aye, you still know how to make an entrance... sir,' said the DC, with an amazing lack of respect for a senior officer of such exalted status.

Johnstone had clearly been so focused on Malcolm that he had failed to register Numan's presence and when he did so the

234

change in his demeanour was startling. He squinted suspiciously at the DC from behind square, black-rimmed glasses.

'Dennis Numan... I might have known you'd be mixed up in this cowboy operation. Aye, it's the best place for you, no doubt the last chance saloon indeed,' said Johnstone before he snapped his attention back to Malcolm. 'Have I made myself clear, Detective Sergeant? You have twenty-four hours to wind up your whole operation on Three Group and send all of your material to my office.' Johnstone leant forward until his face was just inches away from Malcolm's and then his right hand shot up and gave the DS a quick double slap, which had enough of a sting in it to make it clear it was more than a playful gesture. And with that, the human tornado that was Detective Chief Superintendent Johnny Johnstone turned on his heels and left the room.

The room echoed with silence and Malcolm, the grimace disappearing from his face, spread his hands out in front of him to indicate that the matter was over. 'Don't worry, boys, we can get a lot done in twenty-four hours, and besides, Mr Johnstone seems to forget we have the chief constable's personal sanction. A strange little episode though.' Then, turning to Numan and raising an eyebrow, the DS added, 'You two obviously know each other, Dennis, care to elaborate?'

'Johnstone's a nasty bastard all right, gaffer, but a boozebag and hoor-maister into the bargain, and one with a few skeletons in the closet. But perhaps the most interesting thing about the head of the Serious Crime Squad is that I know for a fact he is a former member of the army, cos when he was my section sergeant in the central he never stopped bleating on about the Troubles,' said Numan, a sly smile playing at the corners of his mouth.

'Ex-army, you say, very interesting, very interesting indeed. Do you think you might be able to find out just when he was in Northern Ireland and if he has any links to Rentoul and Three Group, or possibly even Dawson?' asked Malcolm.

'No problem, gaffer, leave it with me,' said Numan, smiling.

'Okay, so we have plenty to be getting on with,' said the DS and then he turned his gaze Thoroughgood's way, paused for a minute to ensure he had the probationer's complete attention and said, 'But there's another matter we need to address, Gus, if you don't mind?'

'Whatever you like, Detective Sergeant Malcolm,' replied Thoroughgood.

'The boys and I have been impressed with you, Thoroughgood. For a rookie you've shown a fair bit of initiative and, given the shit-storm you've been through with your shift, you've also shown some balls just to still be in the job, never mind alive after your run-in with Dawson. You're green, but you have the raw ingredients that can be moulded into a first-class detective and we all think that the unit would be a great place for that process to gather pace.' Looking up at Numan and Hardie, Malcolm then asked, 'That right boys?'

Numan responded first. 'Aye, I'd say you've hit the nail on the head there gaffer.'

'And you Hardie?' asked DS Malcolm.

'As long as he doesnae plan on dressing up in that schoolboy uniform anytime soon!' quipped the DC and the room filled with laughter.

A smile broke across Thoroughgood's face and for the first time in his police service he felt a sense of belonging wash over him.

But before he could say anything, Malcolm held up his hand. 'The plan will be to get you a spell as a temporary aide with us, return you to shift and then bring you back in as a confirmed ADC. But that's all a wee bit in the future, Gus. First, we need two things from you that will go a long way to helping us put an end to the ice cream wars.'

'Name them, Sergeant, and I'll do my best to make them happen,' replied Thoroughgood, tensing.

'First of all you're going to have to tough it out at the shift. We now know that Rentoul was clearly in on the deal with Dawson just as much as Davidson and Jones surely were, despite their sticky ending. You never know what might shake down through some of the other senior cops. But I want you to do everything you can to get on with these guys and foster relations with them. With Davidson and Jones gone you've got a clean slate to start again, so make the most of it. Rentoul is a big player in this and he might be the key to getting to the bottom of Dawson's claims. Then, of course, I want you shaking Collins down for every scrap of info you can get out of the bugger. You think you're up to it?'

'Like I said, I'll do my best, Detective Sergeant Malcolm,' said Thoroughgood, playing the straight bat.

Malcolm wagged a finger the probationer's way before continuing. 'Before I go any further, while you are in our company you can dispense with all that Detective Sergeant Malcolm crap. It's fine when there are other ears about but otherwise it's Cormac. Understood?'

Thoroughgood nodded in the affirmative.

'Good. Now to the second part of your orders. I need you to push Celine Lynott and really see if we can get anything from her on Dawson. I know that is going to be a bit risky but then when you mix business with pleasure which, reading between the lines, is exactly what you have done, young man, then you can bet your bottom dollar there will come a time when the two come into conflict. Well, I'm afraid now might be that time, so are you okay with that, Gus?'

'There's an issue with that, Detective Sergeant... Er, Cormac. Dawson has warned me away from seeing her again.'

Feeling three pairs of eyes boring into him, Thoroughgood knew he was being tested and that there was only one answer. 'Absolutely not a problem whatsoever... Cormac.'

'Right answer,' said Numan, and bounded over to the windowsill where he offered Thoroughgood his hand. 'Welcome aboard, son,' said the DC and a moment later Hardie appeared in his slipstream. 'Likewise, young 'un.'

CHAPTER 57

Celine sat on the white leather settee and cradled her knees, staring up through the skylight and into the darkness of the night. Over and over in her mind she played out both sides of the dilemma she now found herself in.

Confirmation that Thoroughgood had been right had finally been provided by the sight of Dawson deep in conversation with an overweight police sergeant, who bore a bizarre resemblance to the children's TV character Bagpuss, at the rear of Tutankhamun's. The look on Mojito's face when he had caught her lingering just a little too long at the top of the wrought-iron steps of the rear fire exit had made it clear to Celine that she had aroused the crime lord's suspicions, to say the least.

But where did she go from here? Thoroughgood had disappeared and wasn't answering his flat phone. It was all such a mess – and just when her prospects of a decent future had at last appeared real.

The sharp knock on her front door snapped her back to the present and, coming as it did amid an otherwise stony silence, Celine gave a startled twitch. She made her way to the front door, unsure what she was going to do when she got there... For she knew it would be him.

She opened the door and Mojito's brooding presence confirmed her worst fears.

'We, my dear Celine, need to talk,' and with that he pushed the half-open door wide and walked straight past her and into the flat.

Standing under the skylight he turned to face her. 'How much do you think you know?' But before Celine could reply he answered for her. 'The snatches of a telephone conversation heard from the creaky landing outside my office and what you saw from the top of the fire exit stair? All, of course, topped off with whatever rubbish your boyfriend, the wannabe detective, has been filling you with.' In the flat's dim light, the anger in his eyes burned bright.

Keeping her distance, Celine realised that this was the first time she had felt threatened by Mojito's presence, and as she wrapped herself in her own arms, she realised that the accuracy of his accusations meant a denial was futile.

'So tell me, what is the truth, Bobby?'

But Dawson, his anger mounting, strode over and grabbed her by the shoulders. 'The truth? Nothing you would understand, you stupid bitch. What you've done is become a pawn in a game that you should never have become involved in. I had hopes for you, Celine, but now they will never be realised.' And with that, he backhanded her with a vicious blow that sent her flying onto the settee.

Thoroughgood took the stairs two at a time as he climbed the close at Belmont Street, his sense of déjà vu from his last visit to Celine's flat now being swamped by the dread engulfing him.

He winced as he recalled the words he'd used to try and implore her to inform on Dawson. Now, as he reached the landing outside her flat door, Thoroughgood felt anxiety filling his body. For by asking her to inform on Dawson he had now placed her life in danger and immersed her in a deadly contest she should never have become embroiled in.

Dawson had called Celine his 'insurance policy', but what did that mean? Thoroughgood knew he was placing her in danger by turning up at her flat but he'd been careful and made sure, this time, that no one had followed him, scanning the empty street before he'd made for the front door. The bottom line was that he had to see her, had to make sure she was okay.

As he reached the landing, his black suede shoes crackled on top of broken glass and, as he began to bend down to examine the source of the snap, crackle and pop, he noticed the shards trailed towards the door and probably underneath it and inside.

He knocked on the door and with silence the only reply, tried the handle and felt the door give slightly. Encouraged, he put his shoulder to it and forced it open with only minimal resistance given. As it creaked wide, Thoroughgood felt his heart start to pound. The voice in his head confirmed his worst fears: 'Why would Dawson leave her free to come and go if he wants to use her as an insurance policy?' The realisation dawned on him that Celine was now no more than a hostage to make sure he would do as Dawson demanded and inform the IA of his claims. But now he'd done so, was Dawson's use for Celine at an end?

He took tortured steps into her flat and saw more evidence that all was far from well. A smashed picture frame lay wrecked on the wooden flooring of the hall. As he entered the living area he immediately focused on the odd angle of the settee and the upturned cushion on the floor. A half-finished glass of liquid, he assumed it was Bacardi and Coke, did nothing to allay his fears.

She had been taken, snatched by Dawson and his minions, when her use had ended – and it was all his fault.

'Christ why didn't I come for you first, Celine?' he asked himself, his right hand clawing furiously through his mullet of black hair.

All along he had been manipulated by Dawson, just as he had attempted to play Celine.

'What now?' he asked himself, and felt fresh hope spring in his heart that Dawson's use for her may not be at an end. For Celine was the bartering tool he would use to keep the IA off his back and allow him to bring the ice cream war to its bloody conclusion, while pursuing his own private machinations to their brutal ends.

As he stood there in the half darkness of the empty flat, the words of Marillion's 'Script for a Jester's Tear' began to play in his head over again and again. Slowly, Fish's obscure lyrics began to resonate with new meaning to Thoroughgood, within the context he now found himself.

'So here I am once more in the playground of the broken hearts, one more experience, one more entry in a diary, self-penned.'

The voice in his head articulated the current state of play: 'That bastard Dawson is the one who's been setting the agenda all along. It's got to change, he has to be made to play on our terms.'

And the song's words began to unwind in his head again: 'I'm losing on the swings, I'm losing on the roundabouts, the game is over.'

There and then Thoroughgood vowed that it was not, and gritting his teeth, he spat out three words: 'To the end.'

CHAPTER 58

Jammed into one of the famous burgundy leather booths of the university café, Thoroughgood devoured a bacon-and-egg doubler as hunger, for once, overcame the manic workings of his mind. Wiping away a dribble of burst yolk from the side of his mouth, he checked his watch for the third time: 9.30 a.m. Where the hell was Collins?

But his attention was soon snapped into the here and now by the presence of a familiar, anorak-clad figure, who dropped into the seat opposite him. 'I could murder a cup o' tea and a bacon butty, rozzer,' said Collins, grinning his gap-toothed smile.

Moments later, taking a huge mouthful of scalding tea from a red mug, Collins winced. 'Jesus, no sugar,' he muttered, and immediately grabbed three sachets of the white stuff and unloaded them into the mug. Taking another swig, Collins articulated his delight. 'Fuckin' magic! Noo, I've got some right guid info for yous,' said the tout before biting into his newly arrived bacon butty, the grease from which slid down the side of his mouth before he managed to cuff it away on his green Berghaus.

'Will you get on with it then, Collins?' said Thoroughgood impatiently, once again feeling at the whim of the informant.

'It wiznae Frankie McGuigan that took out yer neebers, pal. I've had ma ear tae the ground and if McGuigan's guys wiz on it then I wid have heard, nae danger I wid. Naw, somebody else will need tae swing for the hit on Jones and Davidson.' Collins took a drink from his tea and rolled his tongue around his mouth, savouring the sickly sweetness of the sugar.

Thoroughgood winced involuntarily.

'But there's mair, copper, much mair, and your gonnae need tae get yer finger oot big time, professor,' said Collins with a wink.

Thoroughgood kept his gaze trained on the housebreaker, his face like stone.

'Word is McGuigan wants to cut a deal with yous, he wants tae come in an' talk, but he'll be lawyered up and he's only gonnae spill to yer pals in the unit, cos he thinks every cop in uniform would gie him a bleachin',' said the informant almost nonchalantly.

Thoroughgood couldn't help his eyes opening wide and betraying his shock at Collins' revelation. But the rookie was soon in for another shock and it came in the form of Numan and Hardie, who sat down at the end of either side of the table.

'All right, gents, we were just passing and thought we would look in on you both and make sure everything was okay,' said Numan, grinning wickedly.

Thoroughgood's jaw tightened at the apparent lack of trust placed in him but he kept his mouth shut.

Collins nearly choked on his bacon butty, before managing to croak, 'Ah, for fuck's sake,' as he articulated his disgust at the nature of their newly arrived company.

Numan turned his gaze on the tout and, opening his hand, said, 'It's time for a full debrief, wee man. We just wanted to make sure you wurnae takin' advantage of our young friend's good nature.'

But before he could continue Numan was interrupted by a sharp Glaswegian voice as a middle-aged, heavily made-up waitress asked, 'Yous needin' any refills or a second roond o' rolls?'

'Two sausage-and-onion rolls, with a squirt o' tomato sauce and two coffees, white, no sugar, sweetheart, thanks for askin',' replied the DC, his impatience showing but his wolfish eyes still taking time to linger on the ample curves of the artificially raven-haired waitress, who replied with a sly smile before she slinked off in an over-exaggerated manner that drew knowing smirks from around the booth table.

'To be fair to the wee man he's never let us down yet... after a wee bit of friendly coaxing,' added Hardie, before a belch escaped from behind his moustache.

'Exactly. Now it's time you just repeated everything you have told young Gus, here, Collins, and don't be tryin' to spin a fanny,' said Numan, reaching across the table and enveloping the tout's left hand in his right, before administering a squeeze that forced a pain-wracked cry from the informant.

'Awright, awright, you've made yer point. I reckon Davidson and Jones were set up by Dawson and maybees even Rentoul. That way they take care o' a couple o' bawbags that were leading right back to their door, plus, as I wiz sayin' to the professor here, I wid have heard somethin' if McGuigan had been behind it,' said Collins.

'Well done, Sherlock!' said Hardie before nudging the tout in the side with a sharp elbow.

'Whit wiz that for?' snapped the informant.

'Cos I fancied it. More importantly, if your hypothesis is correct, nice word that, then the finger is pointed firmly at McGuigan and his team.'

Thoroughgood attempted to chip in but Numan held up his hand. 'It still takes a lot to get your head round the whole band-of-brothers thing one minute and the next Mojito is signing off on his own men. But there's more, Gus, a lot more, my boy. We have been very busy workin' through the wee small hours on this, believe me. On you go, Kenny,' he said, but Hardie was otherwise engaged in stuffing his chops with a large mouthful of the sausage-and-onion roll that had just arrived.

Rolling his eyes to the heavens, Numan gulped from his coffee mug and got down to business. 'Bottom line is we're hoping we can approach McGuigan and offer him our protection in turn for a squeal. If he wants to attend at Lennox Hill on a voluntary attendance, then we'll also have the warrant served on him at the High Court quashed. Cos if anyone else gets their hands on him, Rentoul will be all over him and McGuigan is likely to end up filleted one way or another by Dawson and that bastard of his,

Dirty Harry.'

Collins couldn't help himself. 'Yer havin' a laugh, chief. Cos that is exactly the deal McGuigan is lookin' tae cut wi' yous, he'll no parley wi' uniform but come in lawyered up at the Hill and deal wi' yous and yer boy here, thanks to a wee whisper that reached his ears, but aye, the warrant needs to be made to go away.'

Numan smiled. 'Perfect!' He started to rustle through the pockets of his shiny black anorak before fishing out something that to Thoroughgood looked like it had come straight off the set of *Star Trek*.

Seeing the confusion in his features Numan smiled mischievously before explaining. 'Nope, it's no' a brick and I'm no gonnae be shoutin' "Beam me up, Scotty" anytime soon!'

Laughter erupted around the table but the would be siren of a waitress, thinking she was the butt of a crude joke, made her suspicions known. 'Aye, you polis are aw the same. Think ye can come in here and lord it like yer bloody royalty. Well, if your naw wantin' any more ye can finish up and get on yer way, there's the bill!' And she slammed down the tab.

'Ah, come on pet, cheer up,' quipped Numan, and after flashing her a smile oozing with lecherous intent, he added, 'Why don't you do us all another round of rolls and coffee? There's a tenner, that should leave you with enough change for a wee drink tonight, darlin.'

The waitress, her self-esteem boosted by Numan's flattery, smiled and replied, 'Well, thank you, Detective, I don't mind if I do,' and scuttled off towards the kitchen.

'For fuck's sake, that's a bad case of grab-a-granny, Dennis,' laughed Hardie.

'Aye, but I'm no fussy, the older the Stradivarius the better the tune, as they say,' replied Numan and then he brandished the *Star Trek* prop in front of Thoroughgood. 'This, laddie, is a mobile phone and on it I am expecting...' He turned his wrist towards him and checked the time. 'A call from DS Malcolm to confirm whether our feelers have reached McGuigan yet.'

'So while we're waiting for that call, let me explain how this is gonnae work to both of you,' said Numan with a thin smile. 'Gus, we want you at the bar at Lennox Hill when McGuigan comes in. He will need to be booked in and we need someone there who isn't gonnae be on the blower to Rentoul the minute he shows. We will have Lennox Hill Office on lockdown and, depending on what happens after you've booked him in, we will either be taking him straight to Pitt Street or cutting a deal there and then, if there is one to be cut. But we have to make him the offer on what he considers home turf. Are you with me?'

Thoroughgood, putting aside his anger at Numan and Hardie hijacking his meeting with Collins, nodded. 'No problem, Dennis.'

Then Numan leant across the table and grabbed Collins by the front of his Berghaus. 'Now listen to me, Collins, you are officially our property and that is why you've been allowed to stay at the table and listen to whit the big boys have got to say. But now, bud, you're gonnae earn your keep, as my old granny would say. I want you keepin' tabs on Dawson and that new bitch of his. We don't have the man power, or at least men we can trust, to do the job for us, but I think you know whit's gonnae happen if you try and screw us over again. Capisce?'

'Yer no' jokin,' said Collins, as Numan released his grip and pushed him back into the booth.

'Good boy. I want you to find out the exact flat this redhead is staying at and I want it done now.' Numan paused and took out a card from the inside pocket of his jacket and slapped it down on the table in front of Collins. 'Then you phone me on the brick here and we will come and turn it. Plus I want you callin' me with any other titbits that come your way, wee man.'

Collins' eyebrows shot up. 'An' whit am I getting' for daeing yer work for ye, chief?'

'You'll be looked after, Collins, that's all you need to know right now. Now bugger off and get busy cause this is a pay-per-play deal only pal,' said Numan, nodding his head towards the door.

Hardie stood up and waved his hand to show Collins the door. After a short hesitation the tout reluctantly stood up, shuffled out the booth and made for the exit.

'Oh and Collins,' shouted Numan. 'Do a good job and there will be plenty more work for you. Fuck up and…' The DC let his words trail into a threatening silence.

Collins got the message. 'Aye, very good,' he said, and walked out the door.

The ringing of the mobile saw Numan quickly pick up the phone and, as eyes popped in delight, it was clear that the DC liked what he was hearing from down the line. After a minute or so the familiar, slightly lilting tones of DS Malcolm became apparent at the other end of the mobile. 'He's up for it, ya beauty!' said Numan, flashing a thumbs-up sign at the rest of the table. Then he added, '0100 hours, day after tomorrow?' He threw a questioning glance at Thoroughgood, who mouthed a 'yes' in reply.

Moments later the call ended. 'It's game on, boys,' said Numan. 'The aim is to give McGuigan every chance to plead his case and when we're happy with that, in turn for his freedom, temporary though it may be, he will be used as the bait to tempt Mojito into the open. Right now that seems to be our only hope of getting an eyeball on him. Then once and for all we will finish this bloody ice cream war and put Dawson behind bars, 14 Intelligence Company or not.'

'Amen to that,' said Hardie and they raised their mugs of coffee in salute.

Turning sideways to Thoroughgood, Numan smiled wanly. 'Listen, son, I know that wasn't easy for you, us takin' over your meet with Collins. But at this stage of the game, given what a slippery wee bastard he is, we thought it was best, so no offence, wee man.'

'It's no big deal, Dennis… But there is something else,' said Thoroughgood, almost reluctantly.

'Spit it oot then, son,' said Hardie.

'I've been up to Celine Lynott's flat and it was turned over but there was no trace of her. I think Dawson has her,' said Thoroughgood.

'Bloody great, that's all we need. Right we'll get a lookout circulated for her and a mis-per raised but I will guarantee you're right and that Dawson has her tucked up somewhere in his grasp. We will get her back, Gus, believe me.'

'I hope so,' groaned Thoroughgood as Numan and Hardie exchanged knowing glances.

'Aye, he's got it bad, Dennis,' said Hardie.

CHAPTER 59

Rentoul stared into his whisky, his senses numbed, his eyes unseeing. He took a swig of the whisky and slammed the quarter-gill glass down hard on his office desk.

Nineteen years of friendship, loyalty and trust all gone in a matter of moments and it was all his fault. He should have known that McGuigan would never have allowed himself to be shuttled from the High Court in such unceremonious circumstances without a Plan B.

Plan B, that was a fuckin' laugh. Wasn't that the very way he had described his plan to set McGuigan up to Davidson and Jones? Yet instead it had been fatally flawed, allowing McGuigan to be sprung and his minions to take their vicious vengeance on his brothers in arms.

While Rentoul had the balls to deliver their death messages in person to Davidson and Jones's widows, he could not vanquish the sense of guilt that hung over him and laid the blame for their murders firmly at his own feet. He could still hear his hollow words of reassurance to their widows as he promised that their killers would be brought to justice, while Davidson's weans screamed the house down and his wife, Elaine, tried to drown herself in a bottle of whisky.

'Now what?' he asked himself out loud.

He had to get a hold of Mojito and find out what his next move would be, but the brutal murder of two serving police officers had brought a much more powerful spotlight to bear on their seemingly routine involvement in the gangland feud that had become immortalised by the moniker 'The Ice Cream Wars'.

Once again he grabbed his phone and dialled Dawson's private office number; once again it rang out and Rentoul found his imagination beginning to work overtime, running through a series of violent scenes that ended with his own brutal demise.

'Fuck it,' spat Rentoul. 'There is no way Jimmy Rentoul sits back and lets a ragged-arsed corporal call the shots, 14 Intelligence Company or no.'

Rentoul rammed his chair back into the filing cabinet behind him and stormed through the fire doors, past the uniform bar and out through the rear doors into the secure car park at the rear of Bayne Street, a rage for revenge engulfing him as more questions began to flood his mind.

Where the fuck had Mojito been? The ambush had been set for the blind tunnel and that is exactly where it had come, but instead of McGuigan being sprung and spirited away by Mojito to face the ultimate punishment, with Davidson and Jones left nursing cuts and bruises, his men had been brutally slain.

Rentoul waited for the mechanical security gate to slip open and allow him to drive the marked Ford Escort out of the back yard, wondering where it had all gone wrong.

Had McGuigan's minions anticipated their plan and in turn ambushed the ambushers? And if so, was that why Mojito was no longer answering his phone? Where was McGuigan now? Christ, half the force was out looking for him and still the bastard remained at large. Shaking his head furiously, Rentoul worried that McGuigan could have been smuggled out of Glasgow by the network of Provisional sympathisers Dawson had warned him about, who remained active under the eyes of the law.

Gritting his teeth, Rentoul vowed to himself he would get to the bottom of it. But the deaths of his two cohorts left him feeling vulnerable in a way he had not done since he had patrolled the Bogside all these years ago. The difference was that now there was no one to watch his back. 'What about these bastards the IA, and that grassing little shit Thoroughgood?' the voice in his head asked unhelpfully.

'I'll bet my last pound that weasel has painted one hell of a picture for them. Why the fuck did Mojito allow him to walk free? Should've dumped him in the Campsies with a slug in his heid and no one would have been the wiser,' muttered Rentoul out loud.

He promised himself that he would take care of Thoroughgood as soon as he squared things with Mojito. An opportunity had been missed but he would manufacture another one to make sure that the probationer was no longer the thorn in his side that he had become.

Engaging second gear Rentoul drove the Escort up to the traffic lights, flicked the window wipers on and watched the drizzle clear from the vehicle windscreen.

It would take him twenty minutes to get to Mojito's office, and if need be he would wait there all night until he got to the bottom of this mess and left Dawson in no uncertain terms that the importance of his mission was now null and void when it came to sorting McGuigan and avenging Davidson and Jones once and for all.

Rentoul stuck a fag in his mouth, lit up, wound down the window and billowed smoke out of it. Then a crack rang out somewhere in the distance and a split-second later Sergeant James Rentoul's head exploded over the vehicle dashboard as the remainder of his burst cranium crashed onto the police vehicle's horn and its strident tones burst out endlessly into the night.

CHAPTER 60

The front door burst open and Virgilio Celtrani's self-important figure breezed into the paint-peeled, graffiti-daubed foyer of Lennox Hill Office. In his slipstream followed Francis McGuigan.

Keeping his eyes down on the lost property register he was updating, Thoroughgood initially ignored their arrival but inside his heart was pounding. He knew that the IA had placed him in a position of great trust that was far in advance of his callow length of service. Even although Malcolm and Numan were waiting in the prisoner's cell, which also doubled up as an interview room, the job of processing McGuigan's decision to come in from the cold was all his.

Sarcastically Celtrani knocked his knuckles on the reception counter and slowly Thoroughgood raised his eyes and smiled at his 'customers'.

'How can I help, gentlemen?' asked Thoroughgood, feigning ignorance and attempting to take some of the pomposity out of Celtrani.

'My name is Virgilio Celtrani and I am lawyer for Mr McGuigan. We are here by arrangement with Detective Sergeant Malcolm and Detective Constable Numan and attending voluntarily.'

Thoroughgood smiled and immediately pulled out the voluntary attendance book. 'DS Malcolm and DC Numan are waiting on you in the interview room, but first I need Mr McGuigan's signature and details down here to confirm he is attending of his own volition.'

'Let's get this shite over with,' spat McGuigan, grabbing the biro pen offered him by Thoroughgood and signed the VA form with a flourish.

Just as McGuigan looked up, Numan arrived behind Thoroughgood in the uniform bar. 'Aye, its yersel', McGuigan, and you've brought yer best pal with you.' He gestured to the swing doors that led into the corridor running off the uniform bar, which opened right on cue, and from behind them Malcolm said, 'This way, gentlemen, if you don't mind.'

Sullenly, McGuigan headed through the doors first, with Celtrani clearly unhappy he was being relegated to the role of supporting cast rather than star of the show. Moments later the four men sat around the cracked plastic table Thoroughgood had pushed into the prisoner's room earlier.

'So, gentlemen, time is not on our side. I believe you wish to make a formal denial of any involvement in the murders of Constables Davidson and Jones. Is that correct?' asked Malcolm.

'Any chance o' a light?' asked McGuigan and Numan fished out a green plastic lighter and did the necessary.

McGuigan took a long drag on his cigarette, blew the smoke high above their heads, and turned his gaze on the detectives. 'I am completely innocent and yous know as well as I do I've been set up. Now what the fuck are yous gonnae do about it?'

Thoroughgood checked his watch: 0155 hours and still they talked. For the fifth time he walked out into the foyer and opened the door, scanned the dark, foreboding gloom, making sure there was no sign of Rentoul, or anyone else for that matter, up to something they shouldn't be.

The murders of Davidson and Jones, and the outbreak of a flu bug, had conveniently meant that there were no beat officers walking out of Lennox Hill, but by the same token Thoroughgood knew that sometime soon a supervisory check would be required on the Hill in the form of a drive by from one of the Bayne Street gaffers, and there was every chance, given he was home alone, that Rentoul would make sure he was the sergeant who would come calling for a 'sign'.

Yet all was quiet. No doubt no small part of that was down to the fact that McGuigan's gold Mercedes S-Class was sitting right outside the office with its ubiquitous 'QUIGGY 1' number plate, and as such Thoroughgood supposed the locals were bound to keep a low profile.

The rookie was snapped from his thoughts by the sound of a door opening from behind him and the increasing volume of voices coming his way. So a deal had been done. Creeping into the corridor, Thoroughgood couldn't help himself straining to catch the conversation.

It was Celtrani who was in full flow. 'So there you have it, gentlemen, my client thanks you for dealing with the issue of the warrant and in turn you've had his full cooperation with regard to a witness statement in relation to the unfortunate demise of Constables Davidson and Jones. In return we expect you to honour your promise of full protection for Mr McGuigan until the situation is resolved. A good day to you, gentlemen.' As he exited the room he gave a patronising flourish of his right hand and then continued down the corridor towards Thoroughgood.

Next out of the interview room was a stony-faced McGuigan, then behind him Malcolm and Numan stood pensively, the frowns on their faces ample proof that all had not gone as they had hoped.

As the brief drew level with Thoroughgood he snapped, 'Do you mind, Constable?' and the rookie was forced to flatten himself against the wall to let Celtrani and the brooding McGuigan leave the dilapidated confines of Lennox Hill Office.

As they exited the building the front door was slammed shut so hard that it rebounded open before eventually coming to rest closed again. Thoroughgood parked himself in the station constable's chair in the uniform bar and wondered if Malcolm and Numan would come through to put him in the picture, but the temporary silence was broken by the phone ringing out.

Lifting the receiver, Thoroughgood frowned at the sound of a female voice, one which was sheathed in a harsh Northern Irish accent. 'If I was you, copper, I'd get me head down quick.' Then the line went dead.

Heading into the corridor at the rear of the office, Thoroughgood remembered that the redhead who'd met Dawson, according to Collins, had a Northern Irish accent. As Numan materialised at the kitchen door the DC's eyes took in the probationer's puzzled expression and he asked, 'Problem, son?'

'Female with a Northern Irish accent telling me to get my head down,' said Thoroughgood.

Numan's eyes widened in startled terror as the true meaning of this pivotal piece of information hit him, but before words could form in his mouth a massive blast detonated outside the office.

Thoroughgood turned towards the front of the office but as he did so two powerful hands wrenched him back through the kitchen door just as the front walls of Lennox Hill Police station imploded inwards and a deadly rain of bricks, shards of iron shutter and other lethal debris came flying through the air followed by a sheet of flame twenty feet high.

CHAPTER 61

Duncy Parkinson raised the glass, filled with golden fluid, glanced at the clock on the front wall of McGuigan's bar, saw that it read 1.12 a.m. and muttered, 'Hurry up, Frankie, for fuck's sake,' as his impatience at his gaffer's failure to return from his meeting with the unit spilled into words.

The bar was empty and now shut but Parkinson hadn't bothered to lock the doors as he watched expectantly for the return of his gaffer. Swilling the Bell's around inside his mouth he shut his eyes and savoured the sour taste of the blended whisky, but as he did so his ears picked up on the creak of the front door opening and to his amazement a female, her rust-coloured tresses billowing in the backdraft of the door shutting behind her, walked into McGuigan's. Then she leant against the fruit machine just inside the door and gently placed a black rucksack at her feet.

Scenting prey, Parkinson ran his left hand through his slicked-back hair and walked over to the fruit machine, stopped a yard or so away from this strange, alabaster-skinned creature, who was already starting to cast a spell over him and who now, ignoring his presence, was sticking a 10p into the machine.

'Strayed off the beaten track a bit sweetheart, haven't we?' said Parkinson, almost in a whisper, to her back.

The only reaction he got was the fruit machine's arm being pulled down by a pale hand that could have been hewn from the finest marble. Then Devorgilla turned round and raked him with gold-flecked green eyes that pierced him with their searing intensity.

Parkinson felt like a rattlesnake's prey, waiting to have the venom injected, and he threw down the remainder of the glass of whisky in a oner, sighed and wiped the back of his hand across his mouth.

'Are you the boss man?' she asked, a cigarette dangling from the side of her mouth, in a bold Northern Irish voice.

The gangland lieutenant, unused to being spoken to in such a confrontational manner in his domain, was almost left speechless but, smiling wolfishly, he said, 'Naw, Frankie will be back anytime now, but while he's away I run the show. You fancy a wee refreshment, doll?'

At six foot five, the big man was aware of her cold eyes assessing him from a sideways glance. Strangely, Parkinson felt uneasy and he began to fiddle with his black-and-red striped tie, loosening it from his collar.

Then Devorgilla blew smoke in his face and big Duncy was putty in her hands.

Smiling contemptuously through the cigarette fug she saw that Parkinson's eyes were devouring her, but as he did so the towering enforcer missed a shimmer of movement as her right hand slipped under her cagoule and returned into the open with a fistful of steel.

The surprise shockwaved across Duncy's face, but before he could move, a silenced pistol pumped two bullets from point-blank range into his torso and the giant crumpled onto the cheap black linoleum floor, flat on his back as his white shirt ran red from his pumping vital fluids.

'You mad bitch, whit the fuck was that for?' he asked, but as his eyes started to roll the last thing Parkinson saw was the cruel smile that spread across Devorgilla's sculpted features.

'Revenge,' she spat and, smiling, fired a final bullet into Parkinson's cranium.

Then she ripped one of the cagoule pockets open, pulled out a glass bottle stuffed with a rag and swirling full of liquid, and tilted her head to let the cigarette light the frayed edge of cloth protruding from the projectile.

'Your total destruction and annihilation has now been completed, goodbye to the scum of the universe,' she spat and lobbed the petrol bomb at the gantry, watching in satisfaction as it exploded on impact and wreathed the bar in a sheet of flame

Then she kneeled down at the rucksack, zipped it open and flicked the timer switch on. Standing up, she spat the cigarette from her mouth, stamped it dead and walked out the door.

Outside, she jogged across the car park, slipped behind the crumbling brick wall that marked the bar's perimeter and turned to wait for her work to be completed. A moment later the bar erupted in a massive explosion that turned McGuigan's into an inferno and provided Duncy Parkinson with a spectacular funeral pyre.

The first part of her plan was complete and it had been all too easy.

As she heard the sirens start to scream in the distance she jogged round the rear of the ruined bar, scrambled down an embankment and ran down the disused railway line she had previously scouted as the perfect escape route.

She had done Dawson's bidding and avenged his brother, now it was her turn to extract revenge.

CHAPTER 62

'Tell me, what did you expect for your betrayal?' asked Dawson from behind a drawn face devoid of emotion.

'It wasn't me that betrayed you, Bobby, it was yourself,' replied Celine, wincing at the pain pulsing from her bound wrists.

He shook his head in exasperation before continuing in a monotone voice that brooked no argument. 'You had an opportunity to make something of yourself and instead you threw it back in my face – and for what? A rookie cop who lives in a fantasy world?' Mojito shrugged his shoulders as if he had become bored of the whole conversation.

'So what are you going to do with me, Bobby?' she asked, the first signs of real desperation betrayed in the quivering of her voice.

'I,' said Mojito emphasising the word before leaning down and grabbing Celine by her jaw, 'will not be doing anything to you. My life is finished in Glasgow and, unfortunately for you, my treacherous little tart, so is yours. But it will not be me who ends it.' As he completed the sentence, Celine could see that the hatred that had been eating Dawson from the inside had now completely devoured him.

Taking a couple of steps back he folded his black-suited arms in front of him and in the pale light that filtered through the partially shuttered windows his diamond earring glinted.

Then he clicked his fingers and the door to the left of him opened and the hulking presence of Harry, whom she knew as the doorman from Tutankhamun's, walked in. Mojito flicked his head towards Celine and the enforcer walked round behind her and clamped a rag over her face. Moments later she was unconscious.

Standing still in the darkness of the empty room she kept her gaze trained on the front door and waited for Harry to arrive with the body. He did not disappoint.

Nevertheless the abrupt opening of the door, when it came, startled Devorgilla, but as the enforcer's hulking frame came into view she relaxed because, as she had admitted to herself, there had been every chance that Mojito might have elected to set her up in the game of smoke and mirrors he was attempting to play in order to cover the tracks of his escape.

But then he needed her expertise.

As Harry unzipped the body bag and hoisted the corpse over his mountainous shoulders she noticed that the deceased was almost a photo-fit for Dawson: bald, stocky and now garbed in one of his immaculate black suits. Within moments the corpse was placed in Mojito's seat and jammed up against the desk in an upright position.

'You gonnae fix things up just the way the boss wants?' asked Harry with a look of simmering violence that she guessed was the hangover from the killing he had just committed, but which also reminded her of her first IRA commander, who couldn't quite bring himself to believe just exactly what she was capable of... Until she pumped a bullet in his head.

'It's an easy wee job,' Devorgilla said dismissively. 'But what I need to know is where my exit route is.'

'Pull the middle book aff the shelf under the mirror behind Mojito's desk and a concealed entrance opens ontae stairs that'll take ye doon to the cellar. You'll see the door next tae the barrel o' McEwan's Export is unlocked – once you get in the passageway there, follow it until it comes tae its end and ye'll be well away, that dae yous?' said Harry, his contempt and mistrust evident.

She smiled coldly. 'I hope you know what you're doing,' she said, and noticed the setting of Harry's jaw as her jibe sparked his anger.

'Never mind aboot me, darlin', just get the job done and bell me doonstairs, cos the cops should be here any minute noo. I'll make oot as if I'm speaking to Mojito, just as if he's large as life in his office above while you're long gone,' said Harry flatly and then, fixing her with a last look of pulsing contempt, he strode out of the door.

Quickly Devorgilla set to work wiring up the corpse and then loosened the first two floorboards inside the office, where she deftly inserted a pressure fuse to guarantee that the first footfall on it sent the person making it and anyone with him to hell. This would ensure that the remnants of the corpse masquerading as Dawson would be very unlikely to be identifiable, such was the level of carnage that would follow the detonation of the explosive, which she had located under Dawson's desk and was the lethal component of the booby trap at the other end of the firing mechanism.

Then, completing her murderous surprise, Devorgilla afforded herself a wry grin at the etymology of the term booby trap, which came from the Spanish *bobo*, which roughly translated to mean 'stupid daft, naïve or one who is easily cheated'.

CHAPTER 63

His hands – cut, bleeding and raw from the explosion that had destroyed the front end of Lennox Hill Office – gripped the van steering wheel, but as the anger seething within him shot through his veins, Numan felt no pain.

They had been lucky, very lucky, that between them bruising, cuts and badly dented pride had been the only price that they had had to pay for the massive car bomb that had blown Francis McGuigan and his slippery brief, Virgilio Celtrani, to kingdom come.

It had been an act of deadly destruction that had now finally pointed the finger firmly at Mojito. As he rammed the white van into third and sped down Great Western Road, Numan promised himself that this time they would take Mojito down once and for all.

'Fuck's sake, Dennis, take it easy, will you. I don't want to come through the Lennox Hill bombing only to end up a road traffic fatality,' quipped Malcolm as he hung on to the passenger door.

'We've fucked up, Cormac, fucked up big, and now we need to get to Dawson, huckle him and make sure he swings for this. Ice cream wars, my arse. Ask yourself, where the fuck is he getting the expertise to start a bombing campaign in Glasgow?'

'Well, he was in the Paras, as we now know to our cost, but maybe he's had some help from this mysterious redhead. What I can't understand is why we can't get any intelligence on our Irish angel of death. Something isn't right there. You sure the RUC had nothing?' asked Malcolm.

'Not a bloody Scooby Snack and that can only point to one thing. She's working for the Intelligence Services and her ID has been erased by this 14 Intelligence Unit while Dawson plays the organ grinder and makes us look like a bunch of bleedin' monkeys,' spat Numan.

'It's beginning to look that way. It's all adding up, but it isn't, if you catch my drift. The one thing I can guarantee is that when we get to Tutankhamun's we're no' leaving empty handed,' vowed Malcolm, the rapping of his fingers on the dashboard betraying his growing agitation. 'Let's hope Hardie and Thoroughgood get a hold of that bugger Collins and shake something out of him, the little shit has an annoying habit of going quiet when we most need him.'

As Malcolm took in the developing scene at the front of Tutankhamun's whitewashed walls his own disgust found its way into words. 'Just what we don't bloody well need.'

Numan eased the Transit window down and flashed his warrant card at the police vehicle which was stopping traffic a hundred feet down from the nightclub. The cop standing at the roadblock gave him a curt nod of his head and Numan guided the van between the two static marked police vehicles, slipped down through the gears and eased into the side of the kerb just outside the pub opposite Tutankhamun's, rammed the handbrake on, jumped out the driver's door and ran across the Great Western Road with Malcolm in his slipstream.

Satisfied that her work was ready to spring its deadly payload, Devorgilla made the phone call to the bar office downstairs and was met by Harry's rough voice. 'No problem, Mr Dawson,' he said. 'I'll get that seen tae right aways.' Then the phone went dead.

Grimly, she shut the office door, skipping back over the first two floorboards with the grace of a gazelle, aware that whoever walked this way next would indeed become the booby in her trap.

It was at moments like these that her conscience, or the memory of it, pricked her.

As always though, Devorgilla's guilt was fleeting, because her conscience had long since withered and died that blood-soaked day on the Bogside when the only man she had ever loved had been shot dead in cold blood.

'How can I help yous, gents?' asked Harry.

But the telephone conversation he had just completed had given Malcolm and Numan all the help they needed and a smile crept across Malcolm's face. 'We have exactly what we need from you, my friend, now that you have confirmed your boss is home. All we want is to pay him a little visit upstairs...' But before Malcolm could finish his sentence the sound of the front door banging open interrupted him.

Numan's head immediately snapped around. 'Detective Chief Superintendent Johnny Johnstone. Bastard!' muttered the DC under his breath.

Johnstone, his beige raincoat billowing in the draught of the opening door, came to a stop a yard away, took a massive drag from his cigarette and then flicked the butt straight at Malcolm's chest.

'You can stop right there, Malcolm,' he said dismissively, a smile slipping over his waxen features. Then, playing to the gallery of assembled detectives and uniform cops securing the locus, Johnstone took a short step forward and rammed his index finger into the DS's chest. 'I ordered you to hand over all the papers you had on this business within twenty-four hours and you did not comply. Instead you went behind my back and organised a meeting with Francis McGuigan and his brief at Lennox Hill Office – a meeting that should never have happened outside of a terrorist-proof secure building, and it ended with both of them blown to smithereens and Lennox Hill Office levelled. Christ, man, you were lucky to escape with your own lives.'

Malcolm attempted to fight his corner. 'With respect, sir, I...' But before he could make his plea in mitigation, Johnstone sprang at him and grabbed the DS's blouson jacket with his two chubby paws.

'Did I give you permission to talk, Detective Sergeant?' asked Johnstone. He placed a ruddy finger across Malcolm's mouth and added, 'No, is the answer you are looking for, Malcolm.' Then he made a big show of smoothing out Malcolm's crumpled jacket and took a step back.

'Earlier this morning, in the wake of the explosion at Lennox Hill Police Office, the Serious Crime Squad received information that Bobby Dawson would be within his office at Tutankhamun's nightclub and we immediately acted to secure the premises before apprehending Dawson. And, once I have huckled him, I can promise you both one thing, and that is that I will be making my way to the chief constable's door, where he will be told everything about the obstruction to my investigation you perpetrated and the utter recklessness with which you both went about your business. A recklessness that has, in my opinion, led to the murder of Francis McGuigan and Virgilio Celtrani and also been behind the spiralling out of control of this so called bloody ice cream war. In short, you are both finished, Malcolm and Numan.'

Simmering throughout the Johnstone monologue, Numan finally snapped. 'Now wait a minute, Johnstone,' he said, taking a menacing step forwards. 'You're only here because you've been piggy-fuckin'-backin' on our investigation.'

'So, Numan,' interrupted Johnstone, 'your self-control has deserted you, as I knew it would. DCs Fulton and Green, take this man into your custody for insubordination and failing to obey a lawful order. You're finished, Numan, finished for good.' Johnstone's eyes were twinkling with delight at the settling of an age-old score.

Malcolm did his best to pour oil on troubled waters. 'With respect, sir, passions are running high and Dennis hasn't had a wink's sleep in the wake of the Lennox Hill bombing. For goodness sake, sir, but for the grace of God we would have gone the same way as McGuigan and Celtrani, as you yourself have just pointed out.'

Johnstone smiled his contempt. 'Quite frankly, my dear, I don't give a damn. You would do well to remove yourself from this locus, Detective Sergeant.' Johnstone took a step towards Numan and slapped him on the cheek. 'Gotcha! Take him away, boys.' He turned back to his entourage. 'All right, I want two of you at the rear of the building, supplementing the uniform presence we already have there, and I'll take DI Tibbs with me upstairs to formally arrest Dawson.'

Johnstone smiled grimly as he walked over to the bar, where the burly barman, who sported a vicious scar down the right-hand side of his face, was industriously polishing glasses.

Johnstone, who had heard Dawson's presence above confirmed by Malcolm moments earlier, turned to Tibbs and said smugly, 'Serve him the warrant.' The DI duly did as he was bid, but as Tibbs slapped the paperwork on the counter the creak of a floorboard above betrayed movement from Dawson's office that confirmed to Johnstone his prey may be about to try and make his escape.

'Come on, Tibbs, before our bird flies his nest,' said the DCS, and as the two detectives charged up the stairs, Harry discreetly slipped out the back of the bar and down into the cellar.

Manhandled into a panda car, Numan's head was pushed down to avoid a nasty collision with the vehicle roof and he slouched in the back seat of the marked Ford Escort, shoulders slumped in resignation at his impending doom.

Bending down at the vehicle window, Malcolm attempted to reassure him that all would be well, without much conviction. 'Look, Dennis we'll work something out here, believe me...'

But before he could finish his sentence, a huge blast from a hundred yards behind the DS thundered out as tremors shuddered through the very tarmacadam of the road.

'Get fuckin' down,' shouted Numan as the shockwave and deadly rain of the explosion engulfed them.

CHAPTER 64

'Where is the wee bastard?' spat Hardie, sweeping his eyes from the front windscreen to his driver's side window.

'I wouldn't worry too much about that, Hardie. Speaking from experience, Collins always finds you when he wants to,' said Thoroughgood in a manner that immediately rubbed up his senior cop the wrong way.

'From your experience, eh? And what bleedin' experience would that be, boy? We've been drivin' round the Hill for half an hour and there's fuck all sign of the Cat o' nine tails or whatever you call the wee scrote and we don't have time to waste, in case you haven't noticed, Thoroughgood,' said Hardie, his agitation clear but almost immediately replaced by a sweeping sense of guilt. 'Er, sorry about that, son. Christ, you're lucky to still be with us after that bloody McGuigan car bomb business. It's still hard to take it all in. We've been past the remains of the office three times and for all it's smouldering away I still expect to see the battered front door and the rusting shutters every time we make a sweep. You get any sleep since…' Hardie let his words trail off.

But Thoroughgood's attention was already elsewhere. 'There we go, bus stop on the left, male in green Berghaus with hood up,' said Thoroughgood, with a smugness he made no effort to try and hide.

'As if by magic, eh?' said Hardie from beneath arched eyebrows, steering the unmarked red Vauxhall van across the road to the bus stop.

Thoroughgood rolled down his window. 'Well, well, Mr Collins, just the man we were looking for. Why don't you jump in the back of the van? Assuming you have something for us?'

'Nae danger,' muttered Collins and did as he was bid.

From behind the wheel Hardie's eyes fixed on the tout's image in his mirror. 'Okay, wee man, where the fuck is she?'

'A farmhoose,' replied Collins.

'That's very helpful. A farmhouse where, you little shite, somewhere on the road to Tipperary?' said Hardie.

'Naw, somewhere in the Campsies,' replied the tout and then, despite his expectant audience, his mouth clamped shut.

But Thoroughgood realised immediately that Celine was almost certainly being held at the same bolthole Dawson had practised the 'five techniques' on him and quickly he tried to recall every minute detail from his torture session and the surroundings of his confinement.

Despite having been blindfolded throughout his ordeal, Thoroughgood's mind raced as it sought to home in on any scrap of information that might help point them in the rough location of the building Celine was being held captive in. Shutting his eyes, he recalled the damp of the stone he had felt on his hands.

'Okay, so it's not just a farmhouse, it's a deserted one, probably ruined and derelict, judging by the state of the walls I felt on my hands. Slimy stone running with damp,' he said out loud.

'Come on, Collins, help us here, what the feck are we paying you for?' demanded Hardie scornfully.

'Look, I'm sorry but it's aw I got. Anyways, you huvnae paid me yet, boss,' said Collins indignantly but at the same time he stared almost guiltily at his hideously bitten nails.

Thoroughgood, his mind spiralling into overdrive, couldn't help himself articulating his thoughts. 'It isn't a farmhouse, Collins, it's a bloody mill house,' said the rookie triumphantly.

'Okay, smartarse, and how do you know that?' asked the clearly sceptical Hardie.

'Because Dawson has her held at exactly the same place he interrogated me. As I said, the walls were cold and running with damp, which means we are talking somewhere uninhabited, but most important of all there was a really strong sound of water rushing by. It was almost like it was flowing right under the building and that means it isn't a farmhouse he's holding her in, it's an old, derelict mill house, which would, of course, have been operated by a water-powered mill wheel. How many of them do you think are knocking about in the Campsies?'

'You might have a point there, Thoroughgood,' said Hardie reluctantly, as he flattened the edges of his moustache out thoughtfully.

'Farmhoose, mill hoose, whit does it matter, bottom line is, if yous dinnae get there pronto I'd put my last tenner on redhead blowing yer wee bird's brains oot sharpish,' said Collins.

But Thoroughgood ignored his words, rifling through the glove compartment. 'Thank God for that, an operation pack,' said the rookie as he removed the Ordnance Survey map from a drawstring bag and quickly flattened it out on his knees.

'Now, if it is a mill house it can't be in the middle of nowhere, as it would need to be near a road, as well as the river that powered it, so they could get the grain down to the town on market day,' said Thoroughgood, his eyes devouring the map while his index finger traced the thin blue line of a river spidering across it.

'There we are, Baldernock Mill, it's got to be. Long since derelict, right on the River Kelvin and just ten minutes from Glasgow,' said the rookie triumphantly.

Collins, however was unimpressed. 'Aye, well done Sherlock, but noo you'd better get Nigel Mansell here tae put his foot tae the flair or yer damsel in distress will be broon breid.'

'But there's no need for you to be worrying about that, Collins, because you're free ride is over, now beat it,' snapped Hardie.

'Ah, come oan, yous no taking me along for the ride?' asked the informant, only half in jest.

But the anger in Hardie's eyes reflecting from the driver's mirror left him in no doubt that it was time for a sharp exit, and when Hardie slammed on the brakes Collins was sent flying in the back of the van.

'Out,' shouted Hardie, and this time Collins did as he was bid.

CHAPTER 65

'So what do we do now bright spark?' asked Hardie.

'Just like Collins said, we go and rescue the damsel in distress and see who else we can hook in the process,' replied Thoroughgood, acutely aware that the final decision on exactly what they did or did not do would be taken by Hardie.

'It would be a big help if we knew what had happened at Tutankhamun's with Numan and Malcolm. They should have been in touch by now to let us know if they managed to gie Mojito the pokey,' said the senior cop.

'Very true, but in the meantime we haven't got time to spare, Hardie. We need to get ourselves up to Baldernock as quickly as possible and then, if it is the locus we are looking for, we send for the cavalry and they can get themselves up there ASAP,' summed up Thoroughgood, and with a nod of agreement Hardie clicked through the gears and put his foot to the floor.

Ten minutes later they hit the traffic lights on the crossroads that would take them up Baldernock Road and eventually to the old mill.

'Straight ahead past St Paul's Church on your left and just keep going as far as you can, according to the map,' said Thoroughgood. 'Just wondering... Are you tooled up, Hardie?'

The trademark arching of Hardie's eyebrows was the only answer that Thoroughgood got, but as they drove through an old cobblestoned ford, sending a geyser of water shooting over the vehicle, the car radio finally sparked into life. 'OP1 to OP2, come in?' demanded Malcolm's voice.

'Go on then,' said Hardie and Thoroughgood immediately obliged. 'OP2 reading you loud and clear, go ahead?'

'All right, Gus, here's the news: Dawson is presumed dead, blown to hell in his own office, but the unfortunate thing is that DCS Johnstone and DI Tibbs were also killed in the same explosion, all of which leaves us who knows where. What's your position?' asked Malcolm.

'We're about five minutes away from Baldernock Mill, a deserted nineteenth-century mill house, which is where we think Dawson has been holding Celine Lynott. She's almost certainly captive in the same place he held me. What do you want us to do?' asked Thoroughgood, hoping for the right answer.

'Proceed with extreme caution,' said Malcolm, but before he could continue the radio set went dead.

'Typical. Another soddin' blank spot,' said Hardie.

The creaking of a footstep on the wooden gangway that ran along the side of the old mill and ended at the rear door, above the broken and rotting wheel, alerted him to the fact they had company.

Squinting out from behind the frayed net curtain that hung across the fragile glazing of the window he saw that Devorgilla had come, and the sight of her, confirming as it did that the key part of his plan had been completed, produced a smile of satisfaction.

Dawson opened the door for her, attempting to read her impenetrable, almost frozen, features for the answers he sought. 'So?' he asked.

'Your nightclub has a gaping hole where your office once was and from what is left it will be very hard to make any kind of identification of the human remnants. In any case, by the time it has been made, if there is enough dental work left among the remains of the day, you can be long gone. But I'm afraid the collateral damage does not include those you had hoped it would,' she said pragmatically, in her cold and emotionless manner. 'It wasn't the unit that came calling at your office door, it was a DCS Johnstone and a DI Tibbs. I'm afraid Johnstone pulled rank at the last moment and tried to grab all the glory for himself.'

'What about the brat Thoroughgood and those bastards Numan and Malcolm?' demanded Dawson, anger blazing in his eyes and quivering in his voice.

'No sign of Thoroughgood and Harry confirmed that DCS Johnstone handed out a bollocking to Malcolm and Numan and put the latter on a charge.' Then she asked, 'Where is the girl?'

'Waiting for you to put a bullet in her head and finish the job I'm paying you so well for,' said Dawson, pacing the splintered floorboards.

But before Devorgilla could respond the sound of something small and sharp chipping off the window grabbed his attention.

'You sure you weren't followed?' said Dawson.

'As sure as the grave,' replied Devorgilla and then she walked through the doorway into the adjoining room, where she found the dishevelled, bruised and cut figure of Celine, gagged and strapped to a ramshackle bedpost.

Twitching the frayed lace curtain once again, Mojito pulled a handgun from inside his jacket in readiness for any unwelcome visitors, but on checking for any movement and seeing none he relaxed, re-holstered the handgun and told himself to get a grip.

'There he is, I knew it. Dawson's alive, well and holed up here. So no prizes for guessing where Celine is,' said Thoroughgood.

'What now then, Einstein? You know he's gonnae be tooled up but what we don't know is where his angel of death is. Might as well wait for back-up, cos one thing's for sure, if we go blunderin' in there then all hell could break loose and if that happens there's no way your girlfriend's gonnae make it out the other side alive,' said Hardie wincing as the damp seeped through his body from the soaking turf they were kneeling on behind a copse of birches just twenty feet away from the rear of the mill house.

'With respect, Hardie, how can we take a chance on that and risk Celine's life? We need a diversion and I think I know just the job,' said Thoroughgood, pointing over to the passing place in the roadway where they had abandoned the van.

Taking another precautionary squint through the window, Dawson shouted over his shoulder. 'So where is Harry?'

'Lying dead in a pool of his own blood,' came the answer, and after the words had been spoken he felt the metallic chill of a handgun barrel pressing into his skull.

'What the fuck do you think you're doing?'

'Getting ready to kill the man who set my husband up,' she spat contemptuously.

'What rubbish are you talking, you deranged bitch?' demanded Dawson, yet a bead of sweat slipped down his bald dome.

'I'd be very careful how you talk to a deranged bitch with a Walther PP in her hand, Dawson. Did you think I would never find out it was you who put the word out that Peter had tipped you off that the protesters on the Bloody Sunday march were armed? That you did so knowing the ultimate price he would pay for any suggestion he had lied and grassed them up to the British?' For the first time, as he slowly turned his gaze towards her face, Mojito saw that her emotionless mask had slipped.

The handgun still tight against his skin, Dawson desperately tried to talk her down. 'That's garbage, woman. It was me that made sure you got out of the shit-storm that followed Peter's murder alive, me who made sure you were given the chance as a double-agent with 14 Unit, me that helped you stay one step ahead of the Provos, that you were well rewarded by us and there were no leaks from our side to compromise you. Christ, why would I have Peter fingered when he was our star informant?' Dawson asked.

'Because he knew too much.' And as the words left her mouth she took three steps back, levelled the handgun at his right leg and pulled the trigger.

The bullet exploded through Dawson's kneecap and he crumpled in a heap on the floor.

'You needed a scapegoat for Bloody Sunday and Peter was it,' she said, her voice quivering with anger but her eyes filling with tears.

The noise of the handgun discharging was unmistakeable. 'Ah, fuck it,' snapped Hardie, realising that his hand had now been forced and then ramming his penny loafer onto the accelerator.

The discharge of the gun and the sound of the engine gunning at the front of the farmhouse was all Thoroughgood needed to spring into action, and he quickly skirted his way towards the mill, trying as best he could to keep to the cover of the treeline.

His target was the waterwheel, which would in turn give him a leg up onto the roof and allow him, he hoped, to come down through the skylight window he could see glinting on the roof.

As he sprinted towards the wheel his mind raced. The gunshot had filled him with a sense of dread that was gnawing at his very being. 'You're too late, son... Again!' said the voice in his head.

Reaching the side of the wheel he began to haul himself onto a wooden shelf that ran vertically up and over the rotting edifice. Gripping the slimy, splintered wood he winced as a shard of broken timber spiked his hand and drew blood, but the pain was soon forgotten as an almighty clap from the front of the mill house thundered out.

Hardie had smashed the van home.

Clutching his shattered knee, Dawson writhed in agony. 'Treacherous ungrateful scum,' he spat, but as the impact of the van smashing into the front of the building shuddered through the floorboards, Devorgilla lost her balance, and as she staggered he threw himself at her.

Yet the assassin was too quick for him and before he had even come within a yard of her she had retrained the Walther on him. 'Time to pay for your sins, Mojito,' she said, and unloaded a round of lead into his body.

The first bullet exploded in his chest and threw Dawson back against the cracked stone wall; the second erupted in his temple, but as he crumpled to the floor the skylight above smashed and sent splinters of glass raining out across the room. As he hit the wooden floorboards, Thoroughgood rolled over onto a thousand burning needles of pain before coming to a crouch and locking wild eyes on the scene that was playing out in front of him.

Almost simultaneously a crack rang out as the front door burst open and Hardie shouted, 'You okay, Thoroughgood?'

The rookie's eyes switched to the denim-clad figure with the long red tresses, who was standing three feet away and pointing the barrel of death straight at him.

'What, do you think, is the correct answer, Mr Thoroughgood?' she asked in her biting Northern Irish accent.

Aware that his hand was shaking as it cradled his chin, Thoroughgood tried to regain his breath. 'Only you can make that call, Miss…?'

'Devorgilla,' she said, as Hardie materialised in the doorway at the front of the room, and trained a Smith & Wesson at her head.

'And a murdering bitch you are too,' said the cop.

Her beautiful green eyes flitted towards Hardie and a smile, which Thoroughgood thought was almost baleful, switched across her porcelain features.

'Where is Celine? What have you done with her?' asked Thoroughgood, unable to repress his desperation to know what had become of the girl.

Devorgilla returned her gaze to the rookie, the gun still rock-steady in her deadly grip. 'Alive and kicking in the room at the back,' she said flatly.

'So why did you kill Dawson? I thought he was on your side,' said Thoroughgood.

Again that doleful half-smile slipped across her face. 'In this war there are no sides, only betrayal.' And then Devorgilla turned the Walther around, stuck the barrel in her mouth and pulled the trigger.

'Sweet Christ!' said Thoroughgood.

Hardie stood over her corpse and shook his head, his face wreathed in shock. 'Aye, you're right there, son. And like or not we'll never know just why the angel of death turned the gun on herself, but is it no' time you checked on your own little angel?' asked Hardie, a smile, as much of relief as anything, twitching at the ends of his moustache.

With great effort Thoroughgood dragged his eyes away from the ghoulish scene of Devorgilla's self-destruction and Dawson's bullet-riddled corpse, and walked into the back room.

Hunkering down he undid the binding around Celine's wrists and tenderly pulled the tape off her mouth.

Although her face was tear stained her eyes shone bright. 'You came.'

'Cos we're for keeps,' he said, and wrapped his arms around her.

ACKNOWLEDGEMENTS

Firstly, thanks, to you, the reader, whoever you may be, for without you there would be no point.

As always, thanks to my darling wife, Arlene, a lady who has the patience of a saint, and has needed every ounce of it.

Grateful thanks to Andy Peden Smith, CEO at McNidder & Grace, for taking a chance on both Thoroughgood and myself.

My deepest gratitude to Les Trueman, who has helped keep *The Shift* real and 'of its time' – your expertise has been invaluable, sir!

Also to my old chums Faither and SupaMalky for the usual consultancy work!

Further thanks to my friends at WHSmith: Garry 'where's the Trusox' Torrance for helping put Thoroughgood on tour in Scotland at a moment I feared for his future, and Brian 'Silver Fox' McIntyre for 'the nous'!

Finally, if I've forgotten anyone, please accept my sincerest apologies. Enjoy!

The next title in the series

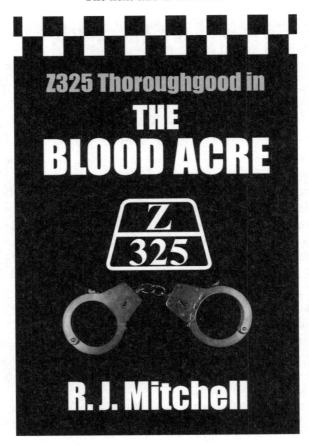

Fresh from his exploits in *The Shift*, Z325 Thoroughgood finds himself assigned to Community Policing in the crime-ridden Balornock Area of Glasgow and realises his DI is in the pay of Glasgow's most feared crime lord, The Widowmaker. Only lies buried in the Blood Acre can help him survive.

ISBN 9780857161581